CW00525107

The Imaginary Wife

T E SHEPHERD

The Imaginary Wife

shepline

First Published in Great Britain in 2018 by Shepline Words, Bicester, Oxfordshire

words.shepline.com

2 4 6 8 10 9 7 5 3 1

The moral rights of the author have been asserted

British Library Cataloguing-in-Publication Data
A catalogue record for this book is available from the British Library.

ISBN 978 0 9571756 9 3
E-BOOK ISBN 978 0 9571756 8 6

Edited by Zedolus Proofreading & Author Services, Bath, England
Twitter: @ZedolusProof

Typeset in Goudy Old Style by Shepline Creative, Oxfordshire
creative.shepline.com

FOR

those we leave behind
but can never forget

'Who are you?' said the Caterpillar. This was not an encouraging opening for a conversation. Alice replied, rather shyly, 'I — I hardly know, sir, just at present — at least I know who I *was* when I got up this morning, but I think I must have been changed several times since then.'

Lewis Carroll, Alice in Wonderland

'And if they're fictional, it is entirely acceptable to cheat on fictional men with other fictional men.'

Jane Rawson, August 2009

'Wouldn't it be weird to discover you were related to someone fictional? You'd start to doubt your own existence.'

David Mitchell, QI, January 2010

Prologue

I gave him up. I had to. I still loved Lewis, but my time with him was at an end. We had met at school when orchestra had brought us together, and we had been close ever since. We had passed through university days very much in love, and we had both got jobs back in our hometown. We were married, and our daughter was born. We were the perfect family.

Lewis had been my world. He and Sarah made my life complete. But then, in just the course of the last few months, it was over, and suddenly it had come to this; me, Amanda Jones, standing, with nowhere to live, and with just two small bags and a battered oboe case, back on the doorstep of my parents' home. I pulled the bell cord again and heard the jangling bells inside.

The shadow of a figure approached me on the other side of the leaded stained-glass panels in the door. I stood on the tiled doorstep, listening as the chain, latches, and lock were removed and drawn back. The door was opened inward by a small grey-haired woman.

'Hello Mummy,' I said.

'Amanda.'

Mummy had never been the warmest when speaking with me. Today of all days I wanted – needed – something more; a hug, some comfort, or just some warm words. Anything. But no, nothing. She just stepped back, and held the door for me as I entered the hallway.

'I suppose you'll be wanting dinner, then?' Mummy asked, in a way that wasn't really a question.

I didn't know what to say. Surely she knew, I had made it clear, that I would be staying; that I had to stay. I didn't have anywhere else to go. I looked down at my bags. Lewis was more than my world, he was my everything; and now he was gone.

Mummy closed the front door and swept off down the long hallway to the kitchen.

'Is – is there nothing I can do to help?' I asked, but my words went unheard and unanswered.

I took my few belongings and slowly made my way upstairs to my old bedroom. Standing in the small room at the back of the house now, there was no trace of my childhood left; Mummy had had the room redecorated as soon as I had left home for university, and any toys I once had were long ago despatched to a charity shop or church fête. I laid my bags down on the quilted single bed – this at least was the same – and began to look again at the room. I was trying to remember how my childhood bedroom had once been, but it was like every trace of it had been wiped from my mind. Every time I thought I had an image, I realised that it was Lewis' I was thinking of, not mine. I'd never thought until now about how much time I must have spent at the Tumnals' back then. I thought of Lewis Tumnal, and my life with him, and I couldn't hold back the sobs any longer. I sunk onto my bed and wept for my past life; the only life that had ever seemed real to me.

Later that evening, I sat in my parents' dining room as we ate our evening meal. My father was leafing through the latest academic papers to have been sent to him for review, and I felt nervous of engaging Mummy in any further conversation. I just sat and ate, feeling the loneliness, and realising that this was how it was going to be from now on.

'We've lost a couple of research assistants recently.'

I looked up towards my father, acknowledging his statement, but unsure. Was he talking to me – or Mummy? I looked back down at my dinner and filled my fork again.

'They've left their rooms. I guess I could pull some strings, and you could move in. I think you would be comfortable.'

I looked up again, feeling a lump in my throat and my heart rushing. I lay down my laden fork and tried to speak. I only exhaled air.

'You will have to observe college rules, of course. And it wouldn't be permanent,' Father continued; I doubted he even knew I was there. 'You only need a room temporarily, though?'

I nodded and shook my head alternately.

'I just assumed—' I began. 'I thought – my old room?'

Father stopped mid-chew. He lifted his gaze to me and stared; I didn't need to be told that I had said the wrong thing, and crossed some invisible line.

'My dear girl, that is out of the question. We need that room for when we have guests. And your mother, she has her monograph... It would be quite impracticable.'

I stared. I think I might have uttered a word or two – something to have voiced my disappointment – but I'm not sure. I was shocked. My marriage was over, and my parents were packing me off to live in a student room?

If this had been a meeting with the Editorial Director at work, I would have known how to defend my career; I knew how to argue my case, and had done so on numerous occasions at work. But this was different. I had nothing to work with here. Not with father...

PART ONE

Lonesome

sconesso e confuso

1

Amanda had the vaguest memories of being here. Years ago, when she had been much younger, she would accompany her father to work. Now she followed him up the staircase of the old college building. The boards creaked under her feet; bowed and worn clean through decades of students making their way to and from their tutorials. Her hand trailed on the banister all the way up to the top floor, and a room under the eaves.

Amanda crossed the room immediately to the window, slipped the catches, and pulled back the leaded lights. There was a small balcony beyond the window – not big enough to sit out on, but, nestled behind the crenellations at the top of the college building, it was maybe big enough for a few plants.

Plants. She remembered her old garden back at Bevington House, and hoped that Lewis would look after what she had achieved there.

'I've had to pull some serious strings to let you even have this room.'

Amanda heard her father's voice in the background, but she was already mentally moved in. She didn't have much to start off with, just the contents of her two small bags; but in her head the room was already her own. She crossed the dark-stained floorboards to inspect the bathroom.

'You may take your meals in the main dining hall, so long as you pay; or, of course, you can eat in town.'

The small suite contained only a small fridge, kettle, and toaster by way of kitchen. Amanda didn't really do cooking – that had always been something that Lewis did since they first met. In her mind, she figured that between the hall here and the staff restaurant at work, she would be just fine.

'You may make use of the JCR, but the senior common room is strictly forbidden. Post can be collected from the porter's lodge – it will not be delivered. You will have to make your own arrangements when it comes to laundry.'

Amanda pulled a wry smile at how much like a rulebook her father sounded.

'I do appreciate this, Daddy,' Amanda told him. 'Really, the room is perfect.'

She watched him, sure that for a moment there was something approaching a smile. Shortly after, her father gave her an awkward goodbye and departed, leaving Amanda to unpack her bags. As afternoon turned to evening, Amanda set the kettle to boil and searched for the tea. There was a little gone-off milk in the fridge when Amanda checked, but no tea or coffee to be found. She picked up a battered paperback novel that she had swiped from her parents, along with her purse, and headed out in search of a drink.

In the college dining hall, not only did Amanda find a large Americano but also dinner. Settling down at the end of one of the long tables, as far from anyone else as she could, she propped her book open and read as she ate. Dinner finished, she put off going back to her empty flat by staying late in the dining hall, reading, and going back twice for a refill of coffee; around her, students and faculty came and went, drifting about her like she was the only constant in the room.

Eventually, Amanda closed her book, downed the cold ends of her coffee, and left the dining hall, to walk back around the quad and climb the staircase to her room. She let herself in, and went straight through the motions of getting ready for bed. It wasn't until she reached her bed that she sunk down and pressed her head in her hands, staring across the room at the sparsely furnished college room as she remembered.

'Lewis.'

Amanda said his name, half-wishing, half-hoping that it would bring him back. For a moment she thought she saw him, moving about the room, quietly busy in the way that he always did. It was a comfort to see him sitting at the desk in front of the window, working on his book – to see him hunched over the pages as his pen moved, sometimes with the furrowed brow of thought, or occasionally looking up to gaze at nothing out of the window.

Amanda woke up. Her neck ached from where she had fallen asleep, slumped into an awkward position, and she massaged out the soreness. Across the room there was an empty desk, bathed in moonlight from the leaded window. Amanda picked herself up, and got ready for bed properly.

When she awoke the following morning, it was to unfamiliar surroundings. She staggered aimlessly around in a daze of confusion before crossing the quad again for breakfast in the great hall, this time sitting next to a group of twenty-something students. Amanda sat and ate her cereal, listening to the students talk and remembering her own student days. The talk seemed to revolve around last night in the JCR, and their dissertation frustrations – the deadline for which must be coming up quickly. Breakfast finished, Amanda returned her tray and retreated to her room to brush her teeth, grab her coat, and find her way to work.

The morning was fresh and bright, filled with clear light and spring blossom. She turned right out of Woodiwiss College and walked up to The Broad. For a moment she considered getting the tram those two short stops to the Radcliffe Infirmary, before cutting through to Walton Street, but eventually decided to walk. Today was the first morning that she had woken in her new college home, and she determined there and then that it would be the first day of a new life.

Amanda walked the length of Broad Street with new eyes; she took in every detail, noticing shops and eateries she had not noticed before. At the church on the corner she turned right instinctively, even though she had no memory of learning this route. Previously she would have kissed Lewis goodbye at the door of their home on the corner of Bevington and Woodstock roads. He would cycle to school, and she would go to work, there to experience the stresses and strains of the day that she would later recount to Lewis back home that following evening. How she got to and from work was unimportant, and no matter how much she thought of it now she couldn't remember.

The route that she now walked was the route that she would follow on a map. Up the length of St Giles, she passed the Ashmolean and The Eagle and Child – places that she knew because Lewis loved them. She turned left into Little Clarendon Street, because that was what everyone did to get to the collegial building on Walton Street that was home to The Press.

Between the corner of Little Clarendon Street and the entrance to her work, Amanda passed her – Kathryn. They had passed before she had recognised who it was, and as she turned and looked back over her shoulder, she wasn't sure if Kathryn had noticed either, but it was definitely her. Amanda quickened her pace, crossed the road, and passed through the turnstiles to the inner quad. She swiped her security pass through a reader next to another door, and continued through to climb the stairs to the Journals office, in the roof of one wing of the old building.

Eleanor and Charlotte were already working in their pod next to the empty production desk. Amanda stopped, and looked at Kathryn's old chair; the computer desk and filing trays cleared of personal items and tidied for a yet to be appointed replacement.

'Problem?' asked Eleanor, looking up from her proofs at Amanda.

Amanda considered the question for a moment before shaking her head. Then she looked up.

'Morning Eleanor, Charlotte.'

Amanda turned and continued on to her office, hung her coat on the hook behind the door, and fired up her computer. At her desk, she now stopped and stared. *What was she to do now?* In earlier days she would go home after work to Lewis, but she never detailed the exact day-to-day nature of her job. The password to the computer was easy, as both she and Lewis shared the same password for everything – the day that they met all those years ago. She figured that she should probably change it, but, she knew this one; it was one of the few certainties left to her.

Once logged in, she fired up her emails and watched as unread messages piled up. Clicking idly through them, she wondered how she was going to get through the day. She was good at her job, she knew that; but as to the minutiae of how she did the tasks that made up her job, she was less than certain.

There was a holiday request from someone. That at least should be easy. Amanda found a file of staff cards, and matched up the name. She sent an email straight back approving the request, and archived the messages. Three messages down, there was another requesting a meeting on Thursday. She accepted, figuring that either she would have worked out what she was doing, or she could use it as a way of finding out what she was supposed to do.

And so the morning passed; cruising old and new emails, working her way back through email conversations, and piecing together to-do items from previously archived documentation. Between what she had told Lewis in her other, former life, and this process of investigation, Amanda was able to piece together an idea of what her job was. From her vantage point in her glass-fronted office she saw people go to lunch, and decided to go herself and investigate.

Amanda stood with her tray in the work canteen, having left the tills and surveyed the people. She spied Eleanor and Charlotte through the door where they were sitting out on the Fairway – the conservatory-like atrium that linked the old and new buildings.

'Mind if I join you?'

Both Eleanor and Charlotte looked up, and Amanda was able to see immediately the level of joint surprise on their faces. Seeing that she was not really welcome, she looked about, saw another empty chair, and began to move off.

'Sure, why not?' Eleanor relented, as she moved to pull her bag from the spare chair.

'Thank you,' said Amanda. She didn't normally do this, she knew now – another piece of the jigsaw of her life fell into place.

'This is a surprise,' Charlotte said. 'You don't normally join us for lunch.'

'No,' said Amanda. 'And it's silly. Work is more than just work. We spend, what, forty hours a week, more than half our working day in these four walls, and I don't know anything about you.'

Amanda moved her gaze to Eleanor.

'So, belated New Year's resolution then?'

Amanda considered Eleanor's question for a moment. She nodded.

'If something has to change, I don't get why you have to wait for some artificial point in the calendar.'

'Fair point,' said Eleanor.

'You are going to – join us – more often then?' asked Charlotte.

Amanda shrugged.

'When I'm not all meetinged out. Have you seen my calendar? It's crazy.'

The conversation faltered. Amanda picked at her dinner with her fork, wondering how to do this; how to enter into the girls' conversation.

'How's the recruitment going?' asked Eleanor. 'Many applications?'

Recruitment? Applications? Amanda pictured the emails in her inbox from some girl in Human Resources. A production editor, to replace Kathryn.

'Yeah, we've got some good people to choose from I think. Michelle seems impressed.'

'Michelle? The HR Intern? I'm surprised she's not applied herself!' Eleanor laughed. 'Glad you're using the best selection procedure!'

'Ellie...' Charlotte hissed.

'Actually, Eleanor, Charlotte, I had a request as regards this.'

Amanda hoped it didn't sound as on-the-fly a decision as she knew it was.

'The two of you probably know the package of journals better than anyone. I was wondering if you would both mind assisting in the recruitment procedure?'

'Really?' gaped Eleanor.

'Sure, I guess—' said Charlotte.

'It would be a big help,' said Amanda. *A big, big help.* If she could get these two to lead on the recruitment, then that would give her yet more time to learn herself what she needed.

'Have you heard at all, from Kathryn? How's she getting on?' Amanda asked. 'In her new job...?'

'Good, I think. No, great,' said Charlotte. 'It's different of course, fiction publishing. The others, they're different.'

'We're all meeting after work on Friday.'

'She should never have left—'

Amanda bit her tongue, as she wondered if her comment sounded a bit too boss-like in tone.

'She didn't have to—'

Charlotte rolled her eyes and sighed.

'We both know that's not true. After what happened.'

Amanda frowned; Charlotte had a point. But what did happen? Her memory of those few months was a haze, from which she was still trying to unpick herself. Friday though – a night out with the girls – if she could just engineer it...

2

Amanda walked home across the city, stopping to pick up some groceries from the local supermarket, and then some fresh things from the covered market. She turned the corner into the lane that ran down beside Woodiwiss College, and was thrust suddenly back into an earlier memory; when she and Lewis, back home from uni for the holidays, walked this lane hand in hand.

'This is our lane,' Lewis told her, with the biggest of grins on his face.

'I know,' answered Amanda, as she always did. 'You say that every time we walk down here. That it's 'Our Liddell Lane'...'

She grinned as she repeated Lewis' own private joke.

'I don't know what I love about it so much—'

Fingers still entwined, he lifted both their hands to point there, and there.

'I think it's the mixture of cobbled gutter and broken asphalt – and that high wall, with the not knowing what's on the other side. If it was either all cleaned up, or twee-ified, it just wouldn't be the same.'

Amanda smiled, a wry grin of agreement at her boyfriend's musing.

Rounding the corner of the lane near the entrance to Woodiwiss College, they passed a girl – maybe a year or two Amanda's junior –

talking to the old porter. The girl was clothed in a blue frock with white lace trimmings and an Alice-band to keep back her long, pale hair. The old man was short and round and friendly-looking, with a bowler hat several sizes too small perched on top of his head.

Amanda laughed, and told Lewis the story that she had just made up about the girl and the man.

The older Amanda turned off the pavement, and stepped through the doorway into the entrance of Woodiwiss College. As she was about to walk on through to the quad, she turned and took a step back, remembering what her father had told her about the porter's lodge, and deciding that she should get into the habit of checking for post.

She stood and stared for what seemed like an age at the rows and rows of pigeonholes. They were organised not only alphabetically, but by some arcane college system that seemed to involve the alphabet, seniority, and subject. She was clueless as to where to find herself.

'Amanda Jones?'

Amanda jumped at the sound of her name so close beside her. She turned to see her – the girl from years ago with the blue dress and the Alice band standing next to her. Not that she was dressed remotely girlishly. Indeed, she was the very opposite of the little girl with the long blonde hair; with hair now cropped short, she wore black trousers, white shirt, and black waistcoat; the very uniform of the college porter, except for the bowler hat.

'How – how do you know my name?'

'You never heard of porter's magic?'

Amanda stared. *No.* The girl grinned.

'New girl in rooms? You see someone staring at the holes you don't recognise? It's what us porters do. Porter's magic is to the college what The Knowledge is to cabbies.'

'Who are you?'

'Watts,' answered the girl simply. 'Alice Watson strictly speaking, but folk 'round here usually just call me Watts.'

Amanda nodded. She liked the simplicity with how Watts worked.

'You worked here long?'

Watts shook her head.

'Just this year, officially. Since my old Dad retired. But before then, I might as well have. You could say I was born and raised in these hallowed walls. This place is more my home than the fusty academics that only leave feet first in boxes, or the students with more pretension than sense.'

Amanda laughed. She couldn't help but think of her own Mummy and Pa when she listened to Watts speak.

'I hope I'm not speaking out of turn or nothin'?' Watts said apologetically. 'You don't seem like neither an academic or a student.'

Amanda shook her head.

'I work at The Press, and my parents are both fusty old academics. I'm only here because my husband, and – I – don't have anywhere else to go.'

Watts gazed back with wide, searching eyes that made Amada remember her own daughter, Sarah. *Was she still her daughter?*

'You're Dr Jones' daughter?' exclaimed Watts. 'Sorry, I – you're the talk of the PCR.'

'P.C...?'

'Porter's Common Room,' Watts said with a grin. 'It's a room in the cellar where we have our tea. Figure if the students and the academics can have their own room, then we can too.'

Amanda nodded. She glanced around at the pigeonholes, and then back to Watts uncertainly.

'Nothing today. Don't worry though, I'll leave anything that comes in your room.'

'Really? I'm not supposed to – my father—'

'Don't you worry about what Dr Jones says. The college don't run itself by the rules that the authorities set. It's us porters that make stuff happen. Come on, I'll walk with you back to your room.'

Amanda felt that she didn't really need accompanying anywhere, but Watts came with her, walking her around the quad to her staircase beneath the twisted stem of a wisteria. However unnecessary the accompaniment was, Amanda did find a comfort in Watts' presence. Since Lewis had turned his back on her in that final act of defiance, she had been wandering lonely and friendless; meeting Watts, with her down-to-earth, no-nonsense approach to the world, felt like the most real thing to have happened to her in a long, long time.

Watts unlocked the door to Amanda's room with her master key, and helped her in with her bits of shopping. As Amanda found homes in the few cupboards that constituted a kitchen, Watts helped her too, by putting on the kettle and getting a couple of cups ready for tea. She swung open the windows to let in fresh air from the quad beneath. All the time Amanda eyed Watts from the corner of her vision, wondering how long her new friend was going to stay.

'Your Dad must have been sad to leave this place?'

Watts turned and stared blankly back.

'When he retired, I mean.'

Watts shook her head.

'Don't reckon Dad could ever leave these halls. He still lives in the old lodge, same as ever. The master insisted – said he couldn't countenance my Dad leaving. Not after so many years' service.'

Amanda smiled.

'That's nice.'

'One of the few decent things the Master has done, if you ask me.'

Amanda nodded. She expected something more by way of explanation, but Watts volunteered nothing more.

'Tea?' asked Watts.

Amanda smiled and nodded. They took their cups and made their way to the seating area for more conversation, which seemed to drift on from one subject to another, until finally Watts set down her mug. She had been rolling the mug around between her hands for the last half hour, but now pronounced it time that she did her evening rounds.

It wasn't until Watts had left, and could be seen from the high leaded window rounding the sides of the quad to the entrance lodge, that Amanda wondered who had been manning the desk for this hour or more. She shrugged. That really wasn't any concern of hers.

As an orange hue seeped into the fading evening sky, the bells of the college chapel clock chimed out seven o'clock. Amanda stopped. Somewhere across the rooftops of Wren Hoe, Lewis would be tuning in, as he always did, to the daily goings-on in Ambridge. Amanda was never a particular fan of *The Archers*, but she turned on the radio now and listened as she freshened up after her day at work. She felt a comfort in it now, for its slow ordinariness and quiet reliability.

As the closing bars of *Barwick Green* echoed around her room, Amanda switched off the radio and left to go in search of dinner. This night, sitting towards one end of the long tables in the college dining room, she looked about at the other people eating their dinners, and couldn't not think of the students and academics in the same mixture of fondness and resentment with which Watts had referred to them. She was a student once upon a time, albeit at a less auspicious university; and there had been a time when she could so easily have followed her parents further into academia. But that was not the path that she – or was it Lewis – had chosen for herself.

Following her second evening meal in college, Amanda retreated to her rooms and read, before turning in for the night before the chapel clock had struck ten. She drifted off into a sound sleep, not for once haunted by images of Lewis drifting through her mind.

When she woke in the morning she was at ease in her new flat, and headed back out to work. At the porter's lodge, Watts was already at the desk and called out a cheerful greeting; Amanda raised her hand and flashed a smile, but didn't stop. At the café on the corner of Little Clarendon Street she bought a coffee to take to her desk, to help her in facing another day working through emails.

Amanda had beaten Eleanor and Charlotte into the office this morning, and was in fact the first to arrive of anyone in their part of The Press. When she looked up from her monitor to see Charlotte settling into her desk, Amanda decided on a break; taking the last of her coffee, she went and sat at Kathryn's old desk.

'Morning.'

Charlotte jumped in her seat.

'Oh, morning.'

'Another day, huh?' said Amanda.

Charlotte nodded. She was ill at ease with morning employer-employee communication.

'Did you have a good evening?'

Charlotte nodded.

'Yeah; nothing special, but good.'

'Keeping yourself for Friday, with Kathryn?'

'Something like that.'

'What's the plan then? Just drinks, or a meal too?'

Charlotte found herself answering even before she had thought about it.

'Cocktails at the Duke, obviously,' she said, 'But yeah, probably a meal after. Dying to know what her new job is like...'

Amanda nodded. She had a venue at least, but not what she would call a concrete invite. She looked up, about to say something more, when Eleanor arrived. She too, was obviously surprised, and taken aback, to find Amanda sitting at their pod.

3

'I swear she's trying to ingratiate herself with us,' said Charlotte. 'The way she was quizzing me about Friday.

She and Eleanor had taken their sandwiches and brought them down to the park across the street.

'You think we should invite her?' asked Eleanor. 'It is just a kind of a meet up with ex-work colleagues.'

'Kathryn would kill us.'

Eleanor nodded.

'It would be like inviting your partner's ex to their wedding.

Charlotte nodded, vigorously.

'I do kind of feel sorry for her though.'

Eleanor looked up, her eyes wide and her forehead stretched.

'Sure she's the boss, and she was a bitch to Kathryn during all that, but—'

Charlotte tried to make sense of her words.

'She does seem to be trying to be different.'

Eleanor shrugged.

'She is different. Don't you think?'

'Can't read her,' Eleanor said, shaking her head. 'At least before, you knew where you were. But now...?'

*

As Amanda left the cloistered world of The Press, she had a mission. She had finished up a freshly made baguette from the on-site deli as she worked at her desk, to give herself the full lunch hour for this mission. Opposite the junction with Little Clarendon Street, in a corner property that was a patchwork of signage and posters and the heart of a nest of tram cables and electrical wires, there was an antiques shop that she meant to investigate. She had seen it on her way in and from work the past couple of days, and she wondered why she had never been in before. It was never important to the Lewis Tumnal story, she guessed.

Amanda left her office with the vaguest notion that it was not unusual for her to eat her lunch at her desk; but she felt that was more because she didn't take lunch breaks. *Was that true?* It was weird how fragments of her past life would work their way back into her consciousness, much as a splinter would pass through an inflamed finger.

She arrived at the shop and pushed open the door, warped and twisted in its frame, and bells jangled above. She pushed the door shut behind her and blinked, to allow her eyes time to adjust to the gloom. The one room at the front was packed with antiques and collectables, cheek by jowl with furniture and glass cabinets containing smaller, more precious items. Moving through it, Amanda discovered that the one room went through to another at the back, and down to a cellar, then up, and across, into who knows how many more rooms.

She returned to the first room that she had arrived in, and began a detailed exploration of this Aladdin's cave of objects. Most she drifted past with little interest, but occasionally some obscure object would pull her in. She would squeeze between furniture to get to the tag, hooking it over in her fingers and reading the description. Often it would result in a shrug, maybe a smile, and then she would move onto the next. Antique shops were so much more fun with someone.

Amanda sat opposite Lewis in the upstairs tea room overlooking the market square of Stow-on-the-Wold. They held hands across the table and smiled each other. On the floor next to them were the bags containing their purchases from the various antique shops that lined the square beneath. Amanda gently nudged Lewis' shoes with her feet and grinned, with a little upward twitch to the shoulders.

'Thanks for the ring,' she told him, looking again at where the diamond rested on the finger of her left hand.

Lewis smiled.

'Yeah, guess what? We're engaged.'

Amanda pushed her hand back through her red hair and beamed. Out of the corner of her eye, she caught the sun glinting on diamond.

Amanda looked down at her hand now. The ring, a little tarnished now, lacked the lustre that it had back then. She eased the ring from her finger now, gulping back her emotions. She pulled her purse from her bag, and dropped the ring in amongst the loose change.

Looking up again now, she saw it: the writing box. It might have been *her* writing box. She squeezed through between the desks and dining tables to the rectangular box made of walnut. She turned the key and opened it. The leather was dark, reddish-brown with faded gold leaf, whereas hers – when it had lived in the lounge at Bevington House – had been green felt. She knew she had to have it and gathered it up carefully in her arms. It was while working her way back out from where the furniture had closed in around her that she saw the barometer on the wall. And then while paying she glanced across, and saw the china in the cabinet...

When the taxicab pulled up outside of Woodiwiss College, Amanda paid the driver before setting about extricating her three cumbersome cardboard boxes from the cab and onto the pavement. Once out she gathered them up and carried them into the college through the entrance lodge, using the boxes themselves as a shield from being seen by Watts, and made her way round the quad to her staircase.

Over the next couple of days, Amanda sought out more antique shops, second-hand and new bookstores – always coming away with boxes and purchases to take back to the rooms on the top floor of Woodiwiss College. She took advantage of lunchtimes to sneak out and browse the Wren Hoe markets, and get the spoils home before returning to an afternoon of work. By the time Thursday evening came, her rooms were looking a lot homelier.

Amanda was busying herself in her room, tending some plants that she had appropriated from the greenhouses at the back of the college, and was planting up some trays of seeds when there was a knock to the open door and footsteps across the floorboards.

'Delivery for you!'

Amanda turned to see Watts standing in the doorway, holding a letter and a small package. Wiping her hands clean on a tea towel, she crossed the room and eagerly took the post. She glanced at the bank statement, casting it aside unopened as she tore open the packet.

'You've transformed this place,' exclaimed Watts as she wandered around the room, stroking the new items of furniture and antiques. She flickered open some books, leafing through lines of Dickens and Shakespeare.

'Fantastic!'

Watts looked up to see Amanda holding the battered paperback novel in her hands.

'I'd forgotten how much I loved this story. Lewis and I would read it together to unwind after exams.'

Watts quizzed Amanda over what the book was, but was flashed only a brief look at the cover as Amanda crossed the room to curl up at one end of the sofa.

'He named his bear after the illustrator,' Amanda said. She smiled, hooking her red hair back behind her ear.

'As wonderful as it is, you do realise your boy's moved on?'

Amanda either didn't hear, or was lost already in the pages of her book. Either way she didn't answer Watts' comment, who continued to inspect everything in the room. She noticed Amanda's oboe on its stand.

'Your oboe?' said Watts. 'You been playing?'

Amanda glanced up, and shrugged a reply. Watts picked up the oboe, placing her fingers on the keys, and her lips around the reed.

'Do you play?'

Watts shook her head and put the oboe back.

'Clarinet; a little, when I was young. How to hold it is about all I remember.'

Amanda closed her book and lay it on the coffee table.

'Friday tomorrow,' she said.

'It is indeed.'

'So what time does Watts finish on a Friday?'

Watts shrugged.

'Porter's magic. As long as the desk is covered, and the jobs get done, the Master doesn't set us hours.'

Amanda looked quizzical.

'So, what's your plan?'

Amanda flinched and set her gaze out the window, chewing on her bottom lip.

'Come on, Miss Jones. You couldn't be more obvious if the Isis was to flood with Siamese and Chihuahuas. Friday night you're hitting the Cowley Road, and you want an accomplice when it comes to murdering a few bottles.'

'I was thinking a couple of cocktails at the Duke of Cambridge, but... yeah.'

'Cocktails, huh?'

Watts stood up tall and straightened the collar of her shirt.

'Not my normal drink, but Alice Watson can do refined.'

Amanda laughed.

'Not sure if Friday night at the Duke counts as refined.'

The conversation faltered. Amanda looked ready to pick up her book again, and Watts was ready to be on her way. Across the quad, the chapel clock rang out the hour.

'You eaten yet?'

Amanda looked up to Watts' question. She shook her head.

'You want to go get something?' asked Watts, with a casual gesture of her arms. 'It's Chilli Thursday.'

Amanda put her tray down on the table and stepped over the bench to sit opposite Watts in the hall.

'Do you eat in here often?'

Watts shook her head.

'Most of the time I just cooks for me Dad in the flat. After a day on the desk, the less that us porters see of the academics the better, we always say.'

'Do you ever – the students – do they become friends?'

Watts shook her head.

'I did once. That was before I was a porter, official like. I thought that we had something in common; you know, with neither of us being learned.'

Amanda forked chilli in with her baked potato. She could see why Watts liked Chilli Thursday – it was good. She looked up again at Watts opposite, listening for the rest of her story.

'Turns out the students in these walls are just like mini-academics,' Watts said, as she forked up another mouthful of chilli. 'More interested in airy hypotheses than living in the real world.'

Amanda frowned. The real world, she mused; that was what she was in now.

'I don't see as I have much choice than to eat here,' said Amanda. 'Not with that pitiful excuse for a kitchen back upstairs.'

'Just steer clear of the high table, and that first block over there—'

Watts pointed behind her, where some students in shirts and ties and tweed jackets, with short-cropped, slicked back hair were eating.

'That's the ones you need to avoid.'

Amanda nodded. She looked across the different rows of tables and the students who sat at them, trying to imagine where Lewis would have fitted in. She decided that he would have been the one on his own with a book for company. Or he and she would be cooking for themselves in their shared flat.

After their meal, Amanda walked with Watts back to the entrance lodge. Watts headed across the grounds to her father's cottage, and Amanda stepped through the gate out into the road for some evening air. She closed her eyes and raised her face to the night sky, breathing in the cool Wren Hoe air. As she stood there listening to the night, she heard laughter in the street, and voices; girl's voices – and one that she recognised.

'Sarah?'

Amanda blinked her eyes open. Could it be? The girls were past her now, but from behind, in jeans and hoody, with her fair hair in a ponytail, it could've been Sarah. *Why was she so uncertain? Sarah was her daughter, but...*

Amanda found that she was crying, and gulping back a lump from the back of her throat. She sighed deeply and stepped back into the college, as the girls rounded a corner onto The Broad.

4

Kathryn carried three cocktails back to a table where Charlotte and Eleanor were already sitting with other work colleagues. She eased herself into the seat opposite and raised her glass.

'Cheers!'

The three friends clinked their glasses together, like it was a seal to a secret pact.

'So, how's Fairyland Books?' Eleanor asked first.

'And more importantly, are there any jobs going?' chipped in Charlotte.

Kathryn grinned.

'Like a dream. A midsummer night's one, that is.'

The others groaned.

'Seriously though,' said Kathryn. 'Alberich is brilliant. He's like the cuddly old grandpa you always wished for but never had. And even though he's... I don't know how old, he's got his finger on the pulse of what children want to read.'

'You're not missing the Journal of Inorganic Soil Composition then?' quipped Eleanor.

'It's like another world.'

Kathryn sipped more cocktail.

'And how is it back in the world of society journals?'

Charlotte shrugged. She glanced at Eleanor, and looked back at Kathryn.

'Same as ever really.'

Across the bar behind Kathryn, Eleanor saw Amanda enter, along with another girl she didn't recognise. She nudged Charlotte gently in the ribs, and surreptitiously nodded across the room.

'So, is Louis joining us tonight?'

'Hmm, not sure. Hopefully,' answered Kathryn. 'He's been really in the zone with his writing of late. It's hard to drag him away.'

Charlotte nodded. She looked at Eleanor, biting her lip.

'Why?' asked Kathryn. 'What's with you two?'

'Nothing. It might be nothing,' said Charlotte.

'It's Amanda...' said Eleanor.

'She's being friendly—'

Kathryn shook her head.

'Why are you – why do you think *I* care? Why do *we* care?'

Kathryn looked first to Charlotte, then to Eleanor, and then, seeing their gazes were across the room, she turned, slowly at first, to see Amanda at a table near the door. She turned again to her friends.

'You told her,' said Kathryn. 'This isn't some coincidence.'

Charlotte shrugged.

'The Duke is where everyone from The Press goes after work on a Friday night.'

'Everyone *but* her,' said Kathryn. She pulled out her mobile. 'I need to text Louis. If he is coming—'

Eleanor reached out to stay her friend's hand.

'If he is coming, you can warn him then. She might not stay.'

Kathryn glanced from friend to phone, and from phone to friend. She frowned and pushed it back across the table, taking up her cocktail instead.

'Is she still there?'

Kathryn's question came during a lull in conversation; a conversation where, as light-hearted and jokey as it was, Kathryn's preoccupation was still evident. Even before an answer came, she was reaching again for her mobile. Charlotte nodded but it was Eleanor who answered.

'She's been joined by someone though. A girl; don't recognise her, but they seem pally.'

Kathryn raised her eyebrows with interest. She reached down to feign getting something from her bag and sneaked a lingering glance across the bar, at where Amanda was sat enjoying a drink with Watts. She flinched away quickly, when she suddenly saw both of them looking in her direction.

'Who is she?' asked Watts. 'She your husband's other woman?'

Amanda's reply came as a frown, even before any words had escaped her lips. She nodded. Watts drank from her pint of bitter and watched as Amanda nursed her long cocktail.

'So what's the story? You think you can still get him back?'

Amanda turned again from her drinking companion, to observing Kathryn's party, to looking again at Watts.

'We did everything together,' said Amanda. 'My whole life, since when I first met him – all my memories they are with him – what we did.'

'Doesn't sound healthy if you ask me,' said Watts.

Amanda shook her head.

'This is different. Since Lewis left me, it's like I don't know how to do *anything*.'

Watts stared.

'You're here. Now?'

'Barely. Only because going out was something that Lewis and I – we – didn't do that often. Sometimes though, I sit at my desk at work and it's like I haven't a clue how to do my job, and I can't tell anyone because I'm this big manager type.'

'I'm not sure I understand.'

Amanda struggled to put the words in the right order.

'It's like the only things I know how to do are things that I would have talked to Lewis about, or that he would have seen me do.'

Watts stared.

'So...?'

Amanda shook her head. She shrugged again, and frowned.

'I need him.'

Watts narrowed her gaze on her friend, looking at her from beneath furrowed eyebrows.

'I know I can't have him. He's here now.'

Kathryn threw a gaze of contempt across the room.

'I've had enough. I'm going over there...'

She was half out of her seat, as both Charlotte and Eleanor moved to stop her.

'Kathryn, don't.'

'It's not worth it,' added Charlotte.

Kathryn looked from her friends, to Amanda – then back. She shook her head.

'No. It's a free country. I'm not moving because of her.'

'That's the spirit.'

Charlotte grinned, standing up with her purse.

'You want another?'

Kathryn picked up the cocktail menu and scanned down the list of drinks. She passed the menu to Charlotte, with her finger marking a spot.

'A Canal Cruiser, please.'

Amanda sat listening to Watts, in that half-listening-but-not-really kind of way. She watched as Charlotte passed through the room to the bar. She saw Charlotte glance over as she gave her order, and waited for her drinks. She found it hard not to stare.

Charlotte turned and leaned across the counter to talk to the barman. Then she was crossing the room straight for Amanda and Watts' table. She pulled up a chair, and took a seat right in front of Amanda.

'Excuse me!' said Watts.

Charlotte flashed her the briefest of glances.

'Can I help you, Charlotte?'

'Yes, you can,' said Charlotte. 'You can find yourself some other bar to have your drinks. We know you are trying to taunt Kathryn by being here, but it's really not her fault.'

'I promise you, I am really not trying to taunt anyone.'

'So why are you here?'

'Not that it's anything to do with you, but I wanted – I *need* – a favour from my husband. My ex-husband...'

'And he's not here, so – why are you?'

Amanda shrugged. She looked at her glass and the little of her drink that remained.

'She's here with me,' replied Watts, with none of the faltering, uncertain voice of Amanda. 'Your drinks are ready I think.'

Watts nodded towards the bar. Charlotte shot them both her meanest and most determined look, as she backed away to collect her drinks and returned with them to her booth. Watts downed the last of her pint, and slipped her arms back into her jacket.

'Come on. Sitting here isn't going to solve anything.'

Amanda stuttered her protestations. She didn't know where to look, as her gaze flickered between Watts, and Kathryn and her wall of protective friends at the other end of the room.

Watts was now standing over her, waiting. Amanda got up obediently, and retrieved her coat and bag.

5

Amanda walked down the length of Cornmarket in the evening, hand in hand with Lewis; her head still buzzed with the film they had just seen, and the infectiously catchy main theme. They talked through the film, reminiscing over the best bits; picking out flaws in the direction, and plot holes in the script. Amanda swooned over the lead actor, trying to get Lewis to admit a liking for one or other of the actresses. She kept looking sideways to where the neon lights from the shops were reflected across Lewis' face.

They stood at the tram stop outside the Ashmolean. This was in the days before the multi-million-pound renovations and extensions to the building, when the museum was a sober, austere frontage onto the lower end of St Giles. Amanda turned to face her boy. She looked up at him and smiled, slipping her hands around his neck, as he, awkwardly, laid his on her waist. Under a flickering street lamp, they kissed, until they were interrupted by a tram rattling into the stop with a squeal of brakes.

'Come on,' Lewis said, and bounded up into the tram. He turned to help Amanda up, like a gentleman, and they took their seats on the slatted benches.

The tram sat for five minutes at the end of the line, though it seemed like longer, chatting and chuntering to itself through the language of the *engine. Amanda laid her head on Lewis' shoulder, enjoying the comfort of his being there. Eventually, the wheels ground and screeched into action and they moved off slowly; Amanda closed her eyes to doze...*

Amanda took a step forward and steadied herself with a hand on the bannister. Her head pounded. That last drink in the pub on the way home had made everything else a blur. She turned and looked back to where Watts remained, a slight and slender figure in college bowler, framed in the light from a Victorian gas lamp. She continued up the stairs, looking back one last time at a turn of the stairs. Watts was gone.

Amanda let herself into her rooms, kicking off her shoes at the door and dumping her bag and shoes on the nearest chair, and continued straight through to her bedroom. She reappeared a few moments later in a state of mid-undress, with echoes of Lewis' voice running through her head, reminding her not to leave her things scattered everywhere. She retrieved her coat, bag, and shoes, and put them away in their proper place.

'Sorry, dear,' she told him out loud, before stopping and realising that this was not Lewis' house. She carried on to the bathroom.

There was a loud knocking on the door. Amanda ducked out of the bathroom, listening. Whoever it was knocked again. Amanda shuffled to the bedroom and retrieved her dressing gown, before crossing the room to answer the door. Turning the latch and pulling the door back revealed Watts, still in her porter's uniform, but without bowler and tie, and her top buttons loosened. She raised a bottle of port from beside her.

'May I?'

Watts gestured to be let in. Amanda shrugged, stepping back to let in her friend. She closed the door after Watts, pulling her dressing gown tighter about her.

'It seems to me, Miss Jones, that in the absence of your husband, we need to find you your own memories.'

Amanda stared, wide-eyed, but accepted her friend's words. She decided that this strange girl was her friend.

'From the Master's cellar,' Watts said, holding the bottle aloft. 'You got glasses?'

'Of course...'

Amanda opened several cupboard doors in the tiny kitchen, before finding two mismatched tumblers. She took them across the room and set them on the coffee table in front of the sofa and armchairs for Watts to pour.

'Won't he miss it, the Master?'

Watts shook her head.

'I'll have to show you the cellars some time. They are like labyrinths under the college.'

'Is it true what they say – about there being secret tunnels from the colleges to other parts of the city?'

'Not that I've seen them, but yes. Not just between the colleges either.'

Watts handed Amanda a generously-filled glass of port. She took it gratefully.

'Here's to the memories of Miss Amanda Jones,' proclaimed Watts, raising her glass.

'Doctor...' Amanda corrected her.

Watts grinned.

'Here's to Dr Amanda Jones.'

Amanda smiled and raised her glass.

'To me.'

They drank, and sat, and drank again. Watts topped up their glasses.

'So, what did you get your doctorate in?' asked Watts. 'Pardon me for asking, but you don't seem old enough to have, what, three degrees, a good job at The Press, and a thirteen-year-old daughter.'

Amanda sipped at her port and considered this fact. She knew it was almost twelve years since Sarah had entered her and Lewis' lives, but she didn't really remember much of her daughter's own early childhood. And Sarah herself was going to be fourteen on her next birthday—

'Amanda?'

Amanda looked up, realising that Watts had been trying to speak to her more than once. She frowned. The dates of her life were not going to reconcile themselves just by staring into her own mind. She shook her head.

'Your doctorate? What was it in?'

Amanda remembered the papers and journals that surrounded her desk at work.

'Geography – geology – I think. At least that's the area I work in, and I remember talking with Lewis about it on holidays. But... you'd think I'd remember doing my thesis.'

'The memory is a funny thing.'

'I guess...'

Watts sat forward, a half-drunk glass in one hand and an open bottle of port in the other.

'But that's not what tonight is supposed to be about, is it? What's forgotten is forgotten. But life, and experiences, that's what happens now. It's the memories of the future.'

Amanda stared across the table at her friend.

'You keep saying that, but I don't know if I understand.'

Watts looked about her, at the college room slowly filling with random books, furniture, and antiques that Amanda had brought in from her shopping trips. The suite of rooms still had something of an institutional feel, with the prominent smoke alarms, and notices about first aid, and evacuation procedures.

'Take tonight, my friend.'

Watts drank port, before topping up her glass.

'You could have just come home, gone to bed, woken up tomorrow morning, and been the same person. But this? Tonight? This is memories in the making. Your memories, formed in *your* home.'

Amanda nodded. A wry smile stretched across her face. It was true, the port was easing the conversation. The randomness of life was coming out, and she had learnt things that she had not known before. She asked again about the tunnels. She was fascinated by them, more so perhaps because her father had never mentioned them.

Watts sat forward, relishing the opportunity to explain. Amanda got the feeling that a fair bit was embellished for the story, but she enjoyed the way Watts told it. As the conversation developed, so more alcohol was poured; minutes ticked into hours, and the hours into the small hours of night.

When Amanda awoke, with the morning sun streaming in through the windows, her throat was dry, and her head was sore. She picked herself up from where she was lying across the covers of her bed, and guzzled a glass of water straight down.

'Coffee...' she groaned, as she made her way across the room to the kitchen. Two unwashed glasses and an empty bottle of port stood on the side, as a testament to last night. Amanda flicked the switch up on the kettle, downing another large glass of water as she waited for it to boil.

She stood and stared at the kettle as it boiled, with the fog of sleep hanging in her head and a throat like sandpaper. When the kettle whistled time, the noise stung her hearing. Amanda found the biggest mug she could find – an enormous Minnie

Mouse one she had found in a charity shop, and which, she felt, was exactly like one she had had as a child.

Cupping the mug of coffee close to her, she took it across the room to stand by the window. With her pounding head and dry throat, and the smell of coffee infusing her nostrils, she felt like a student again. Looking down, she could see students leaving the dining room and returning to their rooms. She saw Watts rounding the quad in her porter's uniform. She waved back, as Watts looked up.

6

It was gone noon by the time Amanda left the cloistered walls of Woodiwiss College. She crossed the city centre with a new-found confidence. In Blackwell's she lost herself in amongst the shelves of books and emerged over an hour later with a bag of books. In an alley behind the playhouse she rediscovered an independent record store, where she found herself listening to a whole album in the retro-style listening booth.

Next door she picked up a filled baguette and took it down through the parks, to eat it by the river and start one of her new books. Across the park, families picnicked and couples lounged. Single people like her read books, or simply lay in the sun listening to music and watching the clouds drift across the sky.

As Amanda read, last night's late-night drinking and talking began to catch up on her. Her eyelids grew heavy, and the words on the page began to slip by. She jolted herself awake and stared at the page, trying to make sense of where she had got to. She had been reading words clear as anything, but those words were not on the page. She sighed and flicked back a page, and another, until she found a bit she recognised. Two and a half pages she must have dreamt! She felt a little sad that she would never now know how that story had ended.

She looked up and across at the river. A family of swans made their way against the current and clambered out onto the bank, the parents with ease while the cygnets slipped and stumbled through the reeds and grasses. A college boy punted his girlfriend down the river, and Amanda smiled. She returned to her reading. It was a good book, a very good book; but she was tired, and the bright sunshine and warmth made her sleepier. She struggled against the weight of her eyelids, and so her mind drifted on to read a different story...

Amanda, a girl of fifteen, lay on her front, propped up on her elbows reading her book. Across the grass in front of her, a family of swans were enjoying an afternoon on the Cherwell.

Just out of reach in the grass, Lewis' jotter pad and pen lay discarded where he had eschewed novel writing for his sketchbook. Amanda hooked a curl of hair back behind her ear and looked up at him, smiling coyly.

'What are you drawing?'

Lewis raised a finger to stay her.

'Don't move!'

Amanda rolled her eyes.

'You've drawn me loads.'

'I can always improve.'

Amanda laughed.

'Cute, I grant you, but... in Maths lessons? Chemistry? I swear, if boys were allowed in the girl's toilets you'd draw me there. There are other subjects.'

'I can't draw them,' said Lewis. 'They think I'm weird.'

'No one thinks you are weird, Lewis.'

'They do, all of them,' said Lewis in a quiet voice. 'Except for you, and Miss Leroy; but she's a teacher and doesn't count. You don't know what it was like, all of them picking on me and teasing me. Until you came along.'

Amanda closed her book, leaving a finger between the pages to mark the place. She looked up at Lewis in a way as to offer him support. She also knew that he wouldn't recognise what she was offering him.

'You've moved again.'

'Sorry, Lewis.'

She returned to her previous position, as best as she could remember it. Again, her gaze fell on the jotter pad in the grass.

'Can I read it?'

Lewis dived forward and pulled it away.

'It's not finished yet!'

'Okay, okay, I know that; but I'd love to read it though. Your stories, they are such a big part of you – which one is this...?'

Lewis flicked between sketching and fingering the pages of his notebook. He mumbled off a title, giving the excuse that it was a working title, and tried to explain the plot. Vaguely Peter Pan-ish, he said – what happens when Brit Pop met Regency England.

Amanda nodded. The explanation as described now sounded terrible, but she knew the plot from other things that Lewis had told her, and she knew it was good.

A breeze rustled through the leaves, and the sun was momentarily obscured by a passing cloud. The adult Amanda was alone, and her eyesight refocused on the words printed on the page. She flicked to the cover. A girl's face against an island scene, with what she had thought were birds in the sky, but now that she looked closer she decided they could be human figures. The title, in a cursive script—

FLYHT

It wasn't so much the title that caught her eye but the author's name: L.E. Summers. She'd just picked this off the table in the bookshop, and the name hadn't registered much to her until now. Why had she not realised? Louis Summers! He was using that daft alternative of his name, with his new partner's surname as his pseudonym. This was Lewis' book, and he had finally finished it!

She stared for some length at the cover again, remembering the man behind the pseudonym. Why had she not realised until now whose book this was? She turned it over to stare searchingly at the back cover. A short blurb and a load of choice quotes, but no author bio, nor one inside either. She sighed and found her place again, wondering now if she should start over and read it for clues.

L.E. Summers. How did Lewis become that persona? And why? What was in the name? She began reading again, but she had to keep scanning back through the book because she thought she had missed something when she was tired. In the end she skipped back to the beginning of that chapter, and began again.

After a deliberately dry preface by a university professor, whom Amanda couldn't help but see as her own father, the novel moved fast with an almost filmic quality. There was a diffidence to Clayton, that she recognised immediately from her own Lewis.

Lewis and Amanda sat on a fence in a field near the river Thames, watching their dappled reflections silhouetted in the river. A cloud drifted across in front of the sun, dulling the intensity of the river reflections and causing the air temperature to drop to a sudden and noticeable chill. Slowly the layers of cloud pushed past to reveal the sun again, a six-pointed star dancing across the surface of the river.

'What are you thinking?' Amanda said, looking up at Lewis.

Lewis shrugged.

'Just watching the reflections. The shapes, and the patterns,' he said. 'I wish I could draw or paint it.'

'You could.'

Lewis shook his head.

'It wouldn't come out right. In here,' he said, pointing to a space behind his eyes. 'I can see myself replicating that colour, the patterns; but from experience I just know that what I would end up with is a big, splodgy mess.'

Amanda laughed, provoking Lewis' giggling almost to the point of falling off the fence. Lewis leapt down, landing in the long grass on the bank of the river. The dark lines of his shadow crashed into the water mirror, and he stopped, squatting on the riverbank; looking down at himself looking up. The auburn-haired Amanda landed by his side, looking down, too, at the reflections. The other Lewis looked back and waved, as a different, fair-haired girl appeared at his side.

Shades of colour were stroked and dabbed onto the paper to create the illusion of the reflections in the water of earlier. Lewis and Amanda worked at an old dining room table, mixing artists' gouache with old poster paints and grubby watercolours.

They worked in the old playroom at the top of Bevington House. Amanda found it weird hearing Lewis – at thirteen – still call it a playroom; in reality, the long room in the attic formed almost a suite of rooms with Lewis' bedroom and his own bathroom, and the floor was somewhere that his parents rarely visited.

'That's brilliant!'

Amanda saw the river and the reflections in Lewis' painting straight away.

Lewis shrunk back shyly.

'Yours is better.'

They tore the pages from their sketchpads and left them to dry, while both started new paintings. Starting with the tested techniques from the first picture, they elaborated the scene. Amanda watched Lewis as he painted, working in silhouettes of their own heads in the foreground, and *then the image of their faces beyond looking back at them. Lewis' face was distorted by ripples, and Amanda's was mirrored still; in the murk behind, there was a third face; the face of an old lady with haunting eyes.*

'Why have you painted Miss Leroy into your picture?'

Lewis turned to Amanda.

'I haven't.'

He looked again at his painting as Amanda came closer, looking into the river patterning. The face was gone; Lewis was right, there was no Miss Leroy; but she had seen it there – hadn't she? She chewed on her lip and frowned.

The older Amanda pushed away a tear, as she leafed through a scrapbook that she had found in the bottom of the small box of possessions rescued from her parents' house. There were scarce few photos of Lewis and her together – mostly they were just sketches on cheap lined jotter paper or Basildon Bond, with a few home-developed prints in which Amanda always seemed to be more like a ghostly afterthought and pulling an odd catalogue pose, or a cover-shot that didn't quite fit.

She remembered him in the dark room at school, spending hours and hours in there with the red light and the smell of the chemicals, and the dodging and the burning of the light from the enlarger. He must have made these then, but she couldn't remember. She did remember long hours herself in the dark room. She had thought that it was the one place that she and Lewis could be alone together in school for – lessons in photographic techniques, it turned out. She smiled as she remembered Lewis; sweet, gentle Lewis. He never took advantage of her, not once. He didn't have it in him, not even if, sometimes, she might have wanted him to.

Amanda remembered the first time she had ever met Lewis. It was during orchestra, after school in the music room. She had been playing for a little over a year, and had recently been promoted to first oboe. Miss Leroy had ushered the small, awkward looking boy into the room a few minutes before the rehearsal began. He had been really nervous, and she had thought he'd needed a quite a bit of coaxing to join the rest of the orchestra. Even then she didn't know why, because he was good, really good, on his flute.

There were of course bits of the score that Lewis didn't understand – even she didn't know some of the terms and symbols, but they each asked the other and helped one another out, through snatches of shared conversation between the pieces, or in hushed voices while the strings were running through something. They bonded.

By the end of the second rehearsal they were friends, and by the third they were inseparable; and not just in orchestra either. Amanda couldn't remember ever having noticed Lewis at school before, but as they became desk buddies in every lesson, apparently they were classmates. She remembered that time through the music they rehearsed in orchestra, and for the amount of conversation they had devoted to Lewis telling Amanda about his life, and Amanda revealing her family.

Amanda stopped, brought up sharp by her reminiscing. That night a few weeks ago, when she had ended up on her parent's doorstep. She knew the way to the house, and what it was like, like it was her home; but as she thought of it now, it occurred to her that she didn't have any real memories of the house. She had memories, yes, of telling Lewis her about it; but none of going there with him. Every day after school they would go back to his home and play, practice their music, paint and draw, or do their homework; and then she would go home alone. Sometimes Lewis would walk her home, but not once did he go in with her. She remembered the streetlight now, an iron one like from Narnia on the corner opposite – that's where they would say goodnight. And then she would cross the street, looking back once before going in. Why did they never go to her house, she wondered. It was like her only memories of that house and her life with her mother and father was what she had told Lewis.

Amanda turned the page, to find a single black-and-white photograph from their wedding. Running her finger across the smooth, hand-developed bromide it was clearly one photograph, but again the faces didn't look quite right. Peering closer, she thought it was weird that her mother and father didn't look at all like the couple in the house who had refused her a room. People change, Amanda reasoned, as they got older; but these were like completely different faces. And her wedding dress? Why did she have no recollection of its style? The single most important dress she had ever worn, and all that she knew was that this was not it.

She flipped the scrapbook shut and shoved it away. What trick was being played with her own memories? Despite what Watts might have told her about making her own memories, she knew that she had to talk to Lewis.

7

The following morning Amanda woke with the dawn, determined to act on her promise to herself the night before. She washed, dressed, and wolfed down a hasty two slices of buttered toast and a mug of coffee, and left her rooms before she could change her mind. Hurrying down the staircase, she emerged into the quad and rounded it quickly. Amanda was just on the point of stepping out through the porter's lodge onto the street, when—

'Hey, Amanda! Wait up!'

Amanda stopped and turned as Watts caught her up, wearing T-shirt and jogging bottoms.

'Watts?'

'Just going on my morning run. You should come.'

'I...'

Amanda looked down at her own jeans, T-shirt, and pumps.

'You'll be fine.'

Watts began jogging on the spot, dancing around Amanda as she continued with her own indecision.

'Really not sure about it being fun,' said Amanda; but she agreed, and set off with Watts as they jogged down to the end of the side street onto The Broad.

At first they ran in silence through the all but deserted morning streets of Wren Hoe. They were barely around the corner before Amanda had to stop, clutching at her hips, bent forward, and wheezing. Watts waited, still jogging on the spot and encouraging her friend on. Steam vented out of the grills in The Broad where it met the chill of the morning air, and after the rumble of the metro beneath, a few early commuters climbed the steps onto the street to make their purposeful way to work.

'Ready?'

Amanda nodded, still wheezing.

'Ready!'

They zig-zagged through the narrow streets between the imposing college buildings and university science blocks, until they reached the open green of the parks, where they paused to allow Amanda a chance to catch her breath. At the far side of the field, some other lone runners were already completing their circuit.

'It is beautiful,' admitted Amanda as they set off again. 'Still don't get the attraction of running, though.'

'It's my only concession to exercise,' Watts laughed. 'It helps me feel better when I'm sinking pints at the old Turf.'

'Of course.'

They worked their way round the paths through copses and more formal planting to the river, where a light layer of mist settled across the water. Dappled sunlight rained down on them through a canopy of soft leaves. Halfway down Mesopotamia Walk, Watts suddenly stopped as Amanda tumbled into her with a squeal. Watts turned, shushing any further noise, and crouched low in silence.

'What are we looking for?' hissed Amanda.

'Otters,' Watts said, her voice hardly audible. 'Sometimes Ratties...'

Watts ducked under branches, treading carefully to watch the river; Amanda stayed still and watched, following her friend's gaze. There was a plopping into the water that turned their heads, but too late; if it was a water vole, it was long gone.

They returned to the path and continued on their run, arriving at the Weirhouse Gate just as a university proctor was unlocking it for the new day. Watts knew the thin, gaunt-faced young man, with the short, slick-backed hair and impossibly dark eyes. Amanda hung back until the conversation was over, and the man was on his way back down Mesopotamia Walk. Something about him made her distrust the man, and she felt confused as to why Watts was pally with him.

'Who was that?'

Watts shrugged.

'No idea. But I know him by sight, like lots of the security guys. This is his round.'

Amanda nodded. She looked over the edge of the bridge at the churning force of the river through the weir.

'Always thought it was a cushy number though, first round of the day – to unlock the gates of the parks. Beats working the doors of the union on a Friday night.'

Beyond the weirhouse they jogged up a narrow lane and across the marshes to Marsh Town Road, where they turned left to skirt round the foot of Headington Hill to take the causeway back across the park.

Back in a town now in the throes of waking up, Amanda was surprised when Watts took her past the turning to college. They slowed to a walk, turning off the main thoroughfares into passages off lanes, to a small café serving the tram drivers and street cleaners of the city. Watts ordered two full English breakfasts with enormous mugs of strong, black coffee, before moving to a table by the window with a plastic gingham table cloth.

'Sometimes it's good to get out of the college climbing room,' said Watts. 'And Molly does the best eggy bread.'

Amanda sat opposite Watts, trying to remember whether she liked fried breakfasts or not. She felt that it was probably not something that Lewis would cook for them.

A kitchen, twenty years ago. A thirteen-year-old Amanda sat at the kitchen table, trying to string coherent sentences together for a homework essay. She struck through whole lines with increasing frustration, before rewriting them afresh. Across the room, Louis did things with pasta and vegetables that she had no comprehension of. Amanda sat, watching Lewis make dinner as she chewed the end of her biro. He often made the dinner for her and his parents. He was such a good cook, and they were very lucky.

The waitress, with a sour face and attitude, brought two huge plates over and deposited them in front of Watts and Amanda. She didn't even wait for Amanda's kindly spoken thanks before slouching back to the kitchen. Amanda managed a wry laugh at the girl, and Watts shrugged.

The chiming of the shop bells, and the forced rubbing of the swollen wooden door in its frame signalled new customers. Amanda glanced over her shoulder, to see the proctor from the parks earlier enter with a couple of his mates; in the university uniform of dark, tailored suits, they could have been identical.

Amanda cut through her bacon and forked it up with a generous portion of eggy bread, beans, and black pudding. She glanced again across to the counter, where the security men were talking in low voices with each other. She turned and leaned over the table to whisper to Watts.

'Why do I think they are watching me?'

'Because they are,' Watts replied, with a mouth full of breakfast. She laughed at Amanda's reaction of fright. 'It's their job. They watch everyone, and report back. It's the rules.'

Amanda waited, frustrated for Watts to continue the explanation only to have her tucking in enthusiastically to the rest of her breakfast. It wasn't until after the plates were cleared and coffee downed, and they had left the café for the network of lanes back to college, that Watts spoke again.

'I thought you knew? The watchers, they are more scrupulous than ever – since *she* left the city. Every Master of every college is vying with every other.'

'I don't understand. Who's she? That's left the city?'

'You kidding me?' gaped Watts. 'Leroy, she that owned the city! Now she's gone there's a throne to be filled, and every college Master thinks it's him that will fill it.'

'What do they care about us, though?'

'We live in the colleges – we might repeat something said in the common room after dinner. The watchers, they feed off this stuff.'

'Now I know why Lewis liked living in the city.'

'You'd think that'd help, wouldn't it?'

Watts shook her head.

'It's not just the others out there in the town – non-university folk – who would like to take the city.'

Amanda tried to probe Watts for more, but they had arrived at their college lodge, and she wasn't going to be getting more out of her friend. They parted, Watts to her duties and Amanda to return to her room across the quad, there to continue to ponder over what Watts had told her. Miss Leroy was gone, and the city and university was rife with a power struggle over who was to replace her; but what interest was she to any of them in that matter?

Yes, she had known Miss Leroy; but that was back in a time before, when she had a life with Lewis. Everything had changed since then, so why did she feel that there was something still very much pressing?

Amanda sat opposite Lewis at the small dinner table in the kitchen of Bevington House. In the background was the warm, comforting sound of some Radio 4 documentary that neither one of them was listening to. She remembered this evening like it was yesterday. It was the day that Miss Leroy had paid them an unexpected visit.

The silence of the meal and the background hum of the radio was shattered by the sudden trill of the doorbell, and the sharp, rhythmic knocking that followed without delay.

'Who can that be?'

Lewis had shaken his head, before leaving his dinner to answer the door. Amanda sat, fork poised over her dinner, listening to every sound from the hall. She could hear as Lewis unlatched the door, dropped the chain, and then the low voices that followed. Amanda sat and picked at her food, preoccupied with who was at the door, and what was keeping Lewis so long. She strained to pick out words from the voices, but couldn't decipher anything more than reserved answers to questions she couldn't hear. Eventually she laid down her fork, and left the table to move from the kitchen, down the hall to where Lewis stood on the doorstop talking to a tall, old lady, with an unmistakable voice.

'Miss Leroy?' Amanda gasped. 'Is everything alright?'

Amanda approached the door, where the conversation was now interrupted.

'What's up? Lewis?'

Amanda looked from Miss Leroy, with her face illuminated by the unflattering porch light against the dark of the night beyond, to her husband.

'Everything's fine, Amanda,' said Lewis, with an unbelievable firmness. 'Miss Leroy was just checking I was okay with some work rotas – with Mr Gibbs on long-term sick. I told you.'

Amanda shrugged. He hadn't told her as far as she could remember. Miss Leroy turned her head, with a clipped precision that perfectly mimicked the sound of her voice as she spoke.

'And how are you, young Amanda?' she asked. 'Lewis is looking after you well, I trust?'

Amanda nodded.

'We look after each other very well, thank you.'

Miss Leroy nodded slowly. Amanda watched her carefully, then looked again to Lewis. Their conversation was at an end, but it was not finished...

Amanda sat at the small desk in her college room and finished writing up the details of her memory. She never had found out what the conversation was about. It hadn't seemed important back then. But now? Was that the first time that Lewis had kept something from her? She pulled out a picture from her purse, creased round the edges, of Lewis. Was that the beginning of what was going to be the unravelling of their relationship?

8

Watts sorted post into the pigeon holes in the porter's lodge, dropping fat brown packages, memos on folded single sheets of A4, and slim white windowed envelopes into fellows' and students' boxes. In the background, Classic FM sang out of the radio. She glanced up through the window and across the quad, to where she could see Amanda silhouetted in the dormer window of her upper floor.

'Boy – do you have my post, boy?'

Watts stopped still where she was. Her uniformed back faced the voice that commanded her. Her gaze drifted sideways to a mirror that only she could see – and to the man who had addressed her, reflected in it. He was an older gentleman, in traditional three-piece suit and cravat; the college bursar. Watts smiled, amused by the way that in lieu of a having been introduced he had just naturally assumed that she was a boy.

'Boy, do you hear me?'

Watts cast her eyes up to the pigeon holes and pulled down a stack of mail, turned around, and handed it over with the driest of smiles. The bursar took the mail and left, without another word or any recognition. Watts watched him go, before going back to her work. Sensing someone new in the room, Watts looked up to see the Dean's new personal assistant standing in the doorway.

'Alice Watson. Quiet evening on the front line?' quipped Matthew Leroy-Song, the young, besuited PA to the Dean, with the dark hair, and the equally dark and seductive eyes. He turned heads in every room, and he knew it.

Watts shrugged.

'Comme çi, comme ça...'

Matthew nodded, with the faintest of grins on his face.

'What's the deal with the new person in the Dodgson Suite?'

'Dr Jones, you mean, sir?'

Matthew nodded.

'Not, what you might call, one of our own?'

'I wouldn't know, sir,' Watts replied. 'I just deliver the post, arrange things, like...'

'Come now, Miss Watson, we all know that you don't *just* deliver post...'

He allowed the words to hang in the air, with just the merest tinge of accusation.

'Porter's Magic, I mean. Don't think that the rest of us don't know what it means.'

Watts returned Matthew's words with a steely gaze, and at that moment an older fellow popped his head round the door. With well-practiced ease, she gathered a bundle of envelopes from a pigeon hole and swiped a room key from the hook to pass across the desk.

'Professor Oakham.'

Watts bowed with a smile. The old professor croaked a reply, before shuffling back out to round the quad.

'My point, exactly,' said Matthew. 'You know what everyone needs without them asking.'

Watts laughed.

'It's only Professor Oakham?!'

'Only? I think you underestimate your skills in recognising the needs of others, Miss Watson.'

Watts laughed in a half-hearted, sarcastic fashion. She went back to her business, looking up again minutes later to find Matthew still there, standing a couple of paces back and watching her. She shook her head and returned to sorting the post. Out of the corner of her eye he was still there; saying nothing, just watching. She looked up with a wearisome gaze.

'Was there something else?' she asked.

At first Matthew did not respond, but he did step forward to the counter.

'There was, actually, one thing.'

Watts stared back, expectantly.

'I've seen you, trying to make sense of things,' he told her. 'There are some things that have taken place, though, that do not need to be made sense of. Things have happened, and they need no investigation. Those involved will play their parts. They do not need any help from you, Alice Watson.'

Watts laughed.

'I have literally no idea what—'

Matthew cut her off. With a short, sharp shake of the head, he continued.

'Do not make me be more specific. Do not chase answers that have *nothing* to do with you. Am I clear?'

Watts managed a nod. She waited until he had stepped back and turned left out of the lodge before shaking her head.

She left the lodge at 10:30 and locked the oak door behind her. Then she turned into the courtyard and walked fast and determinedly around the quad. Inside, she was still seething at what Matthew had said, and how he had said it. It had been working away at her for the last hour of her shift, and she had to talk to Amanda about it. She knew that it was her friendship with Amanda to which Matthew had been referring, and she also knew that none of it was any of his business.

And then she saw it, or rather them; two silhouettes in the square of light reflected down from the high stone college building onto the grassy centre of the quad. She stopped still. Even in reflected silhouette she could make out Amanda's unmistakable profile; and close by, facing her, the outline of Matthew Leroy-Song.

'No!'

Watts didn't mean to scream, but it just leapt from her mouth uncontrollably. She stared at the reflected silhouettes of the figures in the window, unable to move as they came together.

Amanda giggled and laughed, framed in front of the dormer window of her college rooms. She offered up her hands into Lewis' where he stood in front of her. He smiled at her, coy and insecure, just as always, and she smiled back at him with reassurances. They held each other, and looked into each other's eyes. And kissed. Again, and for longer. They came together in an embrace.

Lips touched. The shared warmth of their breath was felt. Amanda felt secure in Lewis' presence. She whispered her love to him, and he kissed her again.

In the quad, Watts knelt, winded by what she saw. Only an hour earlier, Matthew had stood in front of her and warned her off Amanda – basically told her to her leave her alone. And now this. The embraced couple in the window – when did this begin? She stared, transfixed by the reflections on the grass. Slowly, she managed to turn around and look up to the top floor window, just as they moved away, back into the room.

9

'No! Sarah screamed, sitting bolt upright in bed. Her heart beat furiously and her breathing was frantic. The visions of her dreams were still fresh in her mind as her breathing returned to normal. Her eyes began to readjust to the darkness, picking out the outlines of furniture and the windows of her room – the former attic bedroom of Bevington House that had been her father's all those years ago.

Sarah reached over and clicked on the light. The room was as it should be; her jewellery and bottles were on the dresser, and her books arranged on the shelves. Across the room, in the child's wicker chair, sat her father's own Ardizzoni Bear.

Everything was okay again, and Sarah could breathe once more. She allowed herself to drop back down in the comfort of her pillow. Her fingers handled the lamp switch; and then it hit her, the dream. She sat up sharply and swung her legs out of her bed. Throwing on her dressing gown she ran from the room, across the landing, and dived down the stairs.

The bedroom was empty, and down she went again, hardly touching the stairs, swinging herself round the newel post at the foot to skid to a halt in the lounge. Kathryn looked up from where she was curled up on the sofa in her dressing gown, enraptured in her late-night reading.

'Where's Dad?!' Sarah screamed, in a trembling, faltering voice.

Kathryn looked up.

'Seriously? You know it's his Indie Author meet-up tonight. I think he was going to the pub with Beth and Polly after. He should be back soon—'

'No – it's too late...'

Kathryn glanced at her watch.

'It's barely half-eleven.'

Sarah froze. She glanced across the room, at the skeleton clock on the mantelpiece. It's timing was erratic, but it worked. As she stared, the minute hand moved past the six.

'I – I thought—'

Kathryn slipped a bookmark into her book and set it down next to her.

'Sarah?' What's wrong?'

Kathryn sat forward, watching the teenager with concern. She was still trying to reconcile how she should be to the girl. Sister? Or stepmother? Or just a friend? It was a relationship that was never completely obvious, and now, with Sarah troubled and upset, it was awkward.

'Call him,' Sarah said sharply, and suddenly. 'He's not at the pub.'

Kathryn approached Sarah cautiously.

'It's happening again. It's her, I know it is.'

'Sarah, it's fine.'

Sarah shook her head. She spied Kathryn's mobile on the coffee table and snatched it up. She thumbed through the phone and hit dial on Louis' name; then the ringing, the pulses of a connection, and...

Voicemail. Sarah quit the call and slapped the phone back into Kathryn's palm. She shook her head.

'He's with *her*.'

'You mean Amanda? She's your mother,' said Kathryn. 'If anything, I'm the other woman in our relationship.'

'She was using Dad. You *saved* him,' argued Sarah. 'And she's not real.'

'And Louis is not with her, Sarah,' said Kathryn, with a determination equal to that time in the Duke. She remembered Amanda then, and the thought that she had tried something new wormed its way inside of her.

Sarah was staring back, unconvinced, and obviously waiting for proof to backup Kathryn's assurances. All Kathryn could manage was a weak, hesitant frown.

'Sorry—'

Sarah sighed and swung past Kathryn to sink onto the sofa, crashing her head into her arms.

'It was just so real. And then I couldn't find him. I thought...'

'It's fine,' said Kathryn. She moved to sit next to Sarah, offering her shoulder – an arm – for support, but in a way that was stilted and awkward.

A key turned into the latch, and the fumbling at the door echoed through the house. Both Sarah and Kathryn looked up, staring out the lounge and into the hall, as the front door squeaked and scrunched open in the twisted and swollen frame. Louis pushed the door shut with a hefty wallop that shook the house.

Louis carried on putting his satchel down on the hall table, and hanging up his scarf and jacket, before he moved through to the lounge, loosening the top button of his shirt as he greeted Kathryn.

'—and Sarah?' he said. 'Hey, what's wrong?'

Sarah answered with the longest of stares, from the biggest pair of eyes. She gulped and shook her head.

'Bad dream,' said Kathryn. 'It really shook her up.'

Louis lowered himself to look with concern at Sarah.

'Sarah? What's wrong? What scared you?'

Louis followed his question with silence. He watched his daughter carefully, where her head had drooped with her gaze fallen to the floor. He glanced up at Kathryn, sat alongside his daughter and offering the girl a loose cradling of support. He turned again to Sarah and spoke her name, repeating the question.

Sarah looked up sharply, and swiftly struck him across the face. 'You!'

She pulled herself from Kathryn's loose embrace and stormed from the room, leaving Louis teetering on his haunches. He clutched at the coffee table to steady himself, then began to get up, calling after Sarah; but she was gone, stomping her way back upstairs. Louis got up to follow.

'Leave her, Louis.'

'But — I don't understand...'

'Nor do I, not properly. She came down in a state, because she thought – dreamt – that you were with Amanda.'

Louis laughed.

'I'm sorry. I shouldn't laugh, but...'

Louis picked himself up and moved to a nearby armchair.

'No, it's just – the idea, it's just so preposterous.'

Kathryn smiled, and nodded. Eventually she pulled out her book again, and interspersed reading with covert glances at Louis where he sat, clearly brooding and over-thinking the accusation. Suddenly Louis got up out of the armchair and offered his phone to Kathryn, before leaving it on the coffee table while he poured himself a finger of whisky.

'Call Beth,' he said. 'Ask her. Writing group – we didn't get out of there 'til after half nine, and then we all went to The Downloader for a drink after.'

'I believe you Louis,' replied Kathryn. 'But you need to be careful. We need to be careful.'

Louis looked up, with his characteristic expression of befuddlement.

'The other week – when we were at The Duke – before you got there – she was there, your wife, asking questions.'

'She's not my wife, she's—'

'I know that, Louis! But you know what I mean. It's just easier to call her that.'

Louis apologised, sheepishly.

'Anyway, what would we know that she doesn't already?'

Kathryn shrugged.

'You going to pour me one of those?'

Louis smiled. He returned to the sideboard, turned over another glass, and poured a second finger of whisky. Kathryn took the glass and sipped from it. She felt the whisky burn as it went down her throat; it was good.

'I really thought Amanda would have been swept away when we freed ourselves from Leroy.'

'She was a part of my loneliness—' mused Louis.

'Exactly!' agreed Kathryn.

'Amanda was part of your imagination, and Leroy was going to use her to be reborn for the next however many years. Why does she still exist?'

Louis stared vacantly into his glass, turning it slowly in his hand, and watched the room swirl about in it with reflections from the lights.

'We probably should go and see her,' said Louis eventually. He took in Kathryn's nervous response. 'Together I mean. Find out what she wants...'

*

Watts leant back on the door to her room and closed it, letting out the biggest of sighs. She crossed the small cottage, filled with the forty years of her father's life, and sat down on the edge of her bed. Again, she sighed deeply – thinking all the time of Amanda in the window, with that man.

Long day, she considered. Dragging the palm of her hand across her face she tried to squeeze some life out her eyes. She cast her porter's hat to one side, and loosened her tie and the top buttons of her shirt.

Don't think that the rest of us don't know what it means.

Watts heard Matthew's words echo back through her mind. *What game was he playing?* Yes, that was it – a game. Matthew was playing her as a pawn, and Amanda too – but to what end? She thought of him standing at the desk, instructing her how to do her job. And then she thought of Amanda standing in that window; and, impossibly, with her husband.

Louis lay on his side in bed, knees tucked up like a child and eyes scrunched shut, trying to will himself to sleep. He remembered the last time he saw Amanda – just the once, after Kathryn broke the spell at Miss Leroy's funeral. Amanda had been there at a distance from the small party in the city cemetery. She hadn't known anything of what had happened, free of any of her created past.

The sting of Sarah's hand slapping his face woke him again from the verge of sleep. Sarah. She was the gift of his creativity, just like Amanda was before. And Sarah was still with him, so why would a parting at a funeral make the wife any less real?

Lewis?

Louis froze where he lay at the sound of her voice; so much like Kathryn's, but she *never* called him that.

What's wrong?

Louis squeezed his eyes closed, pressing the sound of her voice from his head. Behind him he could hear the sound of her breathing, and reaching across him the gentle touch of her embrace. Louis shivered. He wanted it to be Kathryn behind him in the bed, but he was too afraid to look. It felt like Kathryn's gentle touch, rather than the imagined presence of Amanda; but now, a year on those feelings had merged into one – the imagined replaced by the real.

It wasn't until after the letter had been slipped under the door that Watts woke from her daydreaming. In her dream state she had heard the person at the door, and now lay on her back in bed, listening as the footsteps retraced their steps up the passage across the threshold of the building and round the paved path of the quad.

Eventually Watts lifted herself from her bed and moved to investigate what had come through the door. She saw the letter as she approached, lying on the floor just inside the door where someone had slid it in from underneath. She stooped and picked it up, an envelope of thick, posh paper, and blank. She turned it over to find it blank on the other side too.

Watts stared at it, turning it over in her hands, and considered it. It stirred some memory inside of her.

PART TWO

Together

affettuoso

1

When Amanda left the cloistered walls of the college for work she was surprised to see, not Watts but, the older, gruffly-spoken security guard on the front desk. When Watts was again away from the lodge at the end of the day she found it to be very odd, but supposed that the girl must have had herself a day off.

The next morning Amanda looked in to the lodge again, so sure that Watts would be at her post that she began to greet her friend as she turned the corner. She stopped when faced with the small, bald-headed, tortoise-like old porter.

'Oh, I thought—'

Amanda shrugged, turned, and came face-to-face with a besuited Matthew Leroy-Song.

'Miss Jones?'

'Nothing. Really.' Amanda said, respectfully apologetic. 'Sorry!'

She turned and fled the lodge and ran to the end of the road. For a moment she was fifteen again, chasing, and being chased by, Lewis. She stood, bent double and wheezing on the corner of Broad Street, as a smile spread across her face. She stopped to check her purse was still in her bag like a grown-up, then walked on until she reached her favourite coffee shop.

On a whim, she eschewed her normal latte for the strawberry milkshake of her teenage years and proudly walked with it across town to work, sucking it up through a straw with a beaming grin across her face.

At The Press, Amanda flashed her pass and pushed her way through the turnstiles, feeling like she did on that first day: fresh out of college, with the importance of a new, proper, job. In the quad she stopped to wait for Charlotte as the girl finished locking up her bike, and then walked with her up to the production offices, located under the eaves of the old building. When she slid open the partition door to her office she couldn't remember the details of the conversation, but it had been light-hearted, inconsequential, and just fun. She sat back in her chair as her computer started up and texted him.

After lunch in the work canteen, Amanda walked through the production office, greeting a few colleagues by name, before slipping into her office. After her earlier concerns, the day-to-day nature of her job had fallen into place. She had found that most of her work came to her in the form of emails with links to budget spreadsheets, and schedules to review and confirm, or minutes and reports to take forward. When it came to contract defence and journal bids to the academic societies, she had found the likes of Charlotte and Eleanor were more than willing to be empowered to produce much of the legwork in producing the bids. In this way, all she had to do was present the findings and make decisions that were already all but in place. She still felt sure that the Amanda that Lewis knew would have had more in-depth knowledge, but the gap in her memories in that respect no longer scared her.

Another class filed from the room to go to first period; Lewis checked his phone for messages quickly, smiling at what he read. He pinged off a reply and switched to airplane mode, before dropping it back into his satchel. He sat at his desk at the front of class and looked out at the row of empty desks waiting to be filled. The door to the room clattered open and the first class of the day piled in. Soon he was picking up from where he had left off last week, with the forms and structures of haiku.

Kathryn pulled the front door of Bevington House closed behind her and set off across the garden, her feet scrunching on the gravel. She stopped and looked back at the tall Edwardian house with its crawling matt of ivy shrouding the brick walls. For a moment she was back on that day months earlier when she had come looking for Louis. Above in the holly tree birds sang. She wished that she could tell the songs apart.

She turned again and continued across the gravel, to let herself out through the solid wooden gate in the high stone wall. Some way up the road she could see a tram approaching, but she struck off across the road and down the road opposite. It was a clear, bright morning, and she decided that she wanted the walk.

Crossing the railway and canal she enjoyed a bright sunny walk down the Eastern edge of Port Meadow, before heading back into the streets of Jericho. Without consciously deciding it, Kathryn found herself cutting up from the canal towards Walton Street along Juxon Street, to pass outside her old house. Just as she was passing the door, it creaked open with the foot-thumping help it needed that she knew so well, and Matthew Leroy-Song emerged into the daylight. Kathryn ducked her head, shielded her face with her hand, and hurried on.

'Kathryn! Wait up!'

Kathryn groaned, as she drew to a halt and turned to face Matthew. She crossed her arms and allowed her foot to tap slowly, impatiently, on the pavement. *What had made her come this way?*

'You walking this way?'

Matthew gestured onwards, and they started on their way again.

'Well, obviously.'

'So, how's life? Lewis?' asked Matthew.

'It's Louis,' said Kathryn. 'And life is good, thanks.'

Matthew nodded.

'And you?' asked Kathryn, with mock interest. 'You and Nina still together, I see?'

'She's a good laugh.'

Kathryn nodded. Why was he walking with her, she wondered.

'I'm sorry,' began Matthew. Kathryn fired an incredulous stare at him in return before he could continue. 'We never get to see each other now.'

Kathryn shrugged.

'I felt that we got on well.'

Kathryn stared, so much so that she had to stop walking, dumb-founded. She began walking again with a quickened pace.

'We have *nothing* in common with each other!'

'Oh come on!' Matthew drawled.

'Yes. Really,' Kathryn told him. 'Now if you'll excuse me I've got to get to work, and you're really slowing me down.'

A tram rattled into the Walton Street stop. Kathryn made her excuses and ran across the street, and up the steps into the panelled interior. As the tram set off again, passing by the grand frontage of The Press, Kathryn watched the figure of Matthew shrink into the distance. She tried to figure him out but found it impossible, beyond knowing that she simply didn't trust him.

As Kathryn settled into her office chair at her desk in Fairyland Books, she found the image of Matthew outside her old house that morning still clear in her mind. It annoyed her that he was still there in her thoughts, and that, if she was honest, he was right; she did like him. Or at least, at some level, she liked the idea of liking him. He was, as any girl would have to admit, drop-dead gorgeous and smooth-talking. He was impossible not to like. And that just made her hate him even more.

Lewis packed his pencil case and his books into his satchel and slipped on his corduroy jacket from the back of his chair. Stopping to look down the rows of empty desks and chairs, he reflected on the day. That last lesson had been a really good one; Form B3 were always a really good class who shared some really dynamic conversations, and today had been no exception. He felt his own creative mind buzzing from the last hour. He smiled, shouldered his satchel, and left the room.

After retrieving his bicycle from the sheds at the back of the school, Lewis cycled out of the school grounds and across town, through the centre, and into the Jericho part of town. He dismounted outside the gatehouse to The Press, kissing Amanda in greeting where she stood waiting.

'Good day?' she asked him.

He grinned, answering enthusiastically as they walked on together around the corner, laughing and joking about their respective days. Amanda sat at a table on a terrace overlooking the canal. Her finger stroking the condensation from the outside of her gin and tonic as she waited for Lewis to return. She looked about, at the children on the bank opposite, and the family of swans on the water below. In the early evening light, the day was peaceful. She looked up as Lewis returned from the bar, with new drinks and some snacks. She smiled – her and her man – just the two of them.

*

Kathryn alighted from the tram onto Woodstock Road. She stepped past the front of the tram and crossed the street, letting herself in through the gate with the blue peeling paintwork in the high, creamy-yellow Cotswold stone wall. She crossed the gravel path and let herself in to the house. Sarah was curled in an armchair, devouring a book. Kathryn dumped her bag in the hall and moved through to the kitchen to make herself a drink.

Kathryn took her mug of tea and went to find Louis in his study. After everything that had happened, Louis had decided not to go back to teaching, but to concentrate on his writing. They had converted one of the upstairs rooms into a study – or library as Louis preferred to think of it – where he could sit and work. It had a view out onto the garden from both windows in the gabled corner of the house, and was large enough that in addition to Louis' antique desk, they could furnish it with a large leather armchair for Louis, and a daybed that Kathryn would use sometimes if she joined Louis for a while. It was where she retreated to now after she greeted him with a kiss, to sit cross-legged on the bed and lift the lid of her laptop.

'How's it going?'

Louis nodded. He looked up, gazing idly out of the window.

'Today, I think, has been a good day.'

He chuckled quietly to himself.

'You know how sometimes the words, they just don't come. The story, it goes nowhere?'

He glanced round as Kathryn nodded.

'Today, it's all just worked.'

Kathryn smiled and nodded. Her gaze fell to her computer screen and the stream of new messages coming in.

'I think I finally feel like a writer,' said Louis. 'You know, being in change of all these characters' lives, and where they're going. Instead of—'

'Instead of being a character in someone else's story?' added Kathryn.

Louis frowned, with a nod.

'Or?'

'Yeah, I know; that to.'

Louis looked down at his writing and re-read the last few lines. He turned back a page, or two, scanning the text, then returned to those sentences again and struck through them decisively.

'This is my story now.'

He said it as much for himself as anyone else.

Outside the canal-side bar, Amanda blinked herself awake in the evening light. In front of her, cupped in her hand was her now empty glass of gin and tonic. Dazed and disorientated, she looked about, sure that another had been brought to her. But by whom? She was sitting alone at the table; and by the looks of it, had been for some time.

She finished her drink, and eventually, tired of waiting, left the bar to walk home across town to her college rooms. When she arrived back at the college she still felt weird – like she had forgotten something. She walked through the lodge in a daze, and barely registered that it was still the old porter on duty. She rounded the quad and stomped up the staircase to her room, to collapse in a chair almost immediately.

2

'Wake up, Alice dear!' Amanda said, as she shook her friend's shoulder where she sat slumped on a bench in the Fellows' rose garden. And then: 'Why, what a long sleep you've had!' she added, as Alice began to stir.

Amanda watched carefully as Alice awoke, at first groggy and disorientated.

'Watts? What happened? How long have you been sat here?'

Watts shrugged.

'No idea. I have though – had such a curious dream.'

Amanda stared expectantly, awaiting the explanation as to the dream in question, until–

Amanda lay, staring out across the folds of her pillow. The morning light filtered in through the windows to a room that seemed, from her perspective, to be on its side. She lay there, wide-eyed, trying to cling on to the story that had been unfolding, even as it slipped further from her, like loose pages drifting away in the wind.

Watts? What about Watts? Amanda was suddenly wide-awake again. She flung herself out of bed and threw herself through the bathroom, getting dressed before bounding down the staircase and skidding out into the quad. She slowed to a fast walk round the quad, before turning into a side passage that led to the Fellows' garden.

She broke into a run through the maze of walkways to the rose garden, and to the bench from her dream. Not unsurprisingly, and with some relief, she found the bench deserted. She mouthed her relief and turned again to return to the college buildings. As she crossed the lawns, she saw the little cottage on the far side of the college grounds, and remembered Watts pointing out her father's cottage. A faint plume of smoke could be seen drifting up from the chimney, and there was a light on in one of the windows.

Watts. Amanda made the decision and turned off the path to cross the grounds in as much of a straight line as possible. The cottage sat right on the edge of the college grounds, leaning up against the high stone perimeter wall. Amanda made straight for the front door and wrapped loudly on it with the knocker. When no answer came she knocked again; and, after a further few minutes; tried the handle. The door protested a bit where it had swollen in the frame, but it gave, and Amanda was able to push it open and step inside.

The front door opened immediately into the lounge, and she saw Watts, sprawled fast asleep in an armchair by the fire. Amanda rushed to her and leant close, shaking her awake.

'Wake up, Watts!'

As she shook her friend awake, she remembered how similar her words sounded to the ones in her dream just a few hours earlier. She laughed with gentle mocking as Watts stirred.

'Why, what a long sleep you've had.'

'Ugh,' Watts grunted, squinting open her eyes as she came too. 'I've had such a curious dream.'

'Watts, how long have you been here? Asleep?'

Watts was still dazed, struggling to recognise where she was, or who was with her. Struggling to sit up by herself, Amanda helped her into a more upright sitting position.

'You look dreadful.'

'Thanks,' said Watts. 'You really know how to flatter a girl.'

'Well it's true!'

Amanda stood and crossed the room to find a glass, which she filled with water and returned to Watts.

'How long have you been asleep for?'

Watts' brow furrowed as she narrowed her gaze, trying to remember. Eventually she relaxed the tense muscles and shook her head.

'Got no idea. Don't even know what day it is now.'

Amanda passed the glass to Watts, and she drank it down gladly. She handed it back empty, with an expectant look on her face. Amanda took it and went to refill the glass.

'So, what happened?' she called from the kitchen. 'You been sick? Or on holiday?'

Watts twisted around in her chair to look through to the kitchen, as Amanda returned with a refilled glass. She shook her head.

'I wish I knew. Think I've just been asleep...'

'All this time? It's been days.'

'I don't know. Really! I remember coming home and finding a letter on the floor, and then...'

Watts' voices trailed off. Amanda began tidying the house and tackling what could have been a week's worth of washing that surrounded the sink of the tiny cottage kitchen.

'What was in it? The letter?' Amanda continued to probe.

Watts sat forward, shaking her head.

'I don't know if I even opened it. Really, I don't remember.'

'So where is it?' Amanda asked, emerging from the kitchen with a towel and a pint glass.

Watts shook her head.

'Must be...'

She got up and crossed the room to the front door, stooping to the doormat.

'I would have come in, seen the letter, then – normally I just open it.'

Amanda set both glass and towel down and crossed to the hearth.

'But you were in the chair – so...'

She took up some fire tongs and started poking at the grate.

'Maybe you burnt it?'

Watts didn't answer. Amanda turned and saw her standing, staring straight ahead.

'Watts?'

Watts nodded towards the mantle. Amanda turned and looked – at the oblong of white paper propped up next to the clock. She plucked it off the mantelpiece and turned it over in her hand, before passing it to Watts.

'It's blank.'

Watts shook her head and recoiled from the letter.

'What if what happened before...? I can't touch it.'

Amanda shrugged.

'I'm sure you were just tired.'

Watts shrank back from the letter.

'I – I can't,' she croaked. 'Please, you open it.'

Amanda frowned and continued to offer the letter to Watts, but she looked so frightened and pitiful over it that she eventually took the letter back, shrugged, and tore open the flap. She pulled out a single, folded sheet of crisp, white Basildon bond paper. It was blank. She turned it over. Blank too.

'Curiouser and curiouser,' mused Amanda.

'What is it?' asked Watts. 'Seems like it should be a letter written by the prisoner – to someone.'

'It must have been that,' said Amanda. 'Unless it was written to nobody; which isn't usual, you know.'

'What does it mean?' asked Watts.

Amanda shook her head.

'Why go to the trouble of sending you a blank letter? It doesn't make sense.'

'Being asleep for a week doesn't make sense,' scoffed Watts. 'Someone did this to me.'

Amanda nodded.

'Matthew.'

Watts looked up, not unsurprised by the name that Amanda volunteered.

'He's warned me off talking to you—'

'Same here.'

'Why though? What's our friendship to him?'

Watts shrugged. She took the blank letter and turned it over, then turned it over again.

'Clever though; a blank letter. It's the ultimate in untraceable threats.'

'It's also the first page of an unwritten story.'

3

Louis wasn't sure what it was that woke him, but he lay still in his bed, all but holding his breath, listening to the silence of the old house at night. Pipes gurgled, and woodwork heaved and groaned, almost as if the house was talking to itself. Behind him, came the slow, rhythmic breathing of Kathryn sleeping.

Had he heard something that had woken him? He strained to listen harder, for sounds in the garden or on the street outside. Or had it been his own anxious thoughts that had woken him?

Louis couldn't sleep, and eventually he eased himself out of bed. Careful not to wake Kathryn, he drew a dressing gown around him and stepped out onto the landing. He padded downstairs, one step at a time, and with each step he seemed to get younger.

When Lewis reached the foot of the stairs he was the eleven-year-old boy of his memories, and the house was a cold and foreboding place. Something – a woman's cough – disturbed the silence, and Lewis froze on the spot. Eventually, he turned to scamper back upstairs—

'Lewis? Is that you?' came the woman's voice, clipped and cold.

Slowly Lewis turned and returned to the ground floor, from where Miss Leroy was summoning him. He approached the lounge door tentatively, pushing it open wider. Across the room he could see Miss Leroy, sitting not in a comfortable armchair, but at her leather-topped desk. When he stepped into the room, it was to the school office on the other side of Wren Hoe.

'Yes, miss?'

'I've heard reports, Lewis,' Miss Leroy began. 'That your imagination may be getting ahead of yourself.'

'I – I–' Lewis said, stumbling over any kind of reply.

Miss Leroy clicked the cap of her fountain pen back into place and turned it over in her hands. She lifted her gaze to the small boy standing opposite her.

'You have been given a great gift, Lewis. You must not abuse it by imagining things that shouldn't be invented.'

'I haven't – I don't–' Lewis stuttered.

Miss Leroy remained silent to the protestations, choosing instead to hold the small boy in her gaze.

'Go back upstairs and remember who your relationships are with.'

Lewis shook his head and gulped.

'I don't have a relationship!'

'Not yet, no,' said Miss Leroy. 'But you will. A one true love to guide you; yours without question.

The eleven-year-old boy in front of the headmistress stood and stared, his eyes big and wide and uncomprehending. Miss Leroy continued to hold Lewis in her gaze, breathing the name of a girl through her lips.

Amanda. Amanda...

Lewis stood and stared, transfixed by Miss Leroy's penetrating eyes; and the reflection of a girl with auburn hair, seemingly reflected in her pupils.

Amanda!

Louis jolted awake. Sitting upright in bed he looked down to his side where Kathryn lay sleeping, stirring maybe.

He eased himself back down into the covers and lay there on his side, looking at Kathryn next to him. Kathryn shifted in her sleep, and stirring herself half awake, she questioned if Louis was okay.

'I'm fine,' he said in hushed whisper. 'Just a restless dream—'

He settled back into the covers again and pulled them close around him. As he closed his eyes for sleep, he remembered the afternoon in the rose garden; the metamorphosis of Miss Leroy into Amanda - the music, and the flood in the standing pool. The wave washed through his mind again, bringing Miss Leroy's face rising out of the blackness and breaking over him, before flooding out into foam across the garden to seep back into the ground. As sleep overtook Louis, he was left with thoughts as to whether Miss Leroy could somehow have survived.

By morning, Louis' mind was bustling with related and competing thoughts. Up and down the stairs and corridors of Bevington House, he kept seeing echoes of Miss Leroy, and of Amanda. Some of his thoughts he kept shyly to himself, and some he tried (and failed) to articulate to Kathryn and Sarah variously, as they got themselves ready for work and school.

'I think we should move,' announced Louis, as Sarah was pushing her schoolbooks into her bag; Kathryn had her coat on.

'What?' both Kathryn and Sarah replied simultaneously, and with equal surprise.

'We've just allowed our lives to fall in around us in these walls, but - she's here - they're here - still. We don't have to live here...'

'It's our home...' said Sarah.

Kathryn stared at Louis, almost with a scowl.

'We'll talk about this later, yeah?'

'It makes sense though. I mean, we should never be able to afford this house really. And who's to say we're not still bound by some of Leroy's magic?'

'Later, Louis,' reaffirmed Kathryn. She reached up to a plant a farewell kiss on his lips.

All too quickly, Kathryn and Sarah had scooped up their bags, said their goodbyes, and left the house; Louis was left alone, standing in the large Edwardian hallway, with his brain firing thoughts and memories at him. He returned to the kitchen to clear away the breakfast, but at every turn he found himself seeing echoes of either Miss Leroy, Amanda, or his life living alone.

He reached up to open a kitchen cabinet and felt like he was wiping away dust from when he had shared the kitchen with Amanda. His hand waivered, feeling the presence of Amanda stood behind him, but too scared to turn and face her. He saw his mobile on the counter in front of him and snatched it up.

'Beth, hi!' Louis greeted the voice at the other end, after he had quickly dialled her number. 'Sorry. I know you're about to go into class, but – what do you say to meeting up for lunch? I could really do with a chat.'

By the end of the morning, Louis had managed to clear away breakfast, got two loads of washing through the machine, cleaned the house, and written a passable attempt at the next chapter. A little before noon, he shouldered his satchel over his corduroy jacket and wheeled his bicycle out of the hallway into the garden, ready to set off on his ride across town.

Beth had only just arrived at *The Downloader* as Lewis free-wheeled across the end of the side street, bridging the pavement and the small forecourt. They went into the pub together and ordered a sandwich with their pints, before finding a quiet table under the window.

'So, what's the matter?'

Beth took a large first sip from her ale. Louis placed down his own beer in front of him and leaned closer.

'I think I'm going mad.'

'Only going?' Beth laughed. 'Sorry, what now?'

Louis stared at his friend with a bit of a scowl. He shook his head.

'I thought things were going to be normal. We ended Miss Leroy's control on my life – the imaginary wife thing – but Beth, why do I still keep on seeing her?'

Beth remained quiet, gazing at her friend with uncertainty.

'Things were never going to be normal, Louis,' said Beth. 'And there's Sarah. She's always going to be a reminder.'

'I guess,' said Louis. 'This is different now. I'm happy in my life with Kathryn, and – but I'm still getting memories creeping in; and not of the past, but of the here and now...'

'The now here,' added Beth.

Louis nodded, enthused by his friend's understanding.

'Why is Amanda – my imaginary wife – still informing my life choices?'

'Is she?'

Louis nodded.

'I wake up in the middle of the night and it's still *her* house. It's *her* that I'm writing about in my next book. It's like I can't escape.'

Beth frowned.

'Maybe you need to write her out of your system?'

'Maybe.'

A silence lingered across the table between them, broken only by a barmaid bringing their baguettes to them. Louis sat in front of the crusty granary bread, and Beth watched him before making a start on her own.'

'If it helps, it's weird at school, too.'

Louis looked up as he listened to his friend.

'You know how she ran the school – it's all still there, but with less floral dresses and stiletto heels.'

Beth grinned.

'We call them The Management – men in suits – they make their decisions according to every league table and white paper. We kind of miss the freedom to teach that Leroy gave us.'

'She didn't give us any freedom...'

'From the government's prescribed strategy, she did!' Beth said, getting impassioned now. 'That's why we miss her.'

When lunch was finished, Louis said an awkward goodbye to Beth. As he cycled away from the pub, it felt wrong that he wasn't going back to school. He went the slightly longer route down across the flood plains, and through the university parks. When he arrived home at Bevington House, he had decided what had been on his mind all day. He found the number in the phone book and dialled through on the hall phone. With the booking made for that afternoon, Louis went back to his writing upstairs in the study, until the doorbell chimed shortly after three o'clock.

Alfred Williams was the only surviving member of Ernst & Williams estate agents, and had an affable, slightly bumbling charm that was impossible not to like. He was joined by Lionel, a much younger man about Louis' age, with slicked back hair and a slippery, greased voice; Lionel was so much the antithesis of Alfred's charm, that Louis doubted how they could possibly be related, which, clearly, they were.

Louis offered them both a cup of freshly brewed coffee, and they sat for a few minutes in the lounge as he gave Alfred a potted history of the house for the sales material. Then he began the tour, during which Lionel took over proceedings with his smartphone attachment to take laser room measurements that were fed directly into an app.

Bevington House was a large Edwardian property with multiple doors and staircases, many original features, and some odd quirks from its history of being at times one large house or sub-divided into separate apartments. Showing Lionel and Alfred around now, Louis found the house was almost directing him down which corridor to take them next. He kept on opening doors expecting to find a room, or showing them a cupboard only to find another room beyond. In time Louis removed himself from the tour and hid himself in the comfort of his study, while Lionel and Alfred continued to document the rooms.

'It's quite some building,' Alfred told Louis, after finding him again.

'Did you find everything?' asked Louis. 'Sorry, it just seemed easier to leave you both to it.'

Alfred nodded. The old man glanced around at Lionel, who smiled slyly.

'I think we have everything we need. You've been most helpful.'

Lionel glanced down at his tablet and scanned a couple of screens.

'We'll draw up the contract for you, pop them through the door, then as soon as you're ready, sign them and we'll – proceed.'

'I'm happy to sign now if you want. I've made the decision – I can't change it. As far as I'm concerned...'

'Of course, of course,' Lionel interrupted. 'We'll still need the formalities of the paperwork, but we understand; and I think I have a couple of clients in mind already.'

Louis nodded; in honesty, he had stopped listening. He saw the two men out, watched them depart, then returned indoors. He stood and stared down the length of the hall – a hall that grew in his mind, or one that he shrank into, until he was an eleven-year-old boy standing at one end of a huge, tiled corridor that stretched the length of the house.

'Lewis! What have you done?'

Lewis heard Amanda, and the upset in her shrill girlish voice. He turned and leapt for the latch of the front door. He slipped out the key and pulled it open, before fleeing out into the garden and running and hiding in the shrubbery.

4

Matthew Leroy-Song stood in his college room, looking down at a chessboard on which were placed delicately carved wooden figures. He turned over in his hands, again and again, one remaining figure: that of a girl the image of Amanda, down to the smudged red pigment in the wood that was aligned with her hair. He frowned and placed the figure down firmly on the board next to another slightly smaller, and paler 'Alice' figure. He crossed to the mantelpiece and pulled a bell-pull sharply and deliberately. Minutes later there was a knock at the door, and a young, besuited servant was waiting on him.

'Sir?'

Matthew glanced again at the chessboard.

'I need you to take a message – you know who to. It seems that the pawns are moving. I need to convene a meeting of the others.'

'It is your wish, my lord,' the servant answered him. 'Will there be anything else?'

Matthew bowed his head. Then, slowly, he reached up a finger to his forehead as if to extract a thought.

'Bring me Nina, too.'

'As you wish.'

The servant bowed and left.

Amanda led Watts from the porter's cottage by the hand and ducked under the low branches of elderly trees until they were crossing the wide college lawns. When she seemed about to release her friend's hand, Watts tightened the grip. Closer to the college buildings they joined the throng of students making for the dining room; groups of girlfriends and guy mates and couples, some in the established routine, and others in the first flits of a relationship. Amanda and Watts walked through all of them and round the paved quad, turning to ascend the few short stairs and cross a lobby into the vaulted, candlelit dining hall. In the cafeteria, Amanda released Watts' hand as they took up trays and chose their meals. Back in the hall, they found seats on opposite sides of a brass candelabra on one of the long benches.

'Well, this is romantic!' joked Watts.

Amanda smiled, if awkwardly, constantly scanning the room and the High Table.

'Where is he?' she urged. 'He needs to see us.'

'Matthew? You're sure that it was him?'

'It has to be. His aunt owned this town. He's got to want to replace her. He's got to think it's his right.'

Watts forked up her dinner hungrily, as if only realising now how long it had been since her last meal. She devoured huge mouthfuls at almost twice the rate as Amanda, although Amanda did always have half her attention on the comings and goings around them in the hall.

'Look, there,' Amanda said suddenly, nodding towards the high table. Watts turned to watch, as Matthew made his way onto the raised platform along with several college fellows.

'Stop staring.'

Amanda frowned, and returned her gaze to her dinner. She noticed Watts' own, all but cleared plate.

The dining hall was filling with students now, each finding their own places, either on their own, or in small, large, or rowdy groups. At the High Table, waiting staff began bringing out plates of food from the Master's private kitchens. The background hum of conversation crescendoed slowly, building over time and unnoticed, until suddenly the room was silent. Amanda and Watts both looked up, along with just about every other person in the hall. The ruckus began near the entrance to the hall, when a girl in her mid- to late-twenties was charging into the hall, flanked by a pair of suited security. She was dressed in a tight-top, short skirt, and long black boots, with heels that did not so much as aid her walking.

'I do not need your help!' Nina's voice ripped through the hall. She stopped briefly, flailing again at the security man, before spying Matthew at the High Table. She gathered herself, and marched the length of the hall, her boots echoing out across the sea of heads. She arrived at the High Table and marched right up to Matthew ,where he sat poised over his starter.

'What do you think you are doing?' said Nina. 'Sending your boys to drag me here like I'm your wench!'

Matthew smiled and looked calmly back up at Nina.

'Take a seat. Please join us.'

Nina glanced down at the place set ready for her. She cocked her head to one side and frowned.

'If you wanted me to come to dinner, you could have just sent a text. Like *normal* boyfriends.'

'My apologies,' Matthew continued to smile with unavoidable charm. 'My staff do sometimes get a little, how should I say... over-enthusiastic.'

Nina scowled at him.

'Please sit,' said Matthew. 'People are staring.'

Nina continued to stare back at him, but eventually relented and slid into the high-backed chair opposite Matthew. She looked down at the plate of terrine and toast with a garnish of salad leaves.

'A Chinese would have done—' she said, as she picked at her food.

From down the length of the hall, Amanda and Watts watched the exchange at the High Table. After the initial vitriol of Nina's arrival, the voices were too quick to hear what was said. Even so, they were among the last to lose interest in the exchange after everyone else returned to their dinners and their conversations, and the general hubbub had crept back up in volume.

'He's quite incredible,' Amanda said, shaking her head.

'Yeah,' agreed Watts. 'What was that all about?'

'He's a control freak; getting his henchmen to fetch him his girlfriend, somehow drugging you into a coma—'

'He seduces you in your room into thinking he's your ex-husband...' Watts added quietly, as she remembered that last night before – whatever it was, happened. She looked up to find Amanda staring at her.

'Don't worry, I know it wasn't you – I mean, not *really* you. But that night I was crossing the quad, I saw you; with him, in the window. I remember now.'

'I thought...'

'I know,' said Watts. 'You thought it was your Lewis.'

Amanda screwed up her face and narrowed her gaze, trying to search her memories.

'It was so real. How did—'

'Because you had told me your marriage was over. Does he even know you're living here? And...'

Watts grinned.

'Porter's Magic. I'd know if he had entered these college walls.'

'Fair point. Your world and all.'

Amanda glanced back up the hall to where Matthew, Nina, and the other senior college fellows were only now settling in to their second course.

'Come on,' she said to Watts. 'They're going to be hours yet.'

Watts nodded, and as the next group of students got up to leave their tables, she and Amanda got up and followed the throng out of the hall and down the steps, to disperse out around the quad. As they were passing the lodge, Amanda stopped. Watts turned to wait for her, tossing her head in a *are you coming?* way.

'You have the master keys in there, right?'

Watts stepped closer. She nodded.

'Any chance we can borrow the key to Matthew's rooms?'

Watts shook her head.

'Amanda, we can't.'

Watts turned the key – a large, old-fashioned sort that clunked reassuringly in the lock. She twisted the handle and pushed the door in cautiously, and she and Watts stepped inside.

In contrast to the simplicity of Amanda's own rooms, Matthew's apartment on the first floor of the main block was a suite of rooms filled with opulence; Amanda stepped through the room, taking in what there was, as Watts closed and relocked the door.

'There are back stairs we can leave by, if necessary,' said Watts. 'Best that the door looks like it's not been touched if anyone comes.'

Watts joined Amanda where she stood in front of the fireplace, staring at the portrait that hung above it. It was of a tall elegant lady, obviously painted when she was in her prime. Miss Leroy stared out of the painting with her unnaturally, piercingly bright eyes.

'I've seen this picture before,' said Amanda.

'It's famous,' Watts said, with a shrug. 'There are copies all over the city. I know when we met her she was a lot older, but it was still her. Her that's in the picture.'

Amanda nodded.

'No, I mean I'm sure I've seen this, the original before. Has it always been here?'

'For as long as I've known...'

Amanda shook her head.

'Last year it hung in Song Villas, I'm sure.'

'Maybe,' said Watts. 'He clearly loved his aunt though. I'm not sure I could live with her always in this room with me – when I was trying to veg out on the sofa or something.'

Amanda remained silent, like she was held in the woman's gaze. Decisively, she broke away and continued to move about the room, looking at the papers on Matthew's desk. Watts remained standing in the middle of the room.'

'What are we looking for anyway?'

Amanda glanced round, then went back to gently leafing through papers and scanning rows of books, careful not to leave anything out of place.

'I'm not sure exactly. Some clue, maybe, that shows that he was responsible for what's happened to us both.'

Watts kicked at her heels and ambled around the room, eventually taking a look at some things. She found herself stood over a table in the bay window that overlooked the quad. On the table were sheets of Basildon Bond paper, and clipped to them, photos. Notes were scribbled to the papers in ink.

'Amanda...'

Watts leafed through the clipped papers; files were the best way to describe them. She found a photograph of herself, with a note attached.

> Alice Watson – porter – details unknown. Possible link
> with A.

'You should see these...' added Watts, as Amanda crossed the room to join her. Watts passed her a photograph of Amanda, with the attached notes.

'There's Lewis, too,' Watts said, continuing to look through the papers. 'And I don't know half these people, but I think they are masters of all the colleges.'

Amanda stared at the photograph and notepaper in her hand.

'How can he say this? How does he *know*?'

'Matthew doesn't know everything,' said Watts. 'Here, look.'

Amanda looked up to receive the last file that Watts passed her. Even before it was in her hand, she could see the photograph of her daughter. She snatched it to her and stared, trying to work out where it had been photographed.

'You seen what it says?'

Amanda turned to the accompanying notes. In large, sprawling handwriting was Sarah's name. *Who?*

'I don't understand.'

Watts was about to answer, when she heard the footsteps on the stairs, and the voices on the landing. She froze, and shot a look of terror at Amanda.

'What do we do?' whispered Amanda.

Watts was frozen to the spot.

'Watts?'

Then, as the key could be heard in the lock, Watts was alive again. She grabbed the papers from Amanda and bundled them together back onto the table, ushering Amanda across the apartment to a smaller doorway with a regular Yale lock that released them out on the back stairs. Watts clicked the door back home just as she heard one of the main doors opening. Watts leant against the wall and put back her head. Both she and Amanda sighed with relief.

'Come on,' whispered Amanda. She put out her hand to Watts, and together they raced down the stairs, rushing through fire doors and corridors until they arrived at the back of the porter's lodge.

'That was close.'

'Too close,' agreed Amanda.

5

Lewis, eleven-years old and timid, crouched in the thickest, furthest part of the shrubbery in the fading light of evening. He was surrounded by thorned branches that clawed and scratched at him, as he peered through the garden, and at Bevington House. He could see his mother silhouetted in the warm glow from the windows. He shivered as night stung him.

Watching, he saw his mother's silhouette leave the window, then heard the front door open, and his name being called in for dinner. Lewis stayed crouched in the bushes, with the ache of his limbs pushing through him. He felt the branches claw tighter at his arms and scratch at his face, like the fingers of an unseen hand dragging themselves across his cheek.

Voices. Not just his mother, but a girl's too; an exchange over by the house, and out of sight from Lewis. Then the sound of the door closing again, and silence; except for the birds singing...

Footsteps on the gravel path. A gentle singing from a girl with music in her. Lewis stayed stock still, barely able to breathe. Then he saw her, just a few paces across the garden, in that black skirt just above the knee, and the red shirt rolled up at the arms. She stopped and swung on her feet, one arm supporting the other as she fingered at her auburn hair.

'Lewis!' she called softly.

Lewis tried to answer, but no words came out. He wriggled forwards, freeing himself from clinging branches as others sprung back and caught him again. Across the garden, Amanda heard the rustling in the bushes. She turned, said Lewis' name again, and approached the spot where he was concealed, as he wriggled and crawled towards the edge of the shrubbery.

'Hey Lewis, what are you doing in there?'

Amanda was crouching down on the outside of the shrubbery, looking in with that warm, friendly smile.

'I – I don't know,' said Lewis. 'It felt safe.'

He scrambled forwards on his knees as the branches clawed behind him at his arms and legs, leaving scratches to his face and neck. He burst out of the bushes and into Amanda's arms.

'Hey, it's okay.'

Amanda held him, and pressed a kiss to his forehead.

'Safe? Safe from what?'

Lewis remained silent. Amanda helped him up and he shook out his cold, stiff legs.

'Come on, it's dinner time.'

'Can we not for a bit?' asked Lewis, pointing to the bench on the terrace in front of the house.

Amanda looked back at him and frowned.

'Just for a minute, okay? Then we go in.'

Lewis smiled, happier now. They crossed the lawn and took their traditional places on the bench. He reached across and closed his hand around hers. They exchanged a silent acknowledgement, and just listened to the birds and their bedtime song.

Louis sat on the bench in the garden of Bevington House in the late afternoon sunshine. Next to him was Kathryn. He glanced across at her, at her fair skin and blue eyes; and hair with its little forward fringe, and the traditional ponytail. He followed her gaze back across the garden to the For Sale notice poking out above the top of the wall. His hand moved across their laps and found Kathryn's hand. He closed his around hers.

'What are you thinking?'

'That it reminds me of the time I had lost you; seeing this place for sale, all your stuff gone. It was horrible, and wrong.'

'I know, but this is different,' said Louis. 'This house is me, but it's also part of the whole 'other' me. Miss Leroy, she gifted me my life here, and my life with Amanda...'

'I'm not so sure Louis,' said Kathryn. 'I know that's what we decided last year, but you're stronger than that.'

'We have to leave.'

'And go where?'

'Your old house? I liked it there.'

Kathryn flung her gaze up.

'Hardly practical, Louis! It was barely big enough when we were living there; and there's Sarah now...'

'We get somewhere new—'

'With what? My salary won't cover anything, and you're not bringing in much now.'

'Then I'll go back to teaching.'

Kathryn turned towards him and fixed his gaze with hers.

'That's not the answer, Louis. This is our home,' she told him. 'Put the house on market if you like, go through the motions; but you'll see that this – it's ours.'

Louis was silent, looking quietly from Kathryn to the garden. He frowned. For a moment, the only sound again was that of the birds singing, flitting from tree to tree, and in and out of the ancient wisteria climbing up the side of the house. The silence was disturbed by a clattering at the gate as Sarah entered the garden. She stormed across the gravel path, scattering the birds around her.

'What, Dad, is *that*?'

She pointed up to the For Sale sign. Louis looked up, stuttering and stammering in front of her.

'Dad, you're impossible.'

She turned and stormed off towards the house. Louis made to go after her, but Kathryn stayed him with a gentle hand.

'Leave her,' she said. 'I'll go talk to her.'

By the time Louis came indoors, Sarah had calmed down and settled to reading. Kathryn busied herself in the kitchen with dinner.

'Anything I can do to help?'

Kathryn shrugged.

'You can lay the table if you like.'

Louis nodded and began fetching cutlery.

'How is she?'

Kathryn looked up, fixing Louis with her incredulousness.

'She's fine, Louis. She's adjusting just fine to learning that she is the child of the imaginary friend of a Dad in an alternate reality. *She's* doing great.'

Louis lingered over the place-setting.

'It's her Dad that I'm worried about.'

Louis continued to lay the table.

'I'm fine, Kathryn. Really!'

Kathryn turned to him, leaving a knife and an onion on the counter. She opened her arms to him.

'Are we good?'

Louis smiled and stepped towards Kathryn. In her arms, he pressed his head into the crook of her neck. He could smell her perfume.

'I love you, Kathryn.'

'Love you too.'

Louis pulled back, and Kathryn could see that everything was far from fine.

'Louis,' she said softly. 'Tell me.'

Louis chewed on his lip, and tried again. Again... He put up his hands to grab the side of his head. The words and all the explanations were inside of him, bouncing around inside his head. He could see them clearly, but every time he thought he was ready to catch one, it was gone. He gripped his head between his hands and shook. He shook his head for sense to come out.

'Louis!'

Louis. He heard Kathryn's voice again. Looking up, his vision cleared to see her standing in front of him, her face beaming with concern.

'Louis?'

'I still see her. Amanda,' he said, and immediately wished he hadn't. 'Not like that Kathryn. Dreams, memories – it's like she's haunting me.'

Kathryn frowned kindly and reached out a hand to offer comfort. She helped him over to the table and sat him down, seating herself next to him.

'You've got to believe me, Kathryn.'

'I do...'

'It's not like before; I know who I am. It's the memories, I'm haunted by the memories.'

Sarah had been on her way to the kitchen, calmed and composed again after the garden, and ready for dinner. With her hand raised to the door to push it open, she heard Louis and Kathryn's voices inside, and she froze. For a moment her heart stopped, and then all she could hear was the rhythmic beat of her heart pulsing in time with her breathing. She lowered her hand again and listened more intently to pick out the voices on the other side of the door.

I still see her, Amanda.

Her Dad's words hit her like a gunshot, reverberating through her as she ran from the kitchen, skidding at the end of the hall and fleeing upstairs. She was halfway up the final flight to her attic bedroom when she stopped.

Her Dad, Louis, was still seeing her mother, Amanda...

Mum. She loved her Mum, so why was she glad that she was gone? Mum. She remembered her mum coming to say goodnight to her, and helping her with her homework, and – every time the memories came to her, she realised that it wasn't Mum, but Dad who did all those things. It was Dad at her bedtimes, and Dad with the homework ... and it was Mum standing next to the pool, with an old, mad headmistress trying to drown her Dad. But her Dad, he did say he saw her. She heard his words again as her head sank to the floor.

6

Watts woke with a throbbing, aching head on the soggy sofa in Amanda's college rooms. As her eyesight blurred into focus, she saw the empty glasses and the two drained bottles of the Masters' port on the coffee table. She dragged herself, first to the floor to crawl out into the open room, and then to pick herself up. She groaned and clutched at her head. Across the room, draped across her bed in yesterday's clothes, Amanda continued to sleep off the excess of last night. Watts stood and stared, and then caught sight of her reflection in the mirror. She pushed a hand through her hair and straightened her collar, before stepping lightly across the room and easing herself out of the flat. Closing the door with a reassuring 'click' to the lock, Watts turned and walked normally, if slightly slower, down the flights of stairs.

The chapel clock had struck nine, and the last students were hurrying across the quad to reach their tutorials and morning lectures by the time Amanda stirred in her bed. She blinked her eyes open. Her gaze slowly focussed on the open palms of her outstretched hands. She watched as she twitched each finger in turn and played with the movement, observing the change in light, shade, and shadow, and the patterns that each resulted in.

Amanda sat up and wiped sleep dust from her eyes. She rubbed her head and looked about her, her gaze focussing on the empty bottles of port and the pair of glasses. Watts. Where was she? What had happened last night? She staggered to her feet and got herself to the kitchen, to drown her thirst with a glass of water before heading to the bathroom.

Quarter of an hour later, Amanda emerged from the bathroom refreshed and wrapped in a towel. She continued getting ready for work and had a coffee and cake breakfast. For comfort she switched on the radio and half-listened to a Radio 4 discussion about the history of cheese in Roman Britain and found herself listening intently to something that she couldn't recall a detail of later when she walked through the streets of Wren Hoe to work.

It wasn't until she reached the little café on the corner of Little Clarendon Street where she bought her morning coffee – and today a salted caramel flapjack too – that she remembered. It came to her so suddenly she felt sure she must have done a cartoon face-palming in the shop as she waited for her drink.

She remembered the papers and research that she and Watts had found in Matthew's college rooms – the notes about her life, and the question mark over Sarah. *Sarah.* Amanda thought about her daughter. She remembered the early days of her relationship with Lewis, when they were just boyfriend and girlfriend; and then the latter years, when they were a family unit. Next to her in the queue was a mother with a young boy in a pushchair, and Amanda realised suddenly that it was that that she had no memory of. No pregnancy; no childbirth; no hoiking around of prams and baby things. Amanda found herself frowning at her thoughts as she received her order and waved a cheerier 'thanks' as she left to continue her way to work.

Taking a break from the emails later that morning, Amanda leant back in her chair and allowed her eyes to relax from the screen in front of her. She eased herself up and crossed the office to hang out in the doorway. Charlotte and Eleanor were working at their pod, with Kathryn's desk still vacant.

'Morning girls.'

Amanda dropped herself into Kathryn's old chair. Charlotte looked up.

'Everything alright?' she asked.

Amanda nodded.

'I think so, yes. Just shattered. Had a – some friends – over last night...'

'Late night, then?'

Amanda nodded.

'I can't be doing with late nights on a school night.' Eleanor added from across the divider.

School night. Amanda sat in silence, gazing out into the room contemplating this. She knew the expression, of course, but it just brought back memories of Lewis. She frowned and drank more coffee.

'To be honest, I'm not sure if I can either these days.'

Charlotte and Eleanor looked at one another over the desk, unsure of how to react. They returned to their work quickly. Amanda just sat and stared aimlessly into the middle distance. Eventually she picked herself up and returned to her office, sliding the glass door closed behind her.

Charlotte looked up as Amanda had left them, turning almost immediately to her friend. She let out an audible sigh of relief.

'Awkward,' added Eleanor.

'You don't think she saw...?'

Charlotte flicked the tabs of her browser to the property website.

'What I was looking at?'

Eleanor shook her head.

'If she did, she wouldn't have seen anything. She was wrecked.'

Charlotte nodded. Her gaze slid back across to the screen in front of her, and the property details for Bevington House. She flicked through the photos again.

'This is big. Why didn't Kathryn tell us?'

Eleanor looked up. After a moment she grabbed her mobile and began to thumb through a message.

'There's one way of finding out,' said Eleanor. 'Neither of us have plans for lunch, do we?'

Eleanor carried three drinks back to the table by the window where Charlotte was already sitting, and took her seat. Charlotte thanked her, each taking a sip before returning to their phones and swiping through the newsfeeds on their Facebooks. Not long, after Kathryn arrived at their table; the friends greeted each other, with Kathryn easing into the seat in the window booth. They quickly established that the food has been ordered.

'Hope you don't mind. The usual, yeah?' said Eleanor.

Kathryn shrugged.

'Cool, yeah.'

She looked from one friend to the other, confused by their unusual lack of conversation.

'What?' she asked. 'Is something up? You both got new jobs?'

Charlotte shook her head.

'We've seen it Kath,' Charlotte said, looking directly at her friend. 'The ad. For the house.'

'Oh...'

'Why didn't you to tell us that you guys were moving?' added Eleanor.

Kathryn looked to the ceiling and sighed. With a frown, she looked back at her friends; then from one to the other, and then swigged back a large gulp of lager. She sat forwards, and with a frown began to explain.

'So, you see, we're not,' Kathryn finished. 'For all that Louis says we are, we can't. Doesn't matter anyhow; having your house on the market doesn't mean anything.'

Charlotte sat forward.

'I didn't realise. I thought Louis owned the house. From his parents...'

'No, I don't understand the details but it's some kind of trust. The house is his for as long as he lives there. You remember when he went missing last year? The house wasn't the house I had been used to?'

Both Charlotte and Eleanor nodded.

'It reshapes itself around what Louis needs it to be,' said Kathryn. 'If we leave, we have nothing. And my wage – well, it barely covered the rent on my old room in Juxon Street.'

'So why is he trying to sell?'

Kathryn shrugged.

'He thinks it's linked to Amanda; and that he can't truly, finally, be free of her and Leroy until he loses the house.'

Kathryn eyed Eleanor, then Charlotte.

'How is Amanda?'

'Ugh – she's been really nice, actually–'

'Keen to be our friend,' added Eleanor.

'Which can be awkward,' said Charlotte. 'We've been conditioned into seeing her as the fearful boss lady for so long.'

'And how long exactly is that?' Kathryn leapt on the question animatedly. 'She's been in that job for as long as...'

'Forever?' Eleanor answered, her mouth curling round the words with doubt.

'Yeah! Forever,' Kathryn agreed. 'But when I think about it, I have no memories of her as a boss since...'

Kathryn stared out into the middle distance as she tried to pluck dates from her memories.'

'Since about the time I met Louis...'

Charlotte shook her head.

'Coincidence? You saying that we only have memories of our, like, forever boss since when your boyfriend first met you?'

'It's crazy, isn't it?'

Charlotte nodded at Kathryn's words.

'Makes sense, though,' she said. 'As far as *any* of this makes *any* sense.'

'Louis doesn't need Amanda anymore, but—'

'Amanda needs Louis,' said Charlotte. 'She needs him to fill in the gaps in her life.'

'It's a mess.'

'One, big, confused mess.'

Amanda sat in her office, looking out at the rows of empty desks where her editors had gone for lunch. She picked up the dry, hardened end of a particularly uninspiring baguette, considered it for a moment, and then tossed it in the bin. She took up her phone and thumbed through the contacts: Lewis. She pinged off a text to him and returned to her work. After a few moments, she was staring at a spreadsheet with ever more perplexed expressions. Her phone chimed out a new message, and she swiped it up to read. She beamed brightly upon seeing the contents, then set it back on the desk beside her.

7

Amanda rode the metro that ran beneath the Banbury Road, perched on the wooden slatted benches. She held on to the poles tightly with apprehension as the darkness inside the tunnel rattled past, lit occasionally by security lamps or shafts of daylight coming down from a vent somewhere above. As the metro slowed into the next station she saw him, standing on the platform in his usual chinos and corduroy jacket. Lewis.

The metro doors slid open with the hiss of hydraulics. Amanda stepped out onto the platform and made straight for Lewis. A hug, restrained, but comfortable. She took a step back to just look at him opposite her, like she was used to seeing him – before–

'Thank you for coming.'

Lewis nodded.

'Shall we?'

With a smile this time he turned with her, and they made their way to the exit. They headed up the steps of the Park Town station to the tree-lined street above. They crossed the public gardens into the broad avenue off which Song Villas was situated.

When they arrived at the driveway to the house the gates were closed and chained. Ivy clung to the iron-work and wrapped itself around the stone pillars to either side. When Amanda looked up, she could just make out the stone wrens poking out from shrubs and ivy that was growing around them.

Peering through the iron gates, Amanda could see the tangle of brambles and overgrown trees. Gone were the neatly manicured lawns and neat drive with the clipped line of lime trees. She felt at the latch and tried the gate. The rusted chain clanked dully on the gates, but they gave enough to allow a person through if they squeezed tight.

Amanda glanced around, half-expecting to see Lewis standing behind her and half just checking the street for passers-by. Once she was sure that she was alone she turned again, grasping the iron gates to push one and pull the other, and somehow squeeze through the gap onto the drive.

Having had to duck to get through the gate, Amanda straightened up to find herself shivering in the chill of dusk. Her head shot round to look out onto the street. A minute ago, it had been afternoon... For a moment she considered going back; squeezing out through the gates, and leaving this place. She turned again and looked up the length of the drive, at the imposing grandeur of Song Villas. Again, a chill breeze caught her, and she pulled her jacket around her and began the walk up to the house.

'I don't get how it can be this overgrown,' said Lewis, as he and Amanda walked the long drive up to the house.

'Or suddenly so dark,' added Amanda. 'It's like it's seven or eight o'clock.'

She glanced to her side just as Lewis turned towards her. She frowned and put out her hand. He took hers, and together they continued up the drive. The house, when they reached it, was standing dark and forlorn amongst the overgrown beds and trees. Each window was shuttered on the inside, like the house had been closed up for months.

'How do we get in?' asked Lewis.

Amanda stepped up to the front door and pushed the bell.

'There must be a housekeeper still living here.'

'You think? The grounds staff have clearly been let go.'

They waited and waited. No answer came. Lewis stepped forward and tried the door, but it was bolted shut.

'The kitchens,' he said.

He headed off around the side of the building, picking his way past over-hanging branches, with Amanda following. Pushing through a narrow gap between two topiary birds, Amanda almost walked straight into Lewis where he had stopped and was staring.

'What is it?'

Lewis nodded his head in the direction of where he was looking; at what should be a wide, open, expanse of formal lawn, but which was a waste-high meadow of thistles, ragwort, and bramble bushes.

'How is this possible? It's barely a year since we were last here.'

Amanda shook her head, but didn't – couldn't – answer. Then she heard it; what sounded like a door closing. She swung round and scanned the façade of the house. Then she was off, tripping up the steps and round the raised planting towards the side of the house. Somewhere behind her, Lewis followed.

Amanda reached the kitchen door and twisted the handle. It opened, if grudgingly, and she stepped into the scullery. Onwards she moved through the corridors, past the kitchen proper to the stairs at the back of the house. She stopped for a moment and listened. The house was empty and silent, except for the slow ticking of a grandfather clock in a far-off hall. Amanda shivered. *Who was still winding a clock in an empty house?*

She started to climb the stairs and stopped, hand resting on the balustrade. She looked round at the stairs that descended down and narrowing towards the cellar. Amanda turned and followed her change of mind, stepping lightly into the dark heart of the building.

A little evening light still managed to filter down into the corridor though small windows placed high in the walls. Cobwebs clung to the corners, and there was a faint smell of damp to the tiled rooms. Amanda pushed on, drawn onwards by instinct. At the end of the corridor she arrived at a closed door. She stood for a moment in front of it, considering what she was about to do. Then, slowly, she turned the handle and pushed the door open; a little at first, and never all the way.

The room beyond was windowless and dark. Amanda stood with the door behind her and waited for her eyes to adjust to the dark.

Amanda let out a piercing and involuntary scream. In front of her, crouched and huddled in the corner, was a girl with wild black hair, and with a red cloak pulled around her. The girl whipped round and stared at Amanda, with a piercing gaze from wild, dark eyes. Amanda stepped back as the girl reached out with one outstretched arm.

Amanda took a step forward again, keeping her eyes fixed on the girl in front of her. The girl, with a brightness to her eyes, had cracked and dry skin stretched across her face, and hands making her a creature that was half-youth and half-crone.

'Help. Me...'

Amanda stayed still. She heard her own voice in the creature's, and saw in the thing's eyes something of Miss Leroy.

'Who are you?'

The girl-crone crouched in the corner of the room and stared, wide-eyed, with one hand outstretched, with a look of begging and pitifulness.

Amanda lowered herself to the creature's level and inched closer.

'Why are you here?'

The girl-crone stayed silent and stared back.

Amanda put out a hand as she inched closer, watching the girl-crone in front of her. She saw for a moment the same wry smile that she often showed. *Was this thing a version – an echo – of herself?* And then the creature was stretching out with all the fingers of her outstretched hand, desperate for contact.

Amanda encouraged the girl-crone with gently soothing words. She continued to offer her own hand, freely as the girl-crone reached closer.

'Save me.'

Amanda nodded at the girl-crone's request. She inched forward and touched her hand. The girl-crone snatched her own fingers around Amanda's hand and screeched with delight; Amanda froze, seeing suddenly, clearly, Miss Leroy's face in the girl's. The eyes, once wild and staring, were brightening with life.

'Amanda.'

It was Miss Leroy's voice that came from the girl's mouth.

'No!' Amanda screamed. Pulling away, she fought with her free hand to relieve the girl-crone's tight grasp on her other. The grip only seemed to become harder as nails were pressed into skin.

'Let me go!' Amanda pleaded. 'I want to help you, but you're hurting!'

'You—'

Amanda felt herself at the receiving end of a desperate, anguished stare.

'You left me. Here.'

Amanda shook her head.

'I never...'

Amanda winced, as the girl-crone's nails dug deeper, harder.

'I had no idea anyone was down here.'

She moved closer, hoping to release some of the pressure on

her arm, where it remained vice-like in the girl-crone's grip.

'And anyway, you're not locked down here,' Amanda said softly, unthreateningly. 'You could have left anytime you like – same way as I came in.'

She nodded her head towards the door.

'Come, I'll show you.'

The girl-crone reached with violence, screwing up her face into tight, folded lines, and pulled herself back into the corner. Amanda tumbled after her, but in the kafuffle that followed the girl-crone's grip on her arm was lessoned, and Amanda pulled free as the girl-crone cowered in the dark corner at the back of the room, shrouding herself in the grubby red cloak she wore.

On the floor above, footsteps crossed the boards, and voices could be heard drifting through the house. Dust fell from cracks in the ceiling.

8

Watts, in her porter's uniform, walked the floor of the house, uncovering the furniture from dust sheets, raising blinds, and swinging open the shutters. In the withdrawing room she made and lit a fire, kneeling by it long enough to stoke it into life, before setting a guard about it and moving on to other duties. In the hall the doorbell chimed, and Watts moved to answer. Pulling it inward revealed Matthew Leroy-Song in his customary suit.

'Sir.'

Watts held the door for Matthew as he stepped past her.

'Is everything ready for tonight, Miss Watson?'

'As you requested,' Alice replied with her formal voice. 'Just the dining and withdrawing rooms, yes?'

She received a confirmatory nod from Matthew, and followed him further into the house.

'The college caterers will be delivering the food at eight o'clock.'

Matthew nodded.

'And you haven't breathed a word of this meeting to anyone?'

'No, sir. And all the usual precautions have been put into place. You won't be disturbed tonight.'

Matthew nodded again.

'Once dessert has been served, arrange the brandies and whiskeys in the withdrawing room, and then you may leave.'

He gave his instructions in a softly spoken, yet authoritarian tone.

'You may send the caretakers in tomorrow morning.'

'Of course,' Watts nodded.

Amanda hung back in the shadows at the bottom of the basement stairs, listening to the voices of her friend Watts and Matthew, and what they were calmly talking about. Matthew was her nemesis, she decided, and Watts knew that; so why was she aiding him?

The voices got louder. They must be immediately above her on the stairs. She leaned out and peered up, and yes, she could just about make out their shadows. She ducked back into a corner.

Her heart beat fast and loud, reverberating through her whole body. Amanda felt like she was a living clock with a heavy, thumping pendulum inside of her. She pressed herself back into the corner and tried to listen to the conversation from the landing above, but over the sound of her own heart and breathing she could only make out odd words.

And then the footsteps through the ceiling signalled the meeting was over. Still Amanda did not move from her hideaway, waiting in silence with only the sound of her breathing for company, before finally emerging out of the shadows and stepping quietly up the stairs.

Watts? She couldn't stop thinking about her – her supposed friend. What was she doing working for Matthew here? Was whatever gathering that was happening here tonight part of her college porter's duties somehow?

Amanda reached the scullery door and was about to flee the house, when she stopped in her tracks. *What was going on here tonight?* She chewed on her lip and decided. She had to find out.

She turned and walked back into the house, but this time, passing the stairs down to the cellar she continued on into the house to the grand reception hall in the centre of the house, deliberately pausing for a moment at the foot of the main staircase before heading into the withdrawing room, and on to the dining room. The table was already laid for a formal meal, with baskets of bread at intervals along its length. Down one side of the room were five floor-to-ceiling windows with a large stone fireplace opposite, above which and behind curtains was a small minstrel's gallery.

Without another thought she stole two hunks of bread from the table, and practically threw herself through the doorway. Inside she pushed the door gently closed as she heard footsteps enter the room. She then crept and crawled up the tiny staircase onto the tiny platform above the fireplace. As she tucked herself up into position, Amanda thought to herself how it would be possible for musicians to play here.

As she sat in the small gallery, Amanda reached forward and gingerly poked at the heavy satin curtains; a little at first, and then more boldly, until there was enough of a crack to look through. If she leaned forward, she found that she could see most of the table. And then she sat, quiet as a mouse, watching Watts continue setting the room.

She wanted to call out to her friend, ask her what this evening was all about. But at the same time, she was frightened. She had thought Watts was her friend, her ally, and Matthew had all but threatened her. So why was Watts working for Matthew? Amanda's head spun with doubt and fear. She needed someone to trust and confide in, and that just made her think of Lewis again.

Lewis. The one person she could always rely upon to trust and confide her secrets in. She sat back, leaning against the stone wall of the gallery and picked at the bread. After a couple of small mouthfuls, Amanda realised how hungry she was, and wolfed down the remaining hunks of bread before settling back to wait. As she waited, so tiredness overcame Amanda, and she dozed off to sleep, and dream...

Amanda held him, Lewis. They were squeezed together into the narrow platform between the hard-stone wall and the thick velvet curtains, on the other side of which voices could now be heard. Mainly deep and male, they were all very properly spoken, but one lady's voice, with clipped pronunciation, sang annoyingly over the top of all the others.

Amanda and Lewis looked at one another on their small ledge. They both leaned forward, hooking back the curtain for a moment just enough to see who was talking.

'I recognise her.'

'Lady Foxhall, the mayor,' answered Lewis.

The voices beyond the velvet curtains went on, swishing in and out, eddying between themselves like the tide.

'I can't make it out.'

'Just business networking I think,' whispered Lewis. 'I scratch your back, you scratch mine. It's how this city is – not what you know, but who. And if you go to the right parties.'

Amanda frowned. They never did go to the right parties.

From the sound of the swirling voices, and the low rumble of furniture, Amanda could picture the party taking their seats around the dining table for the meal. In an unstructured cacophony of sound, a distinct conversation that obeyed rules like a game of tennis began to emerge. Polite discourse emerging was accompanied by the clinking of wine glasses and silver accoutrements on the best dinner service.

'Can you make out what they are saying?'

Amanda felt Lewis' breath on her cheek as his words escaped him. She shook her head, but strained to listen closer. She could hear Matthew's voice, clear and strong, talking about college budgets, and then—

Amanda's attention was jolted by another voice. In reply to something Lady Foxhall had asked about this year's charity ball, she heard the clear and unmistakable sound of her mother's voice.

And then it was gone. Drowned out by the sound of a loud guffawing laughter from, Amanda imagined, an older, larger gentleman with a fondness for pastries.

'Of course, of course, we keep the girl under constant surveillance.' Matthew's voice was unmistakable.

'Amelia and I knew that we could trust in you completely,' Amanda heard her father reply.

Were they...? Could they...?

'She let us down once before, but we shall not fail milady again.'

'Lewis!' Amanda hissed, as she leaned forwards to the velvet. Through the crack in the curtains, she could see Watts standing in attendance.

'I think they are talking about...

'Me,' Amanda said emptily, as she turned to discover that Lewis was no longer at her side.

'Excuse me for asking, Matthew dear, but what makes you so sure that her highness can be 'brought' back?' Amanda's mother said, joining the conversation. 'We were all there when her protégé, aided by his pathetic friends, ended the procedure before it had come to fruition.'

Her words hung coldly over a now silent dinner table.

'There is a vacuum at the very top of our city, and we should be looking to fill it in other ways.

Amanda hooked back one curtain with her finger, just enough to see her mother allowing the full significance of her words to rest on her husband opposite.

'If you ask me, Miss Leroy was foolish to trust so much, something so vital, in a man so unstable.'

From the head of the table, Matthew held his glass of wine towards his guest and nodded silently to Dr Amelia Jones.

Professor Jones cleared his throat and took up the conversation.

'What my wife is trying to say is, how can we be sure that what you're proposing is the correct course?'

Again Matthew nodded, slowly, and smiled.

'I hear you,' he assured. 'And yes, were it just for the sake of my aunt, I would agree with you. She gave that boy everything, and all he had to do was keep his half of the bargain.'

'I understand,' Professor Jones replied, in a husky but calming voice. 'However, even so, is it not too late? We all saw the betrayal. She is gone now. There is nothing more to be done.'

'If I thought that was the case, then of course I would agree. However, only a part of my aunt was lost. If every hope had been swept away that night, then your daughter would have been too, and Lewis would remember nothing. Don't you see? If we can bring all the elements back together at the proper place, then we can complete the process.'

'It would be simpler to just find a new leader. Our people need and deserve that,' Amanda's mother stressed.

'My wife is right,' said Professor Jones. 'With the greatest of respect your aunt has failed—'

Matthew slammed his fist down on the table.

'You have no idea what you are saying. For eighty-eight years my aunt governed this city – has been mother to us all – selflessly. Seven times she renewed the deal. We all know that the eight is the most difficult.'

'So, it's time to find someone new to lead things – to govern our affairs. Unless you can give us some guarantee of what you propose – and I speak for the whole counsel—'

Here, Professor Jones paused. Amanda looked down at a dining table where, up and down the length, others were nodding and acknowledging their agreement.

'We must insist that the appropriate action is taken without delay.'

'And if I can give you such a guarantee?'

Professor Jones didn't answer, but laughed Matthew's comment off with a disbelief he shared with his compatriots around the table.

'Can you, Matthew?' Professor Jones added, after an uncomfortable couple of minutes' silence. 'Can you really provide us with such a guarantee?'

Matthew leant back in his chair at the head of the table. Amanda could see the awkwardness evident in his expression.

'Very well,' Matthew said, standing abruptly. 'Those who doubt me, follow now.'

He crossed the room. Around the table, Matthew's guests looked from one to another. Professor Jones and Amelia were first to rise and follow, and the others soon made their piecemeal way after Matthew.

Amanda remained on the ledge over a now deserted dining room, until she was sure they were not coming back. Then she crawled backwards on hands and knees, and down the tiny staircase.

Through the doorway she could see the dinner guests still filing out through the next room into the hallway, and turning to go down the scullery passage. She skipped on across the room, hoping that a man who had just then turned and looked back would not have spotted her.

She had to get out – get away from here. Amanda looked around the room, and her gaze alighted on the French windows. As she approached them, her mind continued to buzz with questions.

The way that her own mother and father were working against her hurt, but it was Watts' betrayal that really stung. She had thought that they were friends, but all along she had been working for Matthew – and through him, her parents?

Amanda's hands grasped the door handles to the French windows and twisted them open. A fresh, welcome breeze swept in and flushed Amanda's face. She pushed the door open further, and stepped out onto the terrace.

'Amanda? What are you doing here?'

Amanda stopped sharply on hearing Watts' voice in the room behind. She turned to see Watts rushing forwards towards her, and readied herself defensively.

'What am I...?' Amanda retorted. 'Why are *you* working for *him*?'

Watts rolled her eyes.

'It's my job. You know, any other duties as required.'

Amanda backed away.

'No. No, you lied to me.'

Watts shook her head. Amanda stared back at her, and nodded vigorously.

A scream ripped through the house from the basement. The girl's fear and pain were guttural. Watts froze for a second, before pushing and ushering Amanda out through the door and across the terrace.

'You should go,' Watts said, her voice breathless.

'But who was that?' Amanda asked, gesturing back to the house. 'And what are they doing to her?'

'Don't ask. You shouldn't be here.'

'But...' Amanda protested, against Watts' firmness.

'I'll explain later. But you've got to leave. Now.'

Amanda allowed herself to be marched over the lawn. Ahead she could see the locked iron gates at the end of the drive. She turned to face Watts, with the house a dark shape against the sky behind her.

'That girl – that thing they are keeping down there, is that Leroy?'

Watts fixed Amanda with her gaze but didn't answer.

'Why does she look like me?'

Watts stopped.

'You've seen her? She – she didn't touch you, did she?'

Amanda froze again. She shook her head, but hesitantly, all the time remembering that animal's hand that grasped her leg.

'Go, Amanda!'

Watts was insistent.

'Get away from here. If *they* find out you've been here...'

Amanda finally understood, or at least enough – she nodded tremulously, then turned and ran, her feet twisting and turning over the lawn until she crashed face on into the gates. She glanced over her shoulder and looked back. Watts must have gone back in; the house was alone against the sky at the end of the drive. dark and foreboding.

Amanda turned again and tugged, pushing and pulling at the gates, working them loose enough so that she was able to slip through. From the safety outside the grounds she turned once again, this time to see a dozen figures standing on the terrace. *Had they seen?* She turned again and ran.

PART THREE

Escape

risoluto con moto

1

Lewis followed Miss Leroy's commanding stature down the long school corridor. They turned a corner, then another, through a plate glass foyer that separated the original pre-war red-brick school with the 1960s extension, where the school's music centre was housed. When they arrived in the main music practice room the orchestra was already tuning up. Private conversations between friends died away on cue with the music teacher's entrance.

Lewis, then a small, shy boy of eleven, followed the teacher across the front of the room, dying with embarrassment as he was paraded in front of his peers. He carried his satchel over his shoulder, and his music bag containing his flute in his hand. Miss Leroy led him to the flute section and introduced him to a couple of older girls with long fair hair and plaits, the names of whom he couldn't remember.

When Miss Leroy had gone, Lewis found himself sat at the end of the flute section next to a single oboe player – a girl about his age, with red hair. She smiled at him. He smiled back, before focusing on assembling his flute and music stand.

When it came to music, Naomi, or it might have been Natasha, passed Lewis some flute music, but they never really introduced themselves. Lewis sat at his stand and played along with the notes as best as he could. A couple of times Lewis got lost, and the girl next to him playing oboe pointed out where they were.

'Amanda,' the girl said with a smile at the end of the piece. Lewis nodded, and after further prompting admitted his own name.

By the end of the rehearsal, Lewis and Amanda knew which classes they were in, and a few sketchy details about their lives. When it was time to leave at the end of rehearsal, the Naomi or Natasha girl gathered in the music, but didn't think to ask Lewis how he had got on.

'Which direction are you headed?'

Lewis looked up at Amanda, where she was still standing near to him.

'Back to the number eight tram,' said Lewis. 'We live on the Woodstock Road.'

'I get the eight, but in the other direction,' said Amanda. 'You want to walk back to the stop together?'

Lewis shrugged, and managed an awkward smile.

They left the music centre and crossed the playground to leave the school grounds.

'Amanda, wait up!'

Both Lewis and Amanda stopped. A girl in trousers and short-cropped fair hair was running after them.

'Amanda!' the girl called again as she ran. 'You haven't forgotten, have you.'

Amanda glanced from the girl to Lewis and back.

'Alice? No,' she said. 'I haven't forgotten.'

Louis sat in his study at his desk with his pen discarded on top of his writing papers. He held his head in his hands with his elbows on his desk, staring out of the window.

'Alice...' he said out loud.

'Huh? Who's Alice?' Kathryn asked as she looked up from her day bed.

'Alice. I don't know.'

Louis turned in his seat to look at Kathryn.

'Amanda, she had a friend, when I first met her; Alice. I never knew.'

Kathryn sighed and put down her photography magazine.

'Maybe because it wasn't important. Amanda only exists now because – you invented her. Whether or not she had a friend when you were little, it doesn't matter.'

Kathryn saw the hurt and the pained expression on Louis' face. She frowned and went to him at his desk and held him, hugging his face to her chest.

'I'm sorry. That sounded crass and uncaring,' she said. 'But Louis, it's true.'

Louis stayed in Kathryn's hold, enjoying the warmth of her embrace and smiling as he listened to the beating of her heart. His mouth twisted with disappointment, as eventually Kathryn released him.

'You've got to forget her.'

'I know.'

Louis turned back to his desk and stared down at his papers and his handwritten script. Words leapt out at him, launching themselves from the page: Amanda, Alice, Miss Leroy... He blinked and cleared the words from his vision, gathered up the papers into a pile and put them away in a drawer. He picked up his novel and placed it down in front of him, opening it where he had left off. Kathryn returned to the day bed, but instead of retaking her seat, she took her magazine and left the room.

Downstairs Kathryn sat in the lounge, browsing the internet on her tablet while a movie played on the television. Across the room, Sarah sat watching the movie; a Norse mythological fantasy with equal measures of violence to sex, and one that she had seen twice already. As she flicked through friend notifications on her tablet, Kathryn found herself watching Sarah; she observed the shape of the face, the way she wore her hair – usually in a pony tail – but at the moment hanging free around her neck and shoulders. She picked out the details of the hair scrunchy on her writ and the clothes she wore. Kathryn began to look at Sarah and her appearance across the room, imagining how Louis would have described it when he was creating her.

'What?'

Kathryn started, suddenly reawakening into the here and now.

'Why are you staring at me?'

Kathryn looked back at Sarah and her perfectly reasonable questions. How could she explain to the girl – sister, friend, step-daughter – that she was sitting across the room looking at her like she was the fictional character she used to be.

'Kathryn? What's wrong?'

Kathryn stared back at the girl. What was her relationship to this girl who by rights should not exist? She tried, twice, to speak. Again, Sarah prompted her.

'I think it's happening again.'

Sarah narrowed her gaze on Kathryn. She reached for the DVD remote and flicked the film onto pause.

'Your Dad. He's still writing about Amanda, your Mum.'

Kathryn's words got tangled in her own thoughts.

'And I think that what he writes comes true.'

'That was his gift,' said Sarah. 'Like Thomas the Rhymer, the Faery Queen made sure that what he imagined became real.'

'But the Faery Queen's dead. We buried her.'

Sarah picked herself up from the armchair and moved to the other end of the sofa where Kathryn sat.

'The magic was strong though. Who knows what happens to that when the Fairy Queen is defeated?' reasoned Sarah. 'I imagine it's like a broken cobweb, with all these strands just hanging there. Broken cobwebs can be repaired.'

Sarah turned to Kathryn, her face, downhearted.

'And one of them must have caught my Dad again.'

'It's scary,' said Kathryn. 'If he's writing about Amanda – about them—'

'About us,' added Sarah.

Kathryn frowned.

'Then it could become real again, like last time.'

Sarah lay in her bedroom under the eaves of Bevington House, listening to the sounds of night outside her window. The buzzing down the cables, and the rattle of wheels on the track as a tram approached the stop just beyond the perimeter wall. The voices on the pavement and the footsteps disappearing into the distance of a couple heading home after a night out.

She couldn't sleep and sat up on the edge of her bed, continuing to listen to the accentuated sounds of the night. After a few minutes she got up and crossed to the window, slid up the sash, and leaned out to breathe in the night. Her face was bathed in moonlight, and a cool breeze struck her face. In one of the large trees that surrounded the house, owls hooted to one another. Sarah leaned further out the window, and down across the façade of the large Edwardian building. The light was still on in her father's study...

Sarah crept downstairs and across the landing to Louis' study door. Her hand hovered over the handle as she stood in the dark and listened. She could hear her Dad's voice. It sounded like a conversation, but only her Dad's voice, and she couldn't make out the words.

Sarah's hand gripped the handle and the door moved a little where it stood ajar. The voices went silent from within and

Sarah froze, hearing only the fast beating pulse of her heart. Then Louis' voice continued. Sarah's grip tightened on the handle and threw open the door to march in on the room and—

Louis turned where he sat, hunched over his desk with pen in hand and paper spread out in front; and no one else in the room.

2

Lewis turned and saw his daughter in her nightie, her eyes wide and bloodshot and full of rage. He gulped as he laid down his pen.

'Sarah, my darling,' he said. 'What is it?'

Lewis frowned and opened his arms to her. She crossed the room and fell into a comforting hug.

'Dad...?'

Lewis held his daughter tightly.

'Where's Mum gone?'

Lewis' face twitched over the question, pleased that, with his daughter's face over his shoulder, she couldn't see his doubt and uncertainty. He remembered the funeral, when they buried Miss Leroy, and the parting afterwards. So much had happened since then – so much change. But – his mind stopped to think of Amanda, and of why she had left. Why had she left?

'Dad?'

Lewis pulled away. Realising he had tears forming in the corners of his eyes, he looked his daughter straight in the eye.

'Your mother had to leave for a little. After Miss Leroy died it troubled her. She didn't know what was what. She needed time...'

*

'You liar!' Sarah screamed, loud enough to wake the whole house up.

Louis all but fell off his chair as the words came spitting from Sarah's mouth. He stuttered and stammered, and tried desperately, to find the words, but every time he thought he had an explanation, the words were gone.

'Dad, stop pretending to yourself,' Sarah said, staring at him defiantly. 'Mum's gone because she never really existed.

Sarah dived forward as Louis clutched his temples between his hands, to relieve the pressure of so many thoughts and feelings, and emotions and excuses. Sarah grabbed up the papers from her father's desk and waved them in front of his face.

'You can't bring Mum back by writing about her! And if you try you'll only drive away Kathryn, the only real person you've ever really known.'

'You don't understand...' Louis whimpered. 'I can't not write about her – Amanda. It's like she's part of me.'

'She's *not* real.'

Footsteps could be heard outside the door, and a slit of light from the landing widened out as the door opened. Kathryn stood in the doorway.

'What on earth?'

Sarah looked from Louis to stare across the room.

'Tell him.'

She looked back at Louis, where he was sinking further into the hardwood of his chair if that were possible.

'He's still writing about Amanda,' Sarah said, waving the papers. 'That's how this is happening. She exists still, because, he – Dad – won't give her up.'

Kathryn shook her head and stepped towards Sarah consolingly.

'It's not that simple, Sarah,' Kathryn said. 'Look at him. He's trapped, and you letting rip like this is not going to help.'

'You knew?'

Sarah raised her fistful of papers.

'You knew that he was still writing about her?'

Kathryn shook her head.

'I suspected. I didn't know.'

'They've got to go,' demanded Sarah.

'No.'

Sarah turned at Louis' sudden pronouncement. Kathryn looked towards her boyfriend. Louis reached out to them; first to Sarah, and then to Kathryn. Kathryn allowed her hand to join with Louis'.

'If Amanda's not real, then Sarah, my love, how are you...?'

'I'll take that risk, Dad,' said Sarah. 'I know I'm as real as you and Kathryn. And if I'm not, I shouldn't exist either.'

'Sarah...'

But Sarah fled the room, with Louis' papers crumpled in her hands. Louis stared after her at the door that swung on its hinges. He turned to Kathryn with despair in his eyes.

Downstairs the front door slammed. Both Louis and Kathryn started.

'Sarah—'

They both said her name at the same time and rushed to the door to fly through the house. Out the door and across the tiled porch they sped, skidding to a halt in the garden.

Across grass, crouched in the dark, Sarah was striking matches into the bowl of a barbecue.

'Sarah...' Kathryn offered.

Sarah didn't answer. She struck a match and failed again to get the flame to take on the paper. Her hands were shaking as she struck another match.

'Please, Sarah.'

This time it was Louis' voice to speak to her out of the dark.

'Don't,' Sarah said, choking on her words. 'Don't try and stop me.'

She struck another, which flared to life between her fingers. With her other hand she grabbed up the papers, but the match burnt itself out before she could get it to more than blacken the edge of the paper. She swore and discarded the dead match into the barbecue bowl.

'Think about what you are doing.'

Louis' words were pleading and desperate. Sarah turned to look over her shoulder.

'I know exactly what I'm doing.'

She turned again and struck another match across the box. It leapt into life, and she held the papers above the flame. The middle of the page blackened, and a hold began to emerge. The flame burst through and caught the paper. Sarah watched the circle of flame spread out across the page, and let it fall into the barbecue. Louis cried out, shouting at Sarah to stop. He crumpled to his knees and clutched at his chest.

'Sarah, what have you done?'

Kathryn rushed to Louis' assistance. She crouched down next to him and held him close. Sarah remained unmoved, staring into the barbecue. She fed another page into the pyre and watched as the flames spread across the page. In the middle of the page was Amanda's name, and the flames curled towards it, a crisp blackened edge that closed around it until, in a brightness that burnt at the back of the eyes, it was gone.

Louis lunged forward and groaned. Sarah fed another page into the fire.

'Stop it!' pleaded Kathryn. 'Sarah, you're hurting your Dad.'

Sarah watched as the flames ate the next page. Again, Louis groaned, and Kathryn interchanged comfort and pleading. Sarah turned towards them. After the brightness of the fire she struggled to pick them out from the night.

'It's the only way.'

'No!' Kathryn protested. But in the dark it was not Kathryn's face that Sarah saw, with her arms shrouding a crumpled Louis. Amanda looked back at her, out of the dark.

'Sarah...' Amanda said meekly.

Sarah stared back. There. She was there.

'Don't do it.'

Sarah glanced down at her pyre, and at her hand with the last few pages held over it. The flames reached up. She looked back.

'I'm sorry,' Sarah said. Beneath the remaining papers that she held, the flames leapt tall and caught hold, dragging them down into the fire.

Sarah saw her mother scream, but no sound came out. The vision of her shattered, and was left with Kathryn comforting Louis. She saw him lurch upright and dive for the barbecue. He kicked it over and stamped out the fragmented remains of his papers, before sinking again to the floor, and taking up one of the few remaining fragments. Sarah saw the word left in Louis' handwriting – *Amanda*.

Time seemed to slow as the burning edge ate the paper. Louis stared at it. Sarah stared at it. On the other side of the fire, Amanda stared at her name as it slowly disappeared.

'I understand,' said Amanda; and this time she vanished quite slowly, beginning with her auburn hair, and ending with her smile, which remained sometime after the rest of her had gone.

'Mum!'

Sarah's cry was agonised. She dived into the fire for the scrap of paper, but the last of her mum's name crumbled between her fingers. She turned around, scrabbling on her feet.

'Dad! Kath?'

Her face was stretched over her agonised emotions, and her voice, choked.

'What have I done?'

Louis sat still, staring, and unable to answer. As Sarah looked at him he seemed like he was about to hug her. Kathryn frowned, and stepped forward to take Sarah in comfort.

'I don't know,' Kathryn said. 'What we should have done before.'

'Is she...?'

Sarah stared up at Kathryn at close range. Kathryn looked down at Sarah, feeling empty and lost. Nearby, Louis sat on the grass, hunched up with his arms around his knees, shaking. She shook her head.

'I really don't know.'

'But...?' Sarah continued to ask.

'She was an invention of your Dad, as you are. She should have disappeared when we freed Louis from his ties with the Faery Queen. But she remained, and you remain now. I – I just don't know.'

3

Sarah sat with Caz in the small café in the Covered Market, staring into her cappuccino. Opposite her, as Caz sucked up her frappuccino through a straw, Sarah couldn't take her eyes off her friend's blue-dyed hair, that was tucked back in a ponytail with a small fringe brought forward. Her friend had always been the rebellious one of the two of them, as she remembered Caz's mum's reaction to seeing the newly-dyed hair.

'I shouldn't exist.'

Caz shrugged.

'But you do. You're here, right?'

'As much as you are.'

Caz smiled a big, broad smile.

'I'm not going anywhere, my friend.'

Sarah sipped from her drink and grinned.

'I'm glad.'

'Seriously though, what's happened to Amanda?'

'Not seen her,' said Sarah. 'Nor has my Dad, that I know of.'

Sarah pushed a bowl of sugar sachets around the table.

'Before, I knew somehow that she was around; and in the same way, I know now that she isn't.'

'She was still your Mum, though?'

151

Sarah frowned.

'I know. And I do feel guilty for it. But her presence was killing my Dad, and my Dad was so much more real when he was there with Kathryn. He was finally happy.'

Sarah stopped suddenly, with the feeling that she was being watched. She glanced, first left, then right, over her shoulders, at the other people in the café. There was a group of kids at a far table, a couple by the window who were obviously on a first date – or the morning after at least; at another table there was a family with an unruly child. They were all normal, unthreatening people though; so why did a shiver run down her spine?

A glance across the room again, and Sarah caught the eye of one of the weasel-faced young woman in the uniform of the university proctors, as she turned back to her colleagues where they were sat along the front of the bar. Again, Sarah shivered and leant forward to Caz.

'Drink up. We're being watched.'

Caz looked up, surprised, but nodded. She glanced around also, but didn't notice anything untoward.

A few minutes later, the two friends pushed out of the café and turned left, then right through the narrow maze of covered streets that made up the market. Caz tried to talk, but Sarah pushed on and out onto the narrow street at the back of the market, and on further until they were swept up into the thoroughfare of Cornmarket. As they passed the end of the street they had left, Sarah turned and glanced back in time to see the weasel-faced proctors leaving the market too.

'Sarah, what's up?'

'Not here. Not yet.'

Sarah pushed her friend onwards, through the fast-flowing weave of pedestrians.

At St. Magdalen's Transport Interchange, Sarah pushed her friend on through the crowds, all the time sneaking looks behind her at the proctors making their way up the street. Sarah ducked them both sideways, and back, skipping past and overtaking other pedestrians making their way to and from their trolley buses and trams. Past the tower of St Mary Magdalen, and the shadow of the Martyrs' Memorial.

Impatiently, Sarah waited at the lights to cross the road. She looked back to see the weasel-faced proctors searching through the crowds, turning people around and checking their faces. Back to the road, Sarah saw a gap in the traffic and she hastened Caz to cross. At the first tram waiting outside the classical frontage of the Taylorium Institute, they clambered up the steps and slammed the door shut behind them. They fell back onto the benches, panting and out of breath.

Beneath their feet the engines throbbed into life, the wheels began to turn, and the tram jolted and grinded into movement. Sarah flung herself from one bench to another beneath the back window of the tram. Slowly she raised herself up to peer out at the tram stop at the end of the line. By now, the tracks and platforms were surrounded by proctors looking at the tram as it rattled off up St Giles.

Sarah twisted round and sunk down onto the bench. Caz soon came and sat next to her.

'So, you going to explain what's going on?'

Sarah shrugged.

'We were being watched. And followed.'

'But why?'

Sarah shrugged again.

'No idea. Not really. But mum – they must know – and want... I don't know...'

Sarah turned her head and looked at Caz next to her, where they were both slouched, almost horizontal, onto the slatted wooden benches. From their position they could see the trees and the gable ends of the houses that fronted Woodstock Road slide past. At each stop they fixed their eyes on the doors and watched, fearful of who might board the tram.

They counted down the stops, not that they needed too as both had travelled this journey enough times to know every tree and telegraph pole, as the tram slowed into the Bevington Road stop. Sarah crept across the tram and peered out one of the side windows. At the approaching corner of the Bevington and Woodstock roads, two pairs of proctors patrolled the pavement in front of the tree-fronted Edwardian façade of Sarah's home. Caz joined Sarah at her side and peered too out of the window, in time for Sarah to pull her back down.

'Get down!' Sarah hissed. 'They're guarding the gate already.'

The tram slowed to a stop to let some passengers off.

'How are you...?'

Sarah shushed her friend to silence. Through the open tram door, she could see two proctors talking to each other outside the blue door that led into the garden at Bevington House.

The door was slammed shut and the tram moved off again, with a rhythmic squeaking of wheels and a hissing of electricity down the cables above. At each stop up the Woodstock Road, Sarah and Caz were ready to get off and make their way home through the lanes and back streets of northern Wren Hoe; but at each stop they were defeated by the patrols of weasel-faced proctors from the university. At each stop they slunk down in their seats and waited with nervous, fast-beating hearts, until once more the tram was underway again.

'They can't be patrolling every stop...'

Caz turned and stared imploringly at her friend, mouthing the words. *Please. Please no.*

Sarah sat impassionedly, quiet and brooding, as she thought back to the events of last night, and of what she had done. Her act of defiance in burning her Dad's papers had seemed so easy back then, in the middle of the night. Her mother was an invention of her Dad's by fairy magic, and, she had thought, had been banished by the burning of her name on those papers. Now she was left to wonder if her actions had been too impulsive.

At the city ring road the tram slid down into its tunnel and emerged again alongside the mainline railway for the next half-mile until it's terminus at the parkway station.

'We have to get off now—' Caz hissed to her friend.

Sarah nodded. They had already ridden the tram far beyond their ticket.

They hung back on the tram as the last passenger disembarked and watched. Sarah scanned the platform and beyond for proctors, sure that they would be patrolling somewhere. And then, she saw them. A pair standing by the bridge that crossed the stream to the car park. She ducked down, pulling Caz with her out of sight, as a London-bound train swished into the station, separating them from the exit.

'Now!'

Sarah took her chance, and leaping to her feet she jumped down from the tram. Checking once that Caz was with her, Sarah ran down the length of the tram and round the back to cross the track, and down behind a hedgerow. Only then did she stop and look back. As Caz joined her she could see back over the hedges at the tram and the train beyond, blocking all sight of anyone watching them.

They continued immediately down the side of the hedgerow, and under the road bridge to the fields that backed onto the canal at the top end of Wolvercote and the river beyond that.

'So how are we going to get home now?' Caz said finally, after they had put distance, and two major roads, between them and the watched tram lines. 'They're not going to stop watching for – how long?'

'How about your house?' asked Sarah.

Caz looked back at her friend. She knew that the question was rhetorical. Sarah also knew that Caz's parents were funny about unplanned sleepovers, and Caz knew that Sarah knew this.

'We can continue down the side of the railway, then cut across the old sidings into the West End.'

Caz shook her head in amusement.

'You had this all planned, didn't you?'

'Not all of it,' Sarah said with a grin. 'But I've had some time to plan.'

The light was failing when they reached the Wolvercote tunnel. By this point some semblance of normality was returning, with Caz chatting about the lives of their other friends, and she was halfway through one such diatribe when Sarah suddenly shushed her, and pushed Caz through a gap in the hedge.

'More patrols?'

Sarah pointed. Caz followed her friend's gaze up to the road where it went over the mouth of the tunnel, and the proctors standing on the road above.

'I should have remembered they'd have their spies up there too. I had thought we'd go up the embankment through those gardens.'

'They're everywhere.'

'They're faeries.'

Caz stared, but Sarah ignored her and instead ushered her on, keeping low behind the hedge.

'There's another break in the hedge further up, you see. We can get through again there. They won't be able to see us from that angle – not unless they look straight down. Then we go through the tunnel.'

'What about the trains?'

'There's a service path. We'll have to keep single file, but...'

Up against the mouth of the tunnel Sarah took a last look up. She couldn't see anyone up above, and the only thing to say the spies were up there was the fading, pale shadows cast out across the tracks. She turned and followed Caz into the dark interior.

Even just metres inside the tunnel, it was pitch black. Caz and Sarah walked on, keeping to the side and trailing their fingers along old, crumbly brickwork. About halfway they heard the quiet singing of the tracks, then felt the breeze rushing towards them down the tunnel, and the noise. Caz pulled Sarah back flat against the wall. Briefly they were lit up in the lights of the approaching train, and then it was gone, leaving a wash of wind and with a whistle that diminuendoed from the lines. The two friends breathed out in relief, and with fast-beating hearts returning to normal, they continued on their way.

Halfway through, Sarah's eyes had adjusted to the darkness. She could make out the outlines of the tracks, and the shapes of the tunnel's walls and roof. Every few metres there was a small side-opening. Twice she felt sure that, out of the corner of her eyes, she saw someone hiding in the shadows – something with eyes, watching them. She hurried on, walking on the heels of her friend, and then she heard it. She stopped and listened. And again, her ears tried to make out the sound. She called to Caz in a hushed voice to stop, and she listened again. Unmistakably, somewhere and not far off there were other feet on the gravel train bed.

'We're being followed?' Caz said.

Sarah rushed forward and urged Caz on towards the tunnel mouth, as it opened out ahead of them. Forgetting who might be watching from the road above, they ran on down the side of the train tracks, not caring as the proctors called out for them to stop, and gave chase.

4

Matthew stood in the master's study, in front of the old man where he sat in his resplendence. The conversation had not been an easy one, as he had had to explain the disappearance of Amanda Jones. Of course, he had explained that this was just a momentary set back. He did, after all, still have the broken remains of the old woman in the cellar of the big house.

He dared not move while he stood before the master, an experience that even with his own seniority made him feel like a schoolboy in the headmaster's office. His eyes twitched, and his gaze flicked to the windows and down into the quad. Students milled around below on their way to lectures. Then the knock at the door came, jolting Matthew back to the present as the master commanded the person to enter. Matthew turned as the master of Heathside College entered the room. The two college masters greeted each other as old friends, but with the kind of reserve of being from rival institutions.

'Thank you for attending to this matter so quickly, Lord Emberton,' began the Master of Woodiwiss. He lifted himself from his desk chair and ushered his visitor to the leather armchair by the fire. He stopped at a cabinet to pour a couple of drinks. Matthew remained standing, feeling more an office junior than the college bursar that he was by the second.

'I assume that you called me here because it is not good news,' Lord Emberton said as he eased himself into his armchair.

'I am afraid so.'

The Master of Woodiwiss passed his friend a glass of brandy.

'I am sorry to say that my bursar has been unsuccessful. We have the vessel, but new life escapes us. I am sorry to say that, for all his assurances, we have lost far too much time.'

Lord Emberton nodded.

'It is true. The council are already selecting their own candidate from The Town, and our spies are organising into factions. Even on my way here, I found it impossible to know whom I could trust.'

Professor Kennet, the Master of Woodiwiss, folded his hands over each other, slowly and deliberately. He held the conversation with his silence before continuing.

'It's clear to me that we should have acted as soon as Miss Leroy had been defeated.'

Here, Professor Kennet looked up briefly to Matthew.

'The question is not when, but how we proceed?'

'The situation we are in is not a new one,' Lord Emberton added. 'The system of birth and rebirth that has worked so well for the Leroy family for so long has not been the only way of controlling things. It has failed before, and thus it will fail again. It is how we deal with this that is important.'

At this moment Matthew took two steps towards the two elderly masters, as he raised his hand and coughed to clear his throat.

'The rebirth can still happen,' said Matthew. 'My aunt's spirit lives on.'

'No!'

Lord Emberton slammed his fist into the arm of the chair.

'Your aunt failed us. The Tumnal boy was weak from the start, and she weakened him further.'

'It was outside influences—'

'She gifted him too much, and he returned to us a child that was a girl and not a boy, and of the wrong age. If it had not failed now, then it would have in eleven years' time.'

By this time Lord Emberton's voice was raised and forceful. Opposite him, Professor Kennet was nodding in complete agreement. Matthew shook his head sadly.

'In which case, I beg your leave, but I can do nothing more for you.'

Professor Kennet looked up and held his bursar in his stern gaze.

'No, Matthew, you can't. I shall call for you when we have other *college* matters to discuss.'

Matthew nodded, turned, and walked briskly to the door and left the room.

'So,' Professor Kennet continued eventually. 'Where do we go from here?'

Lord Emberton nodded gravely.

'Well, despite my age, and although it's not something that I have actively sought, I came prepared to take on the role. For the good of the city.'

Outside the master's study, Matthew lingered for a moment, listening through the door. He frowned and slipped away like a serpent down the stairs.

5

Watts sat slumped in the chair in her father's lodge, clutching a half-drunk bottle of beer and unable to drink anymore. Her head was a fog of confusion over what had happened with Amanda, as well as from the alcohol.

She lifted the bottle to her lips but couldn't do it. Her arm flopped back into her lap, and with her other hand she rubbed her head and tried to think clearly. She remembered the anger with which Amanda had pushed her away. She remembered the wild-eyed betrayal that had flared out of the way Amanda had looked at her. Watts flinched at the thought.

She remembered running after Amanda, and for a moment on the lawn in front of Song Villas catching up with her – pulling her round and facing up to an explanation and an apology, and...

A wind howled across the lawn, whistling and whishing through the trees that lined the drive; black, finger-like silhouettes reaching out across the twilit sky.

Watts sat in her chair in the cottage, staring at the beer in front of her. What had happened? There was an encounter, definitely; she remembered the hurt and anger in the voice. But then there were other parts of her memory that had the mixed-up reality of a dream just before waking.

I thought we were friends.

Watts heard Amanda say again, and she saw her face saying it, with the rawness of eyes bulging with tears.

Watts heard herself too, insisting that they were; and then there was Amanda again—

But you are working for him.

'Of course, I am,' Watts replied. 'He's management, in the college.'

'You know that's not what I meant. I saw you here, taking instruction from him – setting me up!'

'Amanda, you don't understand...'

And then they were across the park, and those dark outlines of branches were actually the skeletal shape of people climbing in the tree. They were clawing out, reaching further, and almost touching her face.

Back in the cottage she shivered. There it was, a heavy knocking on the door; the sound of a fist beating down on solid wood. Watts froze, pinned rigid to where she was sitting. The beating on the door came again, and this time it was accompanied by Matthew's voice. Watts sat and listened. He was angry, and most-likely drunk, and he was demanding to talk to her. Watts stayed exactly where she was, fixed to her seat, as Matthew continued to bash and bellow, until suddenly there was silence once more.

Watts slowly stood and made her way through the house. She approached, if cautiously, a window that overlooked the front door. She could see Matthew sat on the doorstep, facing away from the house and across the gardens. Watts shrank back, quickly and quietly.

Visions sprang back into Watts' head, of Matthew and her in the reception room of Song Villas. He was leading her through, instructing her on what needed to be done and she was following, listening, and – he turned suddenly and was face to face, up close to her. His instructions ceased, and he was staring into her eyes. And she was staring back into his. She could see every detail in those deep, probing eyes; and then suddenly they had their arms flung around each other's necks, and they were kissing.

She pulled back, out of Matthew's embrace, and stepped away. She seemed to be falling. Falling, back, and down through the darkness, she landed, crashing deep down into the armchair with a flump. Looking back up – she could see Matthew still, high above behind the dormer window of a college room; and in silhouette he was standing before Amanda. They moved closer towards each other, and they were kissing.

They last thing Watts remembered before she drifted off into sleep was watching herself, as if from above, slouched or collapsed back into the armchair. She saw her breathing slow, and her eyes flicker and shut. The last thing she remembered was watching herself drift off into sleep.

Matthew continued to sit outside the lodge, looking out into the night. A short distance off across the garden, amongst the trees and shrubs he was being watched. They watched him, watching them.

'I'm sorry. I betrayed you,' he said. 'I thought I could fix it. I thought I could change what happened.'

Figures scurried forwards out of the darkness to gather around Matthew, but it wasn't to his audience of faeries that Matthew looked. Further off, illuminated in moonlight, Miss Leroy was walking towards him, in long dress, twin-set of pearls, and familiar stiletto heels.

'I – I tried,' Matthew said from where he sat, staring down the garden at his approaching aunt.

As she stepped closer he could see that she was slightly translucent, with a radiating outer glow that reminded him of the moon on a foggy night. She shone through and stepped nearer. He carried on talking to her, trying to explain what he had done, and how he hadn't meant for all this to happen. He found his legs shaking and his voice trembling. He felt a strange chill ripple through him on an otherwise warm summer night.

'Matthew,' she said as she was close to striking distance. 'You failed me.'

And at that instant, everything went cold and dark for Matthew.

6

Summer sun warmed the long meadow grass that bordered the river, as Amanda lay face down in the grass reading. She was lost in L.E. Summers' book about the boy and the girl in 1990s Britain, living on a remote island with a Regency way of life, who discover that they are born with the gift of flyht.

She sighed and flopped the book away from her into the grass. *Why,* she wondered, *was she reading this book?* There was a nice idea – clever even – behind the book that she admired, but it seemed overworked. Also, the 1990s setting seemed only there for some specific references to pop culture. She flicked back to the cover, and looked at the author's name. *Who was he? Who recommended the book to her, and why did she buy it?*

She considered passing on the rest of it, but like bad television she felt compelled to continue. She kicked off her sandals and hooked up the sleeves of her dress to enjoy the seasonal sunshine and rising temperatures. As she reached in her bag for a bottle of water to quench her thirst, she listened to the sounds of the meadow. Birds chatted to one another on the river, insects buzzed around the wildflowers, children played in one direction, and students splashed at the water's edge.

Amanda guzzled down water from the bottle and pushed the bottle back into her bag. She returned to the book to pick up the story of Clayton and Lindsay.

She read on into the afternoon, as the meadow heated to baking temperatures, and she felt herself and her hair and clothes begin to stick with a glue of hot sweat. She snapped the book shut and shoved it into her bag. Sitting up, she could see cows from the field on the opposite bank standing in the shallows of the river to cool off. She shook her head and envied them.

Bag in one hand, and sandals in the other, Amanda crossed the meadow and set them down at the bank, as she let herself down onto the small, sandy beach. She stepped, barefoot, into the shallows – not cold, but still refreshing from the heat of the day. Amanda crouched close to the river, cupped her hands into the water and splashed refreshment onto her face and over her head. She flung her head back and felt herself rejuvenated.

'You want a drink?'

Amanda swung round to see a young man with scruffy dark hair and the beginnings of a beard on his face.

'I'm sorry?'

The man grinned, and pointed up river to where a group of his friends were laughing and joking on the bank ahead of her, and turned to help her climb up.

'Thanks,' she said with a grin. 'Sorry, what's your name?'

'Lysander,' he said, smiling back at her. 'But mostly people just call me Xander.'

Amanda nodded.

'Lysander. I like it.'

Lysander led Amanda back to his group of friends, during which time he had quizzed her for her name and seemed to know that she lived in Woodiwiss College. She felt a little awkward in their company, as she joined the group and was passed a large glass of prosecco. She was so much older than these second or third years, and she felt it. Over and over, Amanda found that she had to tell someone her name, and then explain that she was not a student, and so in the end Amanda just went along with it, soon explaining to them about her DPhil research. All the while she drank prosecco, savouring the coldness of the drink on her dry mouth.

The conversation ebbed and flowed around studies and current affairs, to laughter and jokes, and then relationships. The girl next to Amanda – Hermia – was piling through the wine and had a corresponding affection and closeness for Amanda. She seemed to consider Amanda to be her new best friend, but she also had an affection for the blond-haired and well-groomed boy, Taylor. Amanda couldn't decide if they were an item.

Amanda smiled and drank the prosecco, just enjoying the company and fun of people who had no cares. By the height of the afternoon the heat was steaming. Wherever Amanda looked, the meadow shimmered in a haze of heat, and the refined wine glasses were dispensed with, in order to quench their thirsts from shared bottles. Suddenly another girl, Helena, a history of art undergraduate Amanda had discovered, launched herself to her unsteady feet and declared a need to cool off in the river. She dragged another boy, Ethan, to his feet, and they launched themselves hand in hand towards the river. Giddy and unsteady, Helena and Ethan splashed into the shallows and fell into a close embrace. Amanda got handed the bottle and took a long swig as she watched. She wanted a relationship like that – she never had had a relationship like that – had she? She didn't know herself anymore. Somewhere in her memory she thought there might have been someone, once; but if it had been one that had been that free and passionate, surely she would have remembered...?

Some of the others had joined Helena and Ethan wading in the water. Some of the lads had stripped their shirts and tees off, and Jon, a rugby player if ever there was one, had gone diving in the deeper water.

'Hey Xander, give us the bottle!' Helena called.

Lysander, who was left holding the bottle, scrambled to his feet and took a last swig, before stepping towards the bank. He leant over to pass it to Helena. As he did, Ethan gave his free arm a yank and Lysander toppled into the water. Amanda gave an involuntary yelp as she saw him disappear over the edge. She and the others on the bank leaned forward to look as he straightened up. He'd done well to stay upright, although his jeans were soaked through from the knee down.

Lysander cursed and swore, and shoved Ethan over backwards in a splash that ricocheted back at Helena and the others and him. Lysander turned his back on them to climb back out of the river onto the bank. Behind him Helena shrieked with laughter as she swigged prosecco, soaked from head to toe, with her clothes clinging to her body.

Lysander glanced back over, and shook his head as he returned to Amanda.

'Fools,' he cursed under his breath. 'Amateurs.'

Amanda grinned at Lysander's dry humour. From across the now broken circle, Hermia laughed mockingly.

'Oh shut up, Xander! You've done some crazy-wicked things in your time.'

'Get off—'

Lysander shook his head at her, and scratched around in a bag to pull out a new bottle to open.

'And,' Hermia said, pointing a finger at Lysander. 'The river does look inviting. I am sw-eat-ee!'

She swung round and pointed to Amanda.

'You joining me, Mandy?'

Her voice had a touch of a slur about it.

'How about you, Taylor? You want a swim?'

7

It had been such a nice day that Charlotte and Eleanor decided to break off from the office for lunch. They had texted Kathryn to see if she wanted to join them but headed out on their own a little after one o'clock, after they had had a reply to say she was deep in the midst of a commissioning meeting.

Having walked down through the streets of Jericho, they stopped at the Old Bookbinders for a steak sandwich – medium rare and oozing flavours – and a can of Coke to take down onto Port Meadow. Children were playing football in the grass, as dogs ran figures of eights and tried to round up their owners. Rowers sprinted up the river in pairs and eights, as their coaches barked instruction from the bank and scullers slid past gracefully. Elsewhere, people just sat either on their own or in pairs reading, or just chatting.

Charlotte and Eleanor sat on the bank under the dappled shade of an ancient willow tree and ate their lunch and chatted. Then they continued their walk on a circuit of the meadow that was familiar to them. Towards the northern edge of Port Meadow, with the spires of Wren Hoe behind, them they reached a point where they could hear carried on the wind the laughter and joking from a group of students, both on the bank and splashing around in the river. From a distance they could see girls in the river attempting to persuade some of their friends to join them. As Charlotte and Eleanor watched, one girl untied her wrap skirt and peeled off her vest top, before heading down to the river.

Charlotte stopped, yanking Eleanor to a halt.

'Isn't that Amanda?'

Eleanor followed Charlotte's gaze over to where another person from the group, a tall girl with shoulder length hair that shone a fiery-red in the sunlight, got up from the grass and began hoisting up her summer dress to half its length, before making her slow, slightly unsteady way down to the beach for a paddle.

'What's she doing here?'

Charlotte shook her head at her friend's question. They crouched in the grass and watched as the woman waded into the river and took a bottle from another girl. As she turned during the swigging of wine, Charlotte and Eleanor saw the face clearly.

'It is her,' exclaimed Eleanor.

'What's she doing hanging out with students?'

Eleanor shook her head.

'No idea, mate.'

'Looks like she's having fun though,' said Charlotte. 'Maybe it'll lighten her up a bit.'

'The drink definitely will. You see how much she's necking?'

They stayed watching, transfixed like car-crash television.

'Come on,' said Eleanor, pushing herself up. 'We should get on.'

They continued on their circuit through the meadow, cutting back across the other side to the canal and to Jericho.

As the afternoon turned to evening, Amanda stayed with her group of new friends, first as they went for cocktails and then for a meal. She and Lysander had taken to reading out passages from

L.E. Summers' *Flyht*, with increasingly mocking and comical accents. Lysander, it turned out, did an amazing impersonation of a fine and respectable lady of Regency England, worthy of any BBC classic adaptation. At the point while they waited for their main courses to arrive, and they were reading a passage in which Clayton declares his love for his childhood friend Lindsay, Lysander snatched the quickest of kisses from Amanda.

When it came to the end of the meal, Lysander pulled out a wallet full of notes and paid for both his meal and Amanda's even before she got her card out. They piled out of the restaurant onto Little Clarendon Street, with its strings of lightbulbs across the street and the arcade of 1960's concrete architecture. Amanda was swept up with them as they walked, sometimes skipping, up the street and across the town. She found Lysander at her side, and then his arm slipping around her. She took it easily.

The city was unusually warm, almost continental in temperature, and the streets were still busy with people. Trams shrieked on their rails down the roads, and beneath Broad Street the metro could be heard rumbling in and out of the station. The group turned into Turl Street, towards Woodiwiss College.

A college porter was stood by the oak gate into the main quad, talking with a couple of university proctors. As Amanda walked towards them, time seemed to slow for her. She did not know why, but she felt that she must not be seen. In her vision the walk down the road was a series of stills, moving with a slow staccato, towards her. She saw the faces up ahead as snapshot; looking up, and seeing her, and recognising her, and—

Amanda leant closer in to Lysander, burying her head in his armpit, as she brought his arm around her. He looked down towards her, and grinned. He was loving this. Together, wrapped in each other's arms and surrounded by their other friends, they passed through the oak doors and the porter's lodge. From the warm oppressiveness on the street outside there was an odd freshness to the air inside the quad, and Amanda could breathe again. Her feet instinctively turned to the left towards her room, but ended up having to do an odd hop, skip, and jig as she was swept away to the right with the rest.

Round the quad they went, and up to Taylor's second floor suite of rooms. Taylor, it seemed, had one of the nicest rooms – as Amanda looked round she could see how much she didn't have, including such a well-stocked drinks cabinet, which he spent no time in breaking open. Brandy and whisky were poured, and cigars lit. As Lysander drew on one and passed it to Amanda, she wondered how Taylor avoided the college fines.

Morning came with the ringing of the college bells echoing across the quad. Amanda woke, blinking her eyes open, and suddenly acutely aware of an aching pain in her neck and shoulder. She felt the throw that covered her, and, and, as she looked around herself, Lysander next to her on the sofa in someone else's college rooms.

What? How? What had happened to get her here?

Her brain ached as she tried to remember how she came to be here, but so much was fogged with the after effects of excess. Slowly, and gingerly, she eased herself out from under the throw, carefully removing Lysander's arm from where it lay across her. She sat up and rubbed her eyes, and physically straightened her head with both hands. She blinked again and looked around the room, jumping a little when she saw Taylor sitting in an armchair. She felt her head again, for the dull thud of achy pain – her hair she decided must be an absolute state. By comparison, Taylor was as neatly coiffured as he had been yesterday. He wasn't asleep or reading, but just sat, like he was waiting for something.

Amanda waited, expecting him to say something, but he said nothing. He just sat, looking out, but not at anything in particular. In his hands he held his mobile phone, but he just slid that from one hand to the other and back, stroking the edges of his phone and running his fingers across the screen. Amanda watched him, expecting him to speak. He didn't.

Memories from last night, and the afternoon before, started to creep back into her mind. She remembered Taylor, always quieter and more reserved than the others. She remembered him always with a drink, but always somewhat distant; removed, and aloof.

She stood, and turned to lay the throw Lysander, being careful not to wake him. It bothered her that she could not remember what had happened there – how they had ended up sleeping together on the sofa. Now that she looked about her she saw the others around the room, all sleeping still, some slumped in and across armchairs, and others on cushions on the floor. She could see Helena and Ethan under the sheets of Taylor's bed. And again, she looked to Taylor, sitting in the middle of it all.

'Right then,' Amanda said quietly.

Amanda thought that Taylor might respond. He did finally lift his head, turning towards her in a manner that might be about to acknowledge her. She frowned and stepped clear of the sleeping bodies. Relocating her sandals and her bag, she began to make her way to the door. Still, Taylor said nothing. Not until Amanda was at the verge of reaching for the door handle.

'You can't leave, you know.'

Amanda jumped, and turned. Taylor remained sitting where he had always been. Amanda stared, expecting something more, but Taylor offered nothing extra. She shook her head in disbelief, turned again, and grasped the door handle. She turned it, and – it was locked. Her gaze darted up and down for a key, then she tried it again. She whipped round again, and this time saw that Taylor was now standing; in his hands, she could see he was holding a key.

'Give me that.'

Amanda approached him. Taylor stood still and shook his head, smiling thinly.

'Oh no, Dr Jones,' he said. 'We need you.'

8

Watts arrived outside the entrance lodge to the University Press in the late afternoon sunshine. She found the gate manned by a jovial old man whom she recognised, and who she had always had affection for.

'Hey, Codger,' she greeted him warmly. 'How's tricks?'

Codger looked up at her from beneath the brim of his bowler hat. On seeing Watts, he grinned broadly.

'Well, well, if it ain't Young Watts,' he said. 'How's old Watts doing? Not seen him for nigh on two years now.'

'He's the same as ever.'

Codger smiled and nodded.

'So Young Watts, what brings you to The Press?'

Watts opened her mouth to answer, and then stopped herself, as she reordered the words in her head.

'Come to see a friend,' Watts said eventually. 'Amanda Jones. You probably don't know her.'

'Codger knows everyone, Young Watts,' he interrupted. 'But let me see, I don't reckon—'

He continued to mutter away to himself as he tapped two-fingered into an old computer, reminiscing about the old ledger they used to use before they brought in the damn machines. Watts smiled, keeping herself tucked into one side as other staff pushed their way out through the turnstiles.

'Jones, Jones...' Codger mumbled to himself.

The turnstile clanked again. Out of the corner of her eyes, Watts saw someone pass through and she whisked round to look. Charlotte was heading away from the gates. Watts called out and followed.

Charlotte turned and stared as Watts neared.

'Charlotte, wait up!'

'W – Watts, isn't it?'

Watts came up to Charlotte.

'Has Amanda left work?'

Charlotte didn't answer, not straight away. She chewed on her lip and shook her head.

'She's left already?'

'Never showed up,' said Charlotte. 'We haven't seen her for days. Sorry, but I need to get going...'

'I'll walk with you.'

Charlotte shrugged.

'She's not ill...?' asked Watts, as she quickened to catch up with Charlotte's purposeful pace.

Charlotte looked unsure. She shook her head.

'I don't know, sorry.'

Watts stopped for a moment, letting Charlotte walk on. Then she ran to catch up and caught Charlotte's arm. Charlotte stopped, but pulled away from Watts as she turned to face her.

'Where is she? You know, don't you?'

Charlotte shook her head, vigorously and dismissively.

'We saw her – we don't know if it was her – but it looked like her, down at Port Meadow a couple of days ago.'

Watts pricked up her attention at this.

'She was with these students, it looked like; but she was so unlike the Amanda that we're used to.'

'Changed?'

Charlotte nodded.

'I can't help you though – we're not really friends. We've seen you out drinking with her.'

Watts stared, trying to piece together the jigsaw of Amanda's life.

'So, what happened then?' asked Charlotte. 'Why don't you know where your friend is?'

Watts looked about them, beckoning Charlotte to keep walking with her.

'We had a – misunderstanding. I think – no...'

Watts smacked herself in the face and kicked out at the pavement.

'I've been so stupid! And I think, while I was trying to help her, I pushed her into danger,' said Watts. 'She's messed up.'

'She is that. I can quite agree with you there.'

'And you've no idea who the students were?'

Charlotte shook her head.

'Sorry.'

'If you see her, will you tell me?' added Watts. 'Porter's Lodge, Woodiwiss – you can find me there. Or you can leave a message for me with Old Codger.'

She gestured back down the road at The Press. Charlotte agreed, and at the corner of Walton and Little Clarendon streets, they parted.

Watts returned straight to college. Calling into the lodge, she went straight to the pigeonholes and checked under Amanda's room. Nothing. Aside from the usual college memos, it was empty. She then retrieved a room key from under the desk and headed back out. She rounded the quad to Amanda's staircase and quickly ascended the stairs to the top floor. As soon as she reached Amanda's door, she knew something wasn't right, and tried the door. The handle turned easily and opened without any need for a key. She pushed the door open and stepped in.

Matthew, bent over the drawer of Amanda's desk, looked up as Watts entered.

'What are you doing here?' quizzed Watts.

Matthew shrugged.

'I could ask you the same question.'

'Porter's duties. Delivering messages.'

'Really?'

Matthew glanced back at the empty-handed Watts and looked her up and down.

'I don't see any post.'

Watts nodded.

'And Dr Jones, she's given you permission to be looking through her belongings?'

Matthew laughed.

'Alice, Alice, my dear Alice. You should know that I don't require permission.'

'No!' said Watts, as she crossed the room towards her boss. 'You have no right to be here.'

Matthew stood up straight and faced the porter.

'And just what do you propose to do? Tell her that I was here, and I will tell her you've been helping me.'

Watts shook her head.

'She knows.'

Matthew looked up, his interest suddenly piqued.

'But you knew that. You set it up – all of it. Bringing Amanda and I together, then working to set each of us against the other. It's all been by your design.'

Matthew grinned, with an almost discernible laugh from between his lips.'

'You really think that if all this was 'by my design' that I would be searching her flat for clues as to where she is?' he said. 'She's nothing.'

He threw down the last papers he had rifled through back on to the desk and passed Watts on his way to leave.

'We both need her, let's agree on that,' said Matthew, 'And when one of us finds her, let us promise to tell the other.'

9

Louis' phone pinged out a text message from where it sat on the side in the kitchen. He lay down his knife on the chopping board and turned to wipe his hands, before crossing the room to swipe up the message. Reading it, he nodded, and went back to preparing supper.

It was as he was frying off the onions for the spaghetti bolognese that Kathryn came through to join him.

'That Sarah?'

Louis glanced round and nodded.

'She's staying at Caz's tonight – to give us some space.'

Kathryn smiled, standing at the kitchen table, fingers tracing the edges of her laptop.

'You want a sherry.'

'Yeah okay, why not?'

Kathryn, lifted the lid of her laptop to bring it out of hibernation, and then began to fetch two glasses from the cupboard and a bottle of supermarket own brand Fino Dry where it was nestled amongst several other bottles of booze, several varieties of squash, and a bottle of bleach. Kathryn delivered a glass of sherry to Louis and slipped her arm around his middle, giving him a loving squeeze before rounding the table and going back to her computer.

'How's the project going?'

Kathryn looked up as she launched Photoshop and the Lightroom software and began to explain. Louis smiled to himself as he listened to her explain the details of the project, and how it was not just a matter of handling a theme and the technical understanding, but also the theoretical and historical contexts. Last year, projects had meant producing shots as portfolio, but now Kathryn was expected to write substantial and fully referenced essays. Louis tossed equal quantities of pork and beef mince into the pan, as he considered to himself that he had been glad to have left further photographic studies to Kathryn.

He looked round and grinned, raising his sherry glass. A year ago, he had been competitive with Kathryn to make the best, most creative compositions, but now he had realised that she was by far the better photographer, and where he might have a natural eye for a good picture, she understood why.

By now the mince was browning, and he scraped in a chopping board of mushrooms to the sizzling heat. When it came to serving the dinner out into pasta bowls, Kathryn closed the lid of her laptop and moved it to one side of the kitchen table, as the closing bars of Barwick Green signalled the end of another episode of *The Archers*.

They exchanged the usual pleasantries about each other's days. Kathryn began to enthuse about a new book she had been assigned to publish, and Louis thought, as she described it that it did sound amazing. He also found himself thinking that this was right – the meal and Kathryn sitting opposite – this was how it should be. And those thoughts made him wonder why he felt that. *It had always been like this, hadn't it?* He forked another mouthful of bolognese into his mouth and looked across at Kathryn.

'You okay, Louis?'

Louis started. Lost in his daydream, he refocused his eyes onto his girlfriend - partner. He shivered, as if someone had walked through his memories. He shook his head, but knew that it was unconvincing, and Kathryn returned to him that searching, insightful gaze she had when she knew he was lying.

'I don't know. Something's missing—'

Kathryn tilted her head to one side and retuned to him a wry smile.

'And I don't mean Sarah not being here,' he said, before she could. 'It's different to that. Like I've forgotten something.'

'I know what you mean...' mused Kathryn.

Later that evening Louis had gone up to bed, and Kathryn crept back downstairs again with her phone. She swiped through the contacts and pressed to call Charlotte. The phone cycled through several pulses of dial tone until her friend answered.

'No, I'm fine, Charlotte,' Kathryn answered her friend's query. She stopped to listen to her friend's reply.

'No. I don't know,' said Kathryn, 'Charlotte, something's not right. There's something missing—'

Her flow was interrupted by something that Charlotte said.

'No, we're great. It's brilliant, in fact—'

Kathryn grinned.

'But that's the point; nothing's changed, but something has still gone.'

She threw back her head and crouched close and conspiratorial to the mobile. She tried to speak, but ended up just listening to Charlotte, and slunk down onto one of the bottom steps to sit. It was then that she saw it, on the wall in the hall; the little black and white frame. Louis.

Kathryn got up and slunk forward across the floor, plucking the picture from the wall of Louis on his wedding day.

'Kathryn... Kathryn...?'

Charlotte's voice came down the phone, as Kathryn just knelt and stared in silence.

'Why do I feel like I've met Louis' ex-wife?'

'Didn't she die? Like ten years ago?'

'When Sarah was still a baby, yes.'

Kathryn gripped the photo and stared at it with an increasingly furrowed brow.

'I don't think that's right,' said Kathryn.

Kathryn went quiet. Charlotte continued the conversation at the other end of the phone call, and Kathryn added the briefest of responses, but they were merely punctuation to her brooding thoughts. Eventually they ended the call, and Kathryn swiped back to her Facebook.

She continued to a sit on the stairs in the dark, listening to the creaking and groaning of the house at night. Her ears pricked up when she thought someone was moving on the floors above; but no it was just the whine of heating pipes. She relaxed, not realising how tense she had become. And then she heard it. Like a scratching and scurrying behind the walls, and what sounded like the patter of tiny feet. She stopped still and listened, looking out into the dark of the house; at the darker shadows that moved along the skirting and around the corners.

Kathryn glanced down at her phone and clocked the time. Then she got up and moved through the hall to the lounge, and to a shelf where she had arranged her favourite books. She moved by the light of her phone screen, and by her eyes having adjusted to the darkness. She knew exactly where, and by its feel, which book she was after, and pulled it from the shelf. She then moved across to the corner and crouched down in front of an armchair. Switching on the torch of her phone, she opened her favourite compendium of fairy tales and leafed through to one – her favourite, featuring a detailed Rackham-esque drawing of the creature she was sure she had seen scuttering through the dark.

She pretended to read, while all the time listening and watching out of the corner of her eyed, until she pounced. Her hand flew from the book into the dark shadow at her side, and snatched at something thin and bony. The thing gave off a squeal, and a tiny pitiful yelp that surprised Kathryn so much she almost dropped it.

The creature in her grip was lighter than she had imagined, and she was able to crawl across the floor to switch on a table lamp. Just as the sudden brightness almost blinded her, the creature squeaked again as light flooded the room.

Kathryn turned and faced the creature in the grip.

'I'm dreaming.

She slapped her cheek and pinched her arm until she winced. In front of her, the creature continued to look at her. Two floors up in the Edwardian house, Louis sat in his study, his hand moving his pen fast across the page as a story poured out of him, and the paper flooded with words.

When Louis came downstairs the following morning, he found a lamp on in the lounge and Kathryn slumped on the floor in front of an armchair, with her head on the seat of the chair and books discarded around her. He rushed to her, and knelt to check she was alright, only to find her sleeping soundly. Upon being shaken awake by a concerned Louis, she blinked her eyes open and sat up.

'Have you been down here all night?'

Kathryn looked about her, like she was searching for something. She began to gather up her books from the floor.

'I – I must have just dropped off,' she said, still in a bleary-eyed state of confusion. 'I think I found it.'

Kathryn looked up at Louis. The memory of her encounter with faeries crept back into her head. She wanted to tell Louis about it, but couldn't find the words as she didn't know what it was that she had seen.

Kathryn shook her head.

'Shit! Work – I need to get washed.'

She flung herself to her feet and tore from the room.

'I'll sort you some breakfast,' Louis called after her. Her thanks reached him from the second floor landing above.

Fifteen minutes later Kathryn came back downstairs, brushing her still-damp hair. Louis was in the kitchen, finishing off lunch for her with a mug of coffee, a glass of juice, and cereal waiting. She downed the juice with her vitamins and drenched the cereal in milk.

'Thanks for this,' she spluttered between mouthfuls of food.

'You remembered what it was yet?' Louis asked her, as he slid a lunchbox into Kathryn's bag.

'Remembered...?'

Kathryn slurped a hasty swig of coffee, as Louis began to remind her how she hadn't yet told him about last night, but she didn't need any reminder. Her mind hadn't been filled with anything else. Behind every door, in every corner, and under her bed, she had expected to see the little faery sprite. She had even found herself talking to them, hoping that one might be listening and show itself. But they hadn't. Maybe she had she been dreaming the whole time? Maybe they were only creatures that walked at night?

'Kathryn?'

Kathryn saw Louis waiting for a response. She glanced at her watch and rolled her eyes before collapsing into a chair.

'Shit. I'm late anyway.'

'Kathy, what's wrong?'

Kathryn sped out of the kitchen and returned in a moment with the books that she had had out last night. She took a seat at the kitchen table and gestured at Louis to sit too. Kathryn took her time as she worked through in her head what she was going to say. She frowned, and took a deep breath.

'Miss Leroy. She was the Faery Queen, right?'

Louis nodded, and Kathryn could tell he was trying to figure out where this was going.

'So, why have we never seen a faery?' She was this great, all-powerful queen of enlightenment with powers to bewitch you, and take lives to feed her own...'

She gasped for breath here.

'But no actual faeries. I never saw a faery. Did you ever see a faery?'

Louis shrugged and shook his head. Kathryn nodded.

'It's weird, right?' she said. And then: 'Last night, I saw one.'

Louis looked up and stared. He saw Kathryn looking at him, and he knew that she was telling the truth.

Kathryn took one of the books in her hands – she had been stroking the cover and the edges since she had sat down – and turned straight away to the page with the faery. As she slid the book round in front of Louis and prodded the illustration firmly, it occurred to her that that was what she had seen, of his near likeness. She had never seen that picture before. Her active mind picked holes in her memory, teasing and tussling at what she considered the truth.

'You've been dreaming, Kathryn.'

'He's called—'

Kathryn hesitated. She had spoken to the creature, she was sure, and it – he – had told her his name, but for the life of her she could not now remember.

'He lives in this house, and he's friendly.'

Louis shook his head.

'I don't what Miss Leroy was queen of, but *that* is an illustration – an Arthur Rackham.'

'How can you say that?' argued Kathryn. 'We had to use faery magic to break a spell. That's what a bewitchment is. A spell that she had over your life.'

At the same time as she argued her point, Kathryn glanced down at the illustration and compared it to her dream – no, her memory – and tried to piece it together. She remembered the moment it had first appeared; but why was she downstairs... *The phone call with Charlotte!*

'It's a spell, Louis, and some of it is still working. You created Amanda through magic, and she was still in your life through magic. Who's to say your life isn't still bound by magic?'

'But a faery, Kathryn?' Louis reasoned, as he stroked the illustration in the book and shook his head. 'There's bewitchment, or enchantment, faery magic if you want to call it that; but it's a big difference to meeting one of these in the flesh.'

'No!'

Kathryn shook her head and repeated it over and over in a percussion of denial.

'Last night, Louis. You were working late, and I didn't want to disturb you. I was sitting out there on the bottom step, talking to Charlotte on the phone. And then I saw it out of the corner of my eye.'

'Probably a mouse.'

Kathryn ignored the disbelief, trying to remember exactly what happened.

'No, I heard it first. Tiny feet, but definitely not a mouse. Then, when I went through to the lounge, that's when, as I was looking at this picture, I caught him.'

'Him! There you go.'

Louis flung his arms up in disbelief.

'One, how can you tell faeries apart so easily. And two, there's no way you could catch 'him' so easily, or else everyone would have seen them.'

Kathryn shook her head, possibly more in fury than upset.

'Louis, why don't you believe me?'

Louis didn't answer. He shifted awkwardly in his seat and fidgeted with the edge of the table. Kathryn realised how troubled he was, and reached out to stroke his hand, squeezing a little reassurance.

'I just don't understand. Everything about your life has been weird—

'You're not weird.'

Kathryn glared at him.

'You know what I mean. Everything, Louis! Why shouldn't faeries exist? I mean, it's not like I don't know what I saw.'

Kathryn sighed, and breathed out deeply, trying to calm down.

'I've believed everything you've told me - seen stuff in the past year that really can't be believed. Why can't you believe me now?'

'I do believe you. But this not a faery. This—'

He prodded the illustration.

'This is a fairytale.'

'And...?'

'Miss Leroy was queen of the faery magic. And she's gone now. It's over.'

'I'm not so sure...'

'Put it this way,' reasoned Louis, as he turned to face Kathryn more directly. 'How do you know you weren't dreaming last night? You were pretty shattered, and I found you collapsed this morning. Did you actually ever phone Charlotte?'

'Yes!'

Kathryn's response was immediate. She pulled her phone from her bag and swiped onto her call list. Her face soured...

'Kathryn?'

Kathryn sneaked into The Press, checking the door to Amanda's office as she passed, and seeing the door slid shut and the light off within, she settled into her old desk. She looked up over the divides at Eleanor and Charlotte, heads down and focussed on proof corrections.

'Charlotte?'

Her friend looked up, gaping in surprise at seeing her opposite.

'Did I phone you late last night?'

Charlotte looked perplexed.

'Umm... no. Why?'

10

Amanda sat in Taylor's suite of rooms, drumming her fingers on the arms of the chair, alert to every sound in the room. She had been kidnapped, she knew that now. When Taylor had first told her she couldn't leave she had thought, and had assumed, that it was a joke. But when he had remained deeply serious, and hadn't unlocked the door, not even after the others had started to wake and rise, she knew that this was something that they were all in on.

She cursed herself for getting into this position; but then, as she remembered the order of events yesterday, she realised that everything had been part of a meticulously planned sequence of events. She remembered now, when she first settled down to read her book by the river, that they hadn't been there. They had arrived later, chosen their spot by the river, and lured her in.

From that moment, before she had even spoken to them, she was as good as kidnapped. And worse than being kidnapped, she was also alone. There was no one who would miss her, or come looking for her. She thought of Watts, then shook her head as she remembered how even Watts was working against her.

Across the room, Lysander sat on the sofa where they had both slept last night. His hair was a wild, uncombed mane, and his face was unshaven. He caught her eye and winked. She looked away as she tried desperately to remember what had occurred between them. She remembered the kisses, and his warm breath on her neck, and her pulse raced a little at the thought of it. Was all that affection as disingenuous as it now seemed?

Taylor re-entered from an adjoining room, beaming the biggest of smiles and freshly groomed. He slipped his arms into a blue silk jacket, flashing matching braces beneath. Amanda felt her stomach turn. While she could still recognise a warmth and personable nature to Lysander, and even the girls, she had never entirely trusted Taylor. He had a way of being distant and remote, and somewhat sly; and he always watched everything. *Yes*, she decided, *always watching and never speaking.*

Helena and Hermia followed Taylor back into the main room after a short delay. They had both changed into floaty summer dresses, and Helena was tying a garland of flowers into her hair. Hermia made straight for Lysander, bending over the back of the sofa and embracing him with her arms. She held him close and moved to plant a kiss on the top of his head. She pulled back almost immediately and slapped him affectionately across the head.

'Xander, you stink!'

Hermia continued to parade the room, getting nearer and nearer by degrees to Amanda.

'Amanda, sweetie, you're still here.'

Amanda looked up.

'I don't have much choice.'

Hermia smiled and pulled up a chair alongside Amanda. She, too, began to people-watch the college room. From time to time she would look up at Amanda, before sweeping a gaze round to Lysander. She looked back from Lysander to Amanda.

'He really likes you, you know?'

Amanda turned and focussed her gaze on Hermia.

'He's an absolute dish, isn't he?' said Hermia. 'And you really like him, don't you?'

Amanda stared at Lysander, glancing briefly at Hermia too.

'I'd feel better about him if I wasn't trapped here.'

'Don't feel like you're trapped.'

Hermia took Amanda's shoulders in her hands and began to massage them.

'You're amongst friends. We're your friends.'

Amanda enjoyed a few moments of the massage before pulling away.

'I'd feel more inclined to believe you if the door wasn't locked.'

Amanda crossed the room to where Taylor was bent over a pair of old books, consulting, and cross-referencing the words carefully.

'So, when are you going to tell me?'

Taylor looked up eventually, raised an eyebrow to Amanda's question, and went back to his reading.

'You said you needed me,' continued Amanda. 'Why?'

Helena swept across the room, and tugged Amanda by the arm to divert her into the next room.

'Our play, sweetie.' Helena cooed. We're actors, didn't you know – and we need you to be our lead.'

'Co-lead–' Lysander called after them, raising a hand as a point of order.

Helena ignored Lysander and continued to usher Amanda through to the bedroom, which was more like a dressing room of backstage costumes and makeup. No sooner than Amanda was across the threshold, than friends of Taylor's swarmed about her with dresses and outfits.

An hour later, with Taylor sat in his throne-like arm chair and Lysander and Hermia in close consort together on the sofa, Amanda stepped back through from the bedroom. Her hair was newly dressed in French plaits, adorned with flowers and foliage and a tiara. She was dressed in a long, embroidered 1920s gown, with a plunging neckline both front and back.

'Oh yes!' exclaimed Taylor as he looked up at her. 'Don't you look exquisite?'

Taylor beckoned Amanda closer.

'Come, come, let us see you properly.'

Amanda obeyed, if with reticence. Lysander pounced forward off the sofa and kneeled before Amanda. He reached up and grabbed her hand to kiss it, delicately and reverently.

'You are a beauty,' he pronounced, and behind him Hermia laughed. 'You are a fine queen. Queen of all the faeries,' he continued.

'Will I do, then?'

'You are divine.'

Taylor's voice was the essence of saccharine.

'So, what now?' asked Amanda quite bluntly. 'You dress me up, put violets in my hair...?'

'Whatever you want,' said Helena. 'You're one of us now.'

Amanda smiled. She looked around at Helena, and to Hermia, and Lysander – dear Lysander, she still loved him the best – and to Taylor. She remembered the locked door, and the mischievous smile on Taylor's face as he turned the key over in his hands. The sound of a lock clunking loudly in the mechanism reverberated through her mind, echoing in as she pictured her life outside: the barren flat, the loneliness of her office, and the walk between the two; the microwave meal on her own, in an empty student room. The lock turned, clunking over in her mind. Yesterday's party, the drinks, the laughter, the dresses, the flowers in the hair; and Taylor's room of opulence.

'Is – is there a garden we can go to?'

Hermia and Helena looked towards Taylor, who smiled slowly.

'Of course.'

He moved to a side door at the back of the room.

'Come, let us all go. Lysander, come?'

11

Watts took a last look around Amanda's deserted room, seeing the few possessions as the only echoes of her friend. Backing out of the room she pulled the door closed and twisted the key in the lock, before heading down the staircase and out into the quad. She returned to the lodge and her porter's duties.

'Have you delivered to Mr Demetri yet today?' the elderly day porter asked her sometime during the morning's post duties.

Watts shook her head. She glanced up at the pigeon holes and the stack of letters and parcels.

'I'll take them up,' she said. 'I think he still owes us some fees too.'

Later that morning, Watts started out on her rounds with her porter's satchel of post. She moved from staircase to staircase, pushing memos under staff doors. As soon as she entered the staircase to Taylor Demetri's room, she could smell it; the thick smell of incense that lingered.

Watts climbed the stairs to the top landing. Here the air was pungent with the smell of the incense. She knocked at the door and waited for a reply. No answer came, and so with parcels to deliver she slipped the master key into the lock and let herself in. Once inside the room, she set the parcels down on the nearest table and turned to leave again. Something caught her eye though – something odd. She turned again and stepped back into the room.

At first glance, everything seemed normal in Taylor Demitri's rooms, with furniture arranged neatly and the small kitchen area clean and tidy. Watts pushed a half-open door to the bedroom further open, to find daylight streaming in through the windows onto a stripped bed. The rooms were cleared out and empty, like no one lived here.

'Odd...'

She crossed the room and pulled back a wardrobe door. Empty. Watts returned to the lounge area to look more closely for possessions but found none. She lifted the receiver from the telephone on the sideboard and dialled out to the lodge. After a moment it was answered.

'Yeah, I'm in Demitri's rooms. Funny thing though,' said Watts, 'Has he moved out of college rooms?'

Watts waited and listened to the reply, getting more perplexed by what she heard; and as she listened, and answered, and listened again, she continued to look about the empty rooms. And then her gaze was drawn to the mirror over the fireplace.

From the angle that she first saw the mirror, nothing seemed to be odd about it; but when Watts stepped closer, she found that she was never reflected in it, not even when she was right by the fireplace and able to reach out and touch the glass.

Standing in front of the mirror, Watts looked ahead of her at the reflection of the room behind; except that the room that she was looking was one where drunken friends had been untimely ripped from their party, to leave the remnants of excess draped across sofas and any available surface. A door in the corner that led to the back stairs was swinging open on its hinges. Watts turned her head, and looked to where in her room, the door was firmly shut.

'What on earth?'

Watts uttered the words slowly, and under her breath. From down the line of the phone – it's cord stretched – she could hear her colleague asking her over and over what was happening. She reached out towards the mirror-room on the other side of the glass, half-expecting that her hand would go through into the other room and so jumped back, surprised when her palm made contact with the glass. She scuttled back a few steps, but remained staring. Then she saw it, on the back of the chair in the room that wasn't there – Amanda's jacket, left discarded.

'Amanda?' said Watts. 'Where are you?'

Again, Watts saw the little door swinging open in the mirror. She crossed the room again, ignoring the sounds of her colleague on the phone, where the receiver was now left lying on its side on the table. The door was, as expected, locked, but she retrieved a master key and let herself through to the narrow spiral staircase. At the bottom she let herself out into the quiet serenity of the private Fellow's garden.

As she walked through the secure gates into the main quad, Watts passed a couple of elderly fellows discussing Plato, and Shakespeare's sonnets in an otherwise empty garden. From over the high stone wall, the dome of the Radcliffe Camera loomed over them.

12

Louis sat in his study as the blazing sun baked his writing desk. With his pen held over his book and poised to write, he watched the little wren where it bravely flapped and flitted on the sill of the wide-open window.

The Bakelite phone rang on his desk and the little bird flew off. Louis answered the call with his usual emotionless greeting. He listened to the other end of the line, nodding occasionally, his face grave. After the briefest of replies, he hung up.

Looking down at his novel he saw, scrawled across several blank lines, the address and time. He shook his head and crossed them through, then carried on with his story, writing around the notes.

Song Villas, 4pm. Sarah stared at the text, her phone tucked down on her lap beneath her desk in school. She'd felt the vibration of the message alert come in, and had sneakily retrieved it between reading through comparison passages of *Hamlet* and *The Lion King*. For GCSE English this was a ridiculously easy question, and she had already spewed out a good sixteen-hundred words of exam-ready bullshit.

She glanced down at her phone again and re-read the message, staring at the unknown number that had sent it. Suddenly, the shadow of her teacher fell across her desk.

'Keeping you from your social life, Miss Tumnal? Turn it off and put it away in the deepest recesses of your bag, and I'll pretend I haven't seen it.'

Sarah frowned guiltily, and slid the phone to the bottom of her bag.

In her second-floor office over-looking Beaumont Street, Kathryn worked through some proofs for the latest richly-illustrated modern fairy tale that she was publishing. She had just started discussing the pros and cons of a slightly odd sentence construction with a colleague when her mobile rang on the desk. She cursed that she hadn't switched off the ringer as it sang out her ringtone, and hastily flicked it to silent. The caller was unknown. Kathryn garbled an apology to her colleague and continued with their conversation. Barely a minute or so later, the mobile started vibrating a new call on her desk. She glanced down to see that it was the same number and swiped to reject it.

Five or ten minutes later, as Kathryn had settled back into the solitary process of her job, the phone vibrated again, a third time from the unknown number.

She snatched up her phone and barked down the phone, 'What?' And then, as she listened to the person on the other end, her face changed, from one creased with annoyance, to one of pity and concern.

'Oh, okay,' she said. 'Four o'clock, at Song Villas.'

The call ended, and she remained, for a moment, sat forward at her desk, looking at the ended call on her mobile. She frowned and put it aside, trying to put the oddness of the call behind her.

The morning drifted on; colleagues went to lunch and returned. Kathryn headed out to get a sandwich from her favourite deli on the corner and returned to the office to eat it and relax in the small staff lounge. She checked her phone for Facebook and updated and scrolled through her Twitter feed, sitting and staring some more at the call log from earlier. They had been urgent and insistent over the four o'clock rendezvous, but vague too. She shook her head and slammed her phone down, before picking up her baguette and biting down hard into it. She was pleased when she was joined by the sixty-something owner of the company, Edward, who was a kindly, older man, with the distinctive swept back hair, still dark save for a streak of silvery-white that ran through it. He began chatting to Kathryn, not about work but a walk he had been on with his wife, and his dog who was having an operation that day at the vet. When Kathryn returned, if a little late, back to work, she was completely relaxed and refreshed, and had forgotten about the bothersome phone call.

An afternoon of particularly productive work later, and Kathryn headed out onto Beaumont Street, turned left and walked past the Ashmolean and Randolph to catch the metro north from under The Broad. She alighted again at Park Town station, an underground microcosm of elegance with its glass chandeliers, handcrafted oak panels and brass fittings, and the exclusive boutiques in miniature instead of the hand-by-mouth newsagents and cheap groceries found in stations in other parts of the city. She ascended the marble staircase into a shimmering haze of heat and late afternoon sun, and crossed the road to the avenue of big houses that curved away from the Banbury Road.

Kathryn found the driveway to Song Villas just as she had last seen it. The stone pillars either side of the iron gates were half shrouded in ivy and invading creeper, with the two large wrens that graced the tops peeking out as if they were emerging from a nest. Finding the padlock broken and the chain hanging free, she slipped through onto the drive.

Louis had arrived at Song Villas early in the mid-afternoon and slipped in through the unlocked gate. Instead of walking up to the house, he had found himself drawn across the grounds to the secluded rose garden. Like so much of the garden, this too was deeply overgrown. The once carefully-tended beds and pools were a tangled mess of shrubs and weeds that strangled out the delicate roses, and even the roses themselves had passed their best as he picked his way through the lingering fragrance to the sunken garden with the series of rectangular pools. The pools themselves were overgrown, half-empty and stagnant rather than the serenity they had been before. As he stood, gazing at the head of the top pool where he still half-expected to see Miss Leroy, he thought he could hear a tune lilting on the breeze. The flute melody continued, encircling him like it was carried on the wind. Louis thought for a minute that it was the wind, but looking about he could feel the dry stillness of the hot summer's day. Birds flapped and flitted in the tree canopy above.

Louis turned again, finding himself drawn to approach the pond. As the tune continued to repeat through the rose garden, he looked down into the surface of the pool. In the dark water, between the lilies and weed, he saw himself, lips pursed, and playing the flute.

Sarah approached Song Villas from the opposite end of Park Town. Before she reached the main gates, she found the gap in the fence through which she had got into the grounds that evening a year ago. Last summer, she and Kathryn had made their way through the wooded part of the garden quite easily, but today she found herself thrashing and crashing through the undergrowth and brambles, that clawed at her arms and legs and attempted to pull her down by her clothes.

Eventually she stumbled out through the bushes, and almost fell forward into her Dad where he stood looking down into the pool.

'Dad!'

Louis only just had time to catch his daughter as she came crashing out of the shrubbery.

'Sarah? What are you—'

'Doing here?' Sarah finished. 'I got a text. I thought it was from you...'

Louis shook his head.

'I had a phone call. It was *weird*.'

'Any idea who's behind this?'

Again, Louis shook his head.

Just before four o'clock Louis and Sarah crossed the long, sloping lawn, now resembling a tangled meadow, towards the house, and arrived on the terrace to find Kathryn sitting on a bench in the sun. She looked up as they neared and smiled.

'We thought, you...' began Sarah. 'Do you have any idea who's arranged this.'

Kathryn held up her mobile.

'I even tried Googling for the number, but nothing.'

'Where is everyone?' asked Louis. 'This place, it had staff...'

Kathryn shook her head.

'It's all shut up – you know, like in *Pride & Prejudice* when Bingley packs up Netherfield. Except more final.'

The conversation went quiet as they stood around on the terrace in the late afternoon sun. Sarah kicked at her heels as she looked between Kathryn and her Dad.

'So, does anyone know what brings us here?' asked Sarah.

Louis shrugged.

'She had a local accent,' said Kathryn.

'How did she get all our numbers though?' added Sarah.

'Porter's Magic.'

The statement startled all of them, as they turned to see Watts crossing the terrace towards them in her uniform.

'Who—' asked Kathryn.

'Alice Watson,' said Watts. 'You don't know me, and I don't know you; but I know of you, and we need to work together.'

'You what?' remarked Sarah.

Watts ignored Sarah's questioning comment and turned more directly to Louis.

'You must be Lewis...'

'Louis, but yes.'

Watts smiled acceptance.

'I need your help. It's about Amanda. We need your help.'

Louis stared, and Kathryn stepped forward.

'Mum...' Sarah offered.

'Amanda's not real,' Kathryn said firmly. 'And what she was is gone.'

Watts shook her head.

'No. Amanda's as real as you and I – all of us – but she's trapped. I don't know how to explain it, but it's like she only has half a life.'

Watts watched the expressions change on each of their faces. Cross resentment and folded arms from Sarah, and withered annoyance from Kathryn.

'She's gone. Dead, for all we know.'

'No. She's been kidnapped,' said Watts. 'And it's not right. You have to help me.'

Kathryn stared at Watts with disbelief.

'You do know, I take it, what she did – what she tried to do to Louis?'

'I know that she is a woman who is really frightened, in a world she doesn't understand. I know that for her whole life she has been played with by others. She deserves her own life.'

'It's nothing to do with me.'

Louis drew closer to both Kathryn and Sarah and felt for their hands to hold.

'You invented her!'

Louis gasped at Watts' exclamation.

'Yes, Lewis, I know. I know how she was your imaginary friend, and how all of this started. And you know what? I don't care. That was then. Now, Amanda exists. You might have turned your back on her, but others haven't. They still want her to be this and that. And she... she just wants to be Amanda.'

Louis stared at Watts, as did Kathryn and Sarah. Stunned that someone else knew so much about Louis' life, they struggled to answer. As each of them worked in their own heads to put together a retort, Watts turned, and taking a bunch of keys, unlocked the French windows to the house.

Watts stepped back and ushered the others in, before following them inside and closing up the doors. For a moment they just stood in the garden room and listened to the creaking silence of an empty house. Louis shivered. Kathryn noticed Louis' unease and took his hand.

'I can feel it, too.'

'It's like she's still here...'

Louis squeezed Kathryn's hand tighter. Watts signalled with a wave of her hand to follow as she led them through the house to the top of the cellar stairs, where she turned abruptly to face them.

'I've got to show this to you,' Watts said sternly. 'But you've got to promise to stop when I do, and not go any further.'

She nodded in the direction down, and waited for confirmation of agreement from all three of them before continuing on. In the cellar, Watts pulled out her truncheon-sized porter's torch and shone it ahead of them as they stepped into the next room.

Crouched in a far corner, the girl-crone shielded her eyes from the beam of torch.

'Miss Leroy.'

Louis' cry was anguished.

'Amanda!'

Kathryn's call came on top of Louis' words.

'You - you said—' began Sarah. 'You said that Mum was kidnapped. You meant that you had kidnapped her?'

Watts shook her head.

'That's not Amanda.'

Sarah turned to face Watts.

'Then who is she? What is it?'

At the back of the room, the girl-crone was muttering words - words that might have been English, but could have been gibberish. She reached out towards Sarah and screamed.

'Truth be told, I don't know,' answered Watts. 'Matthew - my boss - I think this is his aunt. He had me doing some work here when he was entertaining college and city folk. Miss Amanda - Dr Jones, that is - she found out. I've not seen her since.'

'Did she see...?'

Sarah nodded towards the girl-crone.

'I think so, yes.'

Sarah staggered back, and Louis moved to support her.

'It would have been like meeting a shadow of yourself,' said Kathryn. 'No wonder she fled. Any idea where she went.'

Watts shook her head as she ushered the others out towards the stairs.

'I have suspicions. There are some students in my college, and I think—'

Sarah's ears pricked up, and her eyes widened.

'I saw her - Mum - out at Port Meadow. They could have been students.'

'Taylor Dimitri,' said Watts, nodding. 'Rich kid and his followers. They think they own the city.'

'And you think he's kidnapped Amanda?'

'I'm sure of it.'

'Why though?' questioned Louis.

'Same reason as Matthew, I guess,' said Watts. 'He wants to give life again to the queen of the faeries.'

'You know about the Faery Queen?'

Kathryn's surprise was loud and immediate, coming on the heels of a scream from the other room.

'Of course, I know about the Faery Queen.' Watts returned. 'This is Wren Hoe - it's nowhere *but* a place for weird shit to happen.'

'But mum - how can my mum give life to the Faery Queen?'

Sarah looked from Watts to Louis.

'It was Louis' life that Miss Leroy wanted.'

'It was Louis' life, yes,' interrupted Kathryn. 'But Amanda was his creation - the creation that was going to be her new body. If Miss Leroy's plan had worked, Amanda's life would have fed Amanda to become the new Miss Leroy.'

'That's what that thing is though.'

Watts pointed into the dark of the cellar.

'A half-girl, half-old woman. The remains of Miss Leroy's life.'

'We never finished it,' said Louis plainly.

'The Faery Queen is not properly dead, so her magic is leaderless - just drifting', added Kathryn. 'It's why everything's changing. Louis' gift is that stuff he thinks up comes true, and his thoughts have been the strongest thing in this town—'

Kathryn's voice trailed off.

'Louis, how many dreams and stories have you been having?'

13

Amanda had a glass of Pimms passed to her by Hermia, as she swept by in a dress and a hat that made her look like a cross between a grunge faery and a May Queen in the Fellows' garden. Amanda drifted up and down the grand paths in the summer heat as bees hummed around flowers, and butterflies flitted from plant to plant. Her attention became side-tracked by a conversation between Taylor and Helena across the garden when an arm reached out from behind a tree, and laid a hand on her shoulder. She jumped.

'Oh, it's you,' she said, as she gulped for breath.

Lysander grinned, and swigged beer from a bottle. Eventually he clocked Amanda's questioning gaze and tossed his head and his mane of unkempt hair.

'What?' he protested.

'Is someone going to tell me what's going on?' asked Amanda. 'What are we doing here?'

'Our play.'

Lysander's reply was a line she should know already. Amanda shook her head and mouthed confusion, until Lysander relented.

'Taylor is quite ambitious. He has a play he wants to perform, and he absolutely insists that we are all in it.'

'He doesn't even know me.'

Lysander raised a pointed finger.

'No. But even so, you are to be the star of the show,' he said, taking a swig of beer. 'Taylor has decided.'

Amanda stared at Lysander like he was crazy. She didn't notice Hermia approaching from across the garden before she flung her arm around her and squeezed her like lost friends. In her other hand she carried an oboe.

'Do you play?' asked Amanda.

Hermia looked from Amanda to the oboe and gazed consideringly at it. She held it up, at arm's length from it, and pondered the question.

'No. But Taylor tells me that you do.'

And with a swift bow and courtesy, Hermia presented the oboe to Amanda. Amanda didn't take the instrument, but after giving it a cursory glance, just stared at Hermia. Her gaze flicked briefly to Lysander, who appeared to show dim expectancy.

'Taylor said you'd know what to play,' Hermia said, as she smiled sweetly, and again offered the oboe to Amanda.

Amanda shook her head, but not, she felt, out of complete denial of Hermia's suggestion. She looked away again from Hermia and stared at the reed instrument with slow-forming decision. Slowly, Amanda reached out and took the oboe from Hermia's grip. Her fingers settling easily over the keys. Amanda glanced at Hermia, who nodded. She turned towards Lysander, who grinned back at her broadly. Inside her head, down through her veins and pulsing through her heart, Amanda felt the rhythm of the tune come back to her. She placed the reed between her lips, filled her diaphragm and—

A burst of tune leapt out of the Fellow's garden – four bars of familiar melody. Amanda stopped herself and pulled the instrument from her mouth.

'That's not right.'

Amanda shook her head and backed away.

'It was beautiful, Mandy. Don't stop.' Hermia said.

Amanda shook her head.

'No, it's not right. That's not my tune.'

'It is,' urged Hermia. 'Believe us.'

'Really,' Lysander said. 'It was very beautiful.'

'I – I can't.'

Amanda stood, looking between Hermia and Lysander. She looked back down at the oboe and her own fingers where they remained, ready on the keys. She looked up again at Hermia and lifted the reed again to her mouth.

The four bars of tune sounded out, and a further four in a variation of a repeat. From around the garden, more of the friends began to gather; Helena too. Lastly, Taylor Demetri paraded out of a downstairs room in ostentatious finery, and with a superior look about him.

Amanda continued to play, surprising herself at how quickly it was all coming together; it was a tune – Lewis' tune, she now remembered – in four bars repeated over and over, with variations and sibilance. She stepped forward into the open garden as she played, and Helena, Hermia, and Lysander encircled her with their other friends. At the head of the group, Taylor stood, proud and pleased as her tune came to a close.

'Beautiful, beautiful,' Taylor said as he stepped up to Amanda, embracing her loosely and kissing her on each cheek. 'It really works. Truly. This will be the icing on the cake to our little play.'

'When is it?' asked Amanda. 'The play,' she added when no answer came.

Helena approached Amanda and pushed a glass of chilled white wine into her hand. Amanda took the glass and sipped from it. One sip led to another, and the afternoon passed in a haze of sunshine, heat, and drinks in the Fellow's garden.

Lysander sat at Amanda's side while she slept in the dappled shade of a cherry tree. Helena brought a bag over to him and knelt on the other side of Amanda. She opened the bag and began to fetch out small bottles and vials.

'You really like her, don't you?' Helena asked, without expecting an answer.

Lysander looked up, and then back down at Amanda. He stroked his fingers through her hair. Helena watched Lysander; the gentle touch of his hands, the tiniest movements of his mouth at the corner of his smile, and the way his eyelashes twitched as he gazed down upon Amanda. Helena eased Lysander aside to apply her oils and fragrances, across Amanda's brow, and behind her ears, and down the line of her cheek bones.

'You want her to be one of us, don't you?'

Lysander looked back at Helena, held her gaze and smiled. He nodded, deftly.

14

The key turned stiffly in the lock, and Watts pushed open the door to Taylor's rooms. She led Louis, Kathryn, and Sarah in, but stopped them almost immediately.

'What?' hissed Sarah.

Watts shook her head. She had felt certain she had heard someone running from the room. She made straight for the mirror and looked through, to see the corner door firmly closed.

'Nothing. Just I thought I heard something.'

Louis shrugged.

'Why are we here?'

'This is Taylor's suite – well, his father's private residence really, which is why he gets to live here in the summer,' explained Watts. 'And I'm sure this is where he's keeping Amanda.'

Louis stared back confused. Kathryn just stared.

'There's no one here!'

Watts shook her head.

'Not here, no. But through there.'

She pointed through the mirror and stepped back to let them see.

'See how it's different? Somehow they've got somewhere that's not here, but still here.'

'They're here now?' Sarah said.

'Now here,' said Kathryn.

'Nowhere,' added Louis.

The words from each of them lingered in the air. Kathryn shivered as a chill surrounded them.

'Is – is that – Nowhere?' Sarah asked, pointing to the mirror.

Louis stepped closer to the fireplace. Up close, the huge mirror was just like any other, reflecting back himself and his every move. Behind him, too, he could see his friends and Watts. But the figures in the mirror were definitely in a different room – a room where there were clear signs of the recent party; clothes were strewn on chairs, and bottles and glasses covered every surface.

Louis turned to the others and pointed down deliberately at his feet.

'Wren Hoe,' he said, and pointed behind him at the mirror. 'Nowhere.'

Watts brought a round of drinks over to the table where Louis, Kathryn, and Sarah were gathered. They had retreated from the cloistered walls of Woodiwiss College to the narrow pub over the road, half-below street level.

Kathryn and Sarah sat either side of Louis watching him, fountain pen at the ready in front of a fresh blank page of notebook. As Watts eased herself into the seat opposite and distributed the drinks, Louis lurched into movement. He poised his pen to the page and smoothed the paper flat with the palm of his other hand. For a moment, he looked ready to write.

Louis pushed back away from the notebook and dropped his pen, where it splattered a mist of tiny dots onto the page.

'The first page is the hardest, Dad.'

Louis shook his head.

'I can't do it. I can't just write her onto the page.'

'You have to, Lewis,' said Watts. 'You created her. You gave her the life that's now been stolen from her.'

'It doesn't work like that,' Louis said adamantly. 'I never wrote Amanda's life out. She was just there – part of mine.'

'You never wrote anything down?'

'Some diaries maybe?' Louis said with a shrug.

'So, write those.'

'You can't write diaries on demand,' snapped Louis. 'Anyway, I don't want her back.'

Watts stared at him across the top of her pint of ale.

'You don't have a choice, Lewis.'

'Louis!' Louis snapped back at Watts.

The sharp words left a silence between them all in their wake. Sarah looked to Kathryn, Kathryn looked to Watts, and Watts glared back at Louis. Kathryn looked to Louis and reached out a hand across the table towards him.

'I think you have to,' Kathryn said, breaking the silence with cautious words as she took Louis' hand in hers. Louis looked back at Kathryn, then pulled back and shook his head.

'If you don't, then someone else – Matthew, or this Taylor person – will use her to bring the Faery Queen back, and we will be where we were last year.

'She's right, Dad. We have to end it now.'

Louis looked back at his daughter, glancing also at Watts and Kathryn. He looked down again at the blank page in front of him and the pen in his hand. He placed the nib to the paper and began writing, suddenly and hastily.

Lewis was sat at his usual table in the window of The White Horse, *furiously writing and oblivious to the almost complete pint of local ale* next to him, and the mobile phone on the table that slowly blinked an unread message. He didn't notice when Amanda entered the bar and arrived immediately at his table. She slid her bag down onto the bench seat next to Lewis and retrieved her purse from her bag.

'I'll get my own drink then,' she said firmly, but with an 'I'm-used-to-this' grin.

She moved off to the bar as Lewis carried on writing. Only then did he look up, too late to respond.

'Sorry, I was – in the zone,' Lewis said, when Amanda returned to the table with a large glass of prosecco.

'It's fine, no worries.'

She laughed as she pressed a kiss on his cheek and took a seat next to him.

'It's great to see your writing is going so well.'

Lewis' pen scribbled out more narrative as Amanda sat with him, watching his writing and drinking prosecco. Looking up briefly he glanced at her and smiled, then went back to his writing, Amanda fished around in her bag and pulled out a book.

The afternoon passed, with Lewis writing and Amanda reading. Lewis was comfortable in her companionship. At some point, Amanda ordered more prosecco and some bread and olives.

'Lewis. Why am I even here?'

Lewis' pen paused over the page and he looked up.

'We're having fun.'

Amanda shrugged.

'You're productive. Me, I could be doing this anywhere.'

'I like having you here.'

Amanda followed Lewis' simple statement by looking at him, waiting for him to say more.

'I know you do,' she added, with a pained grin. 'But what am I here for?'

*

Amanda lay, reclined in the sun and leaning into Lysander's lap. She felt his fingers through her hair as he plaited and re-plaited it, loosely and just for fun. Amanda drifted in and out of a dozing sleep. She drank Lysander's wine and joined in with her friend's conversation, but found herself pulled into herself – away from her friend's – to a pub, and to Lewis and his writing.

Amanda pushed her head back and gazed up at Lysander, crowned in the dappled dancing of the summer foliage above, and the glare of the sun.

'Kiss me.'

Lysander leant closer, casting his shadow across her, and obeyed. She tasted the wine-soaked lips—

'Amanda!' Lewis said sharply. He reached forward to support his wife, where she swayed back on herself and looked ready to topple.

Amanda started, woken again into the present. She sat forward and stared at Lewis, and he was drawn in as ever by her beguiling, dream-filled eyes.

'Lewis, what's happened?' asked Amanda. 'What's happened to us?'

Lewis returned her gaze blankly. Amanda pushed on.

'We never seem to know what to talk to each other about. You sit and write – I work – we don't even play music together anymore.'

Lewis gulped, and his hand went to the wedding ring that hung on a chain around his neck.

'We – we do more than that–' Lewis mumbled quietly.

In the garden, Hermia brought the oboe to Amanda, presenting it to her as an offering. Amanda took it and sucked on the reed, to moisten it ready for playing.

'Do you remember?' asked Hermia.

Amanda nodded. In her head she heard the haunting melody that had been the soundtrack to her life. She wriggled herself up and folded her legs under her before readying herself to play. The tune was in her head, and she nodded the rhythm to herself. She placed her fingers to the keys, breathed in, and played.

It was a fragment of a melody: four bars of a tune that had haunted her life. She paused and played it again and again, over and over, her fingers moving over the keys, as she played the same lilting notes. Lysander sat up, listening to the music with each hand cupped gently on Amanda's waist. Hermia kneeled nearby and felt the music, and Taylor and Helena stopped to listen.

Lewis' pen scratched to the end of a sentence. His head was filled with music – his music. He looked up at Amanda – their music. He reached across at Amanda and snatched her hand.

'Lewis!'

He shook his head.

'I love you.'

'Louis?' Kathryn asked, as she reached to steady Louis. His face was pale, and he was swaying backwards and forwards in his chair. 'Help me lay him down!'

Sarah and Watts sprang to Kathryn's assistance, and pulled the table out to allow room to ease Louis down onto the floor and lift up his legs, as his body went rigid and his eyes became wide and empty.

Kathryn was screaming Louis' name and trying to bring him round from the fit he was having. Next to her, Sarah was panicking for her father, and Watts was bringing them a jug of water and a new glass. She poured one quickly and passed it to Kathryn.

Slowly Louis came around, groggy and confused. He reached for his head, and then the glass of water that Kathryn offered to him and helped him sip from.

'What was that?' Kathryn asked, as she heard some mumbled sounds.

Louis swallowed another mouthful of water and hummed the phrase again, a repeated fragment of notes. Kathryn recognised the tune. She shook her head and reached to close his mouth.

'No, Louis,' she told him. 'Don't sing it.'

Amanda's posture dropped in the sun-soaked Fellow's garden. Her lips released the reed, and her grip loosened over the oboe as it sunk back into her lap.

'You almost had him, didn't you?' Hermia asked.

Amanda nodded.

'I could feel him.'

PART FOUR

Free

semplicemento

1

The heatwave that had gripped the nation continued into the first weeks of September, until a sudden and sharp drop in temperature plunged them into autumn. The trees that had all kept their leaves suddenly displayed a brilliant array of bright colours that made the city streets seem almost like a second spring.

After fervently writing Amanda back into existence, Louis had been careful to only write a few pages a day, to keep the link there. Beyond that he worked on his second novel, attended the local Indie Author meetups, and enjoyed long walks in the countryside with Kathryn.

'What are you thinking?' Kathryn asked, looking up from her laptop where she had it perched on her knees as she sat on the day bed in Louis' study. Louis was gazing dreamily out the window.

'Louis?' she said again.

He started and turned towards her.

'You okay?'

He shrugged and looked back to his writing.

'It's like we're in limbo, isn't it?' Kathryn continued. 'We're just waiting.'

Louis turned again.

'I'm done with this. I just want it over.'

Kathryn frowned.

'I know.'

'Why can't we just go sort it now?' Louis snapped. 'It's so frustrating.'

'Watts seems to think we have to wait—'

'Spring and autumn are times of change, yadda yadda yadda – yeah, I get that...'

'It *does* make sense.'

'And it's autumn now! Kathryn, what *are* we waiting for?'

Kathryn frowned again and glanced back down at her photo editing as he went back to his writing.

'Our move, Louis,' she muttered under her breath, in a low grumble.

Watts advanced her knight forward, taking her opponent's rook in the process, and set the piece down on the table. She took up her glass of whisky in exchange.

'Check,' she said, and grinned at her adversary across the table. She sipped a mouthful of whisky.

Across one of the long college benches of the Woodiwiss dining hall she played Matthew. Alone in the vaulted hall they could hear the creaking silence of the ancient roof timbers, as Matthew leant forward and studied the board carefully. Eventually he moved his own bishop across the squares and took Watts' knight.

'Hasty, Watson,' he said and leant back away from the table, as he folded his arms behind his head. 'Too hasty.'

Watts shook her head and struck a last pawn across the board.

'Think you'll find that's checkmate, sir.'

Watts knocked back the last of her whisky and stood. She flicked Matthew's king over, where it bounced twice and rolled to a stop on the chess board.

'Goodnight.' Watts added, as she stepped away from Matthew and walked the length of the hall. As she left, she turned back briefly to see where he remained, sitting over the finished game.

Walking down the steps outside of the Woodiwiss dining hall, Watts crossed the quad in the fading light of autumn there was freshness to the warm evening air. She turned towards the lodge and soon passed through the gates to the road.

Cutting diagonally across the road, Watts quickly turned down the narrow alley that led out onto The High, to be caught up in a throng of fair-goers. She weaved her way in and out of the crowds as she made her way up through the main street, closer to the pounding and relentless music, the spinning neon lights, and the sickly smell of candyfloss and burger vans.

Just before the church of St Mary Magdalen loomed into view, where it rose up out of the middle of the annual St Giles Fair celebrations, she joined Louis, Kathryn, Sarah and a girl she vaguely recognised where they were standing just away from the main thoroughfare and crowds.

'We thought you weren't coming,' Louis said, as Watts stepped up to join them.

'I said I'd come,' said Watts. 'And it was my idea. If we are to find Amanda, then tonight at the fair is the time. She has to be here.'

'And you think Taylor and his friends will be here.'

Watts nodded.

'Sure of it. Call it Porter's Magic if you like. They won't be able to resist.'

Louis nodded agreement. After a few moments they all began to move off again into the crowds.

'Caz! Stop staring!' Sarah hissed, as she saw her friend staring at Watts.

'Why are we helping her? Isn't she a friend of Amanda's and of the Leroys?'

'She's a friend of my mum's. She's trying to break Amanda free of both the Leroys and us – but to do that she needs our help.'

Sarah was jostled closer to Caz as they re-joined the flow of people up the main street. Watts followed them, and Kathryn after her, with her hand firmly holding onto Louis'.

Gunshots echoed through the medieval streets, and both Kathryn and Louis jumped visibility. Somewhere a short way off, the crowd roared, and Sarah and Caz had stopped to point. Through a parting crowd, Lysander could be seen returning a rifle to the coconut shy and receiving the biggest of cuddly bears in return. He turned and presented it with an embrace and a kiss to Amanda.

'There, look—'

'She looks so different.'

They watched as Amanda and Lysander moved off further into the fair. Amanda looked almost unrecognisable in one of Hermia's dresses and with her hair braided into plaits and woven with flowers.

'Hey, Katherine! Louis!'

Kathryn spun round to see Charlotte and Eleanor pushing their way through the crowds towards them. She tugged at Louis' hand to halt him and called back to Watts and Sarah to wait, as the seething crowds of fairgoers seemed ready to wash them apart.

'Did you see Amanda there?' Kathryn asked her friends.

'Yeah, and she's changed a bit since her extended leave.'

'She's not been at work either?' Kathryn asked, as she looked back round a bit to Louis to see if he had heard.

Charlotte and Eleanor joined the others and they continued on up through St Giles. The tall, grand façades of the Ashmolean and Morton College flanked the fair like the sides of a canyon. Lights swirled, and rides lifted screaming children high over the roof tops. PA systems threw out their music as Kathryn and Louis pushed on through the crowd, with their friends and Sarah and Caz following. Sometimes they seemed to lose sight of one another, but they would soon re-emerge, bobbing to the surface of the crowd.

'Can you see them?'

Louis turned towards Kathryn's face and tried to lip-read the question that he couldn't hear for all the noise. She ducked closer and repeated the question in his ear.

'—Amanda and Taylor – they can't just have disappeared.'

Then Sarah and Caz were in front of them – explaining something – and pointing.

'You what?' Kathryn shouted back over the din.

Sarah pointed again, through to where the old helter-skelter loomed up in ribbons of colour and painted wood.

'We've got to get above the crowd!' Sarah shouted again.

This time Kathryn understood, and they all began to ease themselves between the eddies of tightly bunched shoals of friends. Soon they were in the queue for the ride and slowly moving forward to the entrance, with coins for the boy on the gate. They took their mats and waited to climb the stairs and emerge at the top of the tower above the crowds, above the height of the neighbouring stalls. Even with the determination of the matter in hand to find Amanda amongst a sea of bobbing heads, they could not fail to thrill at the fun of it.

Caz launched herself down the spiralling, accelerating ride, screaming with delight as she went. Sarah followed, but just as she slid off the starting platform she heard Kathryn call out.

Looking up she saw Kathryn's arm pointing and turned to follow with her own gaze as the mat pulled her off onto the spiral down the helter-skelter. Her gaze was flung out across the crowd, and for the briefest of moments she caught sight of the auburn hair of her mother. And then the ride twisted her round, and flung her about and down, and she tumbled out the bottom.

It hardly seemed any time before Sarah was leaping clear as Kathryn tumbled to the bottom of the ride and scrambled to her feet to join her.

'She was over there—' Kathryn said, pointing through the fair.

Once everyone was back together they began to head that way, weaving through the crowds until they saw Amanda, standing in the queue for a ride and chatting with her student friends.

Sarah launched herself forward.

'The queue is not long. We should be able to get in the same group—'

Caz followed, with Watts, and Kathryn and Louis followed them too. In front of the imposing sandstone frontage of a Wren Hoe college building was the House of Mirrors – hardly recognisable as the truck that it unfolded from. Kathryn winced and clutched at her side, as her old wound resurfaced. She stopped.

Louis turned and looked.

'What's wrong? Kathryn?'

Kathryn shook her head. She stood and stared at the gaudy-painted fairground ride, remembering the mechanical workings behind the maze of mirrors, and her sliced hand, and how close she had come to greater harm two years previously. She shivered.

'Louis, I can't,' she said. 'I can't go back in there.'

Louis stepped closer, reaching out to hold her close to him.

'It's okay, you don't have to.'

The queue shuffled forward. Up ahead Taylor handed over a wad of notes to cover admittance for all his friends, and Amanda followed them through the turnstiles. The queue moved on accordingly, and Kathryn moved with it. She stared, her gaze fixed, on the ride up ahead, and the frontage of primary colours that proudly announced the house of mirrors.

Slightly at first, then with more determination, Kathryn shook her head. She turned and stepped away, pushing her way out of the queue.

'I'm sorry. I can't do this.'

Sarah swung round and craned her head to look at where Kathryn was headed.

'But Amanda? We have to—'

Sarah caught Louis' eye. He shook his head at her.

'You go,' he said, and then looked round at Watts. 'Watts too. You know what to do. We'll wait for you here.'

Louis turned and pushed his way back to re-join Kathryn and hugged her tightly. Caz and Sarah were suddenly at the front of the queue with Watts, and Eleanor and Charlotte too, and the man on the gate was demanding entry fees.

2

Kathryn stood with Louis in the St Giles Fair, staring through the lights and haze of people at the House of Mirrors ride. Her head was filled with a monotonous and all-consuming buzz that pressed upon her other senses. She watched as one by one her friends entered the ride. She flinched away, and squeezed her eyes tightly shut as she buried her face in Louis' shoulder, feeling his warm embrace surround her. Eventually Kathryn emerged from her comforting snuggle, and slipping into his arms she edged away from the ride with Louis in the direction of a coffee van.

Sarah followed Caz into the House of Mirrors with Watts, Eleanor and Charlotte following. A warped, thinly-stretched version of herself greeted her at the door. In another mirror, a squidged-fat butler welcomed her with a cackling voice. They stepped through into another passage, past more mirrors of ever-more inventive shapes that twisted and distorted reality.

'There,' Sarah said.

She saw Amanda further on and rushed forwards, following them around a twist in the corridor to be confronted by a wall of mirrors.

'Where did she go?'

Sarah turned, and turned again, looking and searching, her mouth gaping. Caz tugged on her friend's arm and pointed. In the mirror in front of her, they could see Amanda walking away from them down a long, tiled corridor.

'How?' asked Caz, but she expected no answer.

The whir of machinery and cogs turning signalled the walls shifting, and a glass mirrored wall shifted into position behind them.

'Sarah?'

Watts' call came from the other side of the glass. Before they could answer, the floor beneath them started to turn, twisting in a clockwise motion to counter the turning in the opposite direction of the mirrored walls. Shrieks of fright and excitement echoed through the walls from elsewhere in the ride, as the machinery came briefly to a stop. Dust fell in eddies, falling from the boarded ceiling of the truck. The cogs started turning again, and Sarah and Caz swung round to face the mirrored wall as it opened up into another chamber. They stepped forwards, and the mirrors snapped shut behind them.

'Watts?' Amanda asked as she stared back. 'What are you doing here?'

She reached out and her fingers touched the other side of the glass. Watts stared with confusion as she looked into the mirror, not at her own reflection but that of Amanda. Her arm had reached out towards the mirror, a perfect reflection to the pose that Amanda held; their fingers all but touched, separated only by the thin layer of glass mirror.

'Amanda?' she replied. 'Where have you been?'

To either side of her, Watts could see reflections of herself from every angle reflecting onwards and onwards. Behind Amanda, Watts could see her own reverse reflection, and that reflection was facing another of herself in every mirror.

'How have you done this?'

Amanda shook her head and lifted a finger to her lips. Somewhere, far off in the kaleidoscope of reflections, a door opened in one of the reflections and Lysander let himself through. He pushed his way past each Watts-reflection in turn, until he arrived at Watts' side and took her hand in his.

'Hurry,' he said. 'You can't be late.'

Amanda turned and followed Lysander through each reflected room in the maze of mirrors. Watts watched their path through the reflections and wondered how to follow them. The machinery cranked into action again, with the sound of wheels scraping metal against metal, and the mirrored Watts turned again. Watts kept her gaze fixed on the door through which Amanda and Lysander had left, determined to keep it in sight as the reflections moved and slid about her.

Watts.

Watts heard Amanda's soft voice calling her from somewhere far off through the mirrors. Elsewhere there was the sound of the fair, and excited children in the ride ricocheted around in a way that Amanda's voice hadn't.

Watts.

Amanda's voice called out again.

Watts saw the door, reflected about six mirrors back in the maze of glass. She heard the motors grinding to life again and chose her moment. Determined to find Amanda, she prepared herself and took a step forward, towards her own reflection, and through. The world seemed to turn around her as she was suddenly somewhere else in that endless repetition of repeated and mirrored worlds. She continued to step on, keeping her gaze focussed on the door, on and on until she was standing in front of the door. Around her the wheels in the mechanism scraped and squeaked, and she grasped the handle and flung the door open, stepping through as the mirrored panels turned again.

Watts found herself in a long wood-panelled corridor, with a checkerboard of red and white Victorian tiles. She stopped and looked up and down the length of the corridor, which seemed to go on for ever in either direction with no sign of anyone in it.

'Amanda?'

Watts walked in one direction and then the other. *Which way to go?* There were no side doors to this corridor as far as she could see. She turned and looked for the door through which she had come but couldn't find any trace of it.

'Damn!' Watts cursed herself.

Sarah and Caz turned and turned again in the house of mirrors. As one panel opened another closed behind them, always pushing them on through the maze. Sometimes convex and sometimes concave, every mirrored panel warped and twisted their reality. Sometimes the panels were completely flat and tightly packed, in a multi-sided and completely segmented heart to a never-ending repetition of themselves.

'Where did Amanda go?' asked Caz.

The mechanism grinded again and fed them further on into the maze, and a mirrored panel snapped shut in front of them. As the quivering image came to a standstill, they saw Amanda standing in front of them.

'Sarah. You've come!'

'Mum?'

Behind Amanda, Lysander and Hermia were waiting for her, urging her to follow impatiently. Amanda smiled at Sarah.

'Come with me.'

Sarah watched the end of her hand as she reached out. Amanda mirrored her daughter's moves. At the smooth glass of the mirror, they touched. Beyond the glass, Sarah felt the warm pulse of her mother's fingers. They slipped between one another's into a hold.

'Mum,' Sarah said. She nodded and beckoned her mother to step closer.

'Join me,' Amanda answered and tugged on her daughter's hand.

'You come here,' said Sarah firmly.

'Sarah please.'

Amanda smiled with that coy look she was so good at. She tossed her head back and flashed rays of auburn hair. Alongside her, Lysander and Hermia encouraged Sarah.

For a moment Sarah hesitated. She knew that the secret to what was happening lay with her mother, and so she should take this opportunity to be where Amanda was and work on her.

'Please Mum.'

The creaking-cranking of the ride workings shuddered into movement again, signalling another all-change in the mirrors. Amanda's grip tensioned, and she yanked at Sarah's arm just as the mirror shuddered into movement and began to turn. Sarah found herself flung forward and crashed not through to join her mother, but smack into the face of the glass. From the corner of her eye she could see her own eye looking back at her, and her cheek squashed flat against the glass as the mirror moved. Caz shrieked her friend's name and pulled Sarah away in time, before the panels snapped open, rotated, and shut again, pushing Sarah and Caz on through the maze of mirrors.

The next floor to ceiling panel snapped shut in front of her and the machinery went silent once more. Amanda shivered. She looked around her, to her left, and to her right; Lysander and Hermia were gone. She gasped unconsciously and looked around again. She jumped again, physically startled as she saw in front of her in the mirror, her own mother and father standing to either side of her own reflection.

'Mother? Father?' she asked. 'What are you doing here?'

'Amanda, dear. You don't believe for a moment that we care nothing for you.'

Amanda staggered back, recoiling from her father's voice.

'Because we do care for you,' Amanda's mother added. 'Of course we care.'

'You abandoned me in a college room!'

'Nonsense. We've been following your progress,' Professor Jones added. 'Had you needed us, we would have been there.'

'I did need you!' Amanda screamed back at them. 'You left me alone when I had no one. And nowhere to go—'

'And you're now here...' Amelia Jones added. 'You had a good job with a future. Now what are you doing? Fraternising with students.'

'When have you ever cared who I *fraternise* with?' Amanda smashed the answer back across the net to her mother. 'You didn't care how much time I spent with Lewis when I was at school. Did you ever wonder why I spent so much time at his house?'

'What your mother is trying to say is that we never worried about your choices with Lewis. You should never have left him.'

'He left me,' said Amanda. 'Why do you not understand that?'

'You let him leave,' her father told her, and her mother nodded agreement.

The mechanism geared into movement again, and the image of her mother and father flickered as the panel began to move on. Behind her a panel snapped open, and Lysander and

Hermia were here to lead her on into the maze as her parents were snapped away from her again.

Louis and Kathryn waited near the exit to the hall of mirrors ride, holding cups of hot chocolate close to them in both hands and watching as the latest group of ride-goers started to leave the exit, whooping excitedly from their experience. Louis nodded his head towards them, as they started to recognise the faces of people who went in before Amanda and Sarah.

Then came Taylor himself, arm in arm with Helena, followed by Hermia, and after her Lysander and Amanda. They stepped down off the ride and dispersed into the crowd.

'We shouldn't lose her now,' said Kathryn, glancing between the House of Mirrors and where she could still see Amanda in the crowd.

'Sarah, though.'

Kathryn nodded.

Charlotte and Eleanor were next to leave the ride and were quick to re-join Kathryn. Then Caz, and Sarah. As Kathryn and Louis looked on, they knew something wasn't right.

'Freaking weird.'

Caz kept on repeating her review over and over as Louis and Kathryn met up with the two young friends.

'What happened in there?' asked Louis. 'Did you see Amanda?'

Sarah nodded. Her composure was agitated and out of kilter. 'What else?'

Kathryn smiled compassionately, but her gaze was probing.

'It didn't make sense,' Sarah tried to explain. 'The mirrors – they reflected us sometimes, but, sometimes they weren't reflections; and the way they moved, it really messed with our minds.'

'We never caught up with Amanda—' added Caz.

'But she saw us,' said Sarah. 'We spoke to her. She wanted me to – I almost—'

Sarah turned towards Louis and buried her face in his chest as she embraced her father.

'I'm sorry. It was too tempting.'

Louis patted his daughter and hugged her, reassuring her with warm words.

'That ride is evil,' Kathryn said. 'I don't like it.'

Eleanor and Charlotte were suddenly back with their friends, talking on top of each other.

'We know where Amanda is—'

'We saw her. She and her friends, they—'

'They've gone to the *Eagle*...'

'They didn't,' Charlotte said from behind. 'They were going to, but I heard them change their mind. It's *Cloisters* – you know, down Friar's Entry...'

Louis and Sarah both looked at each other and nodded.

'We should go,' Kathryn said.

As they all began to move off, Caz stood firm. She called after them in her thick Wrenshire accent:

'What about your friend?'

They stopped, and each turned around.

'Watts...?' Kathryn said. She scanned the crowd. The exit to the house of mirrors was sealed again for the next ride, and they could hear the shrieks of excitement and terror coming from within.

'Did anyone see her leave?'

Louis shrugged, and Sarah shook her head.

3

Watts walked the long walkway that seemed to stretch on forever with no doors to either side. The walls were lined with portraits in gilt frames, themselves framed by the ornate plasterwork and coving. Her footsteps echoed on the tiled floor, with iron grilles running down each side to hide the heating ducts. Around her, the hallway reverberated with a humming; a continual slow-beating *lub-dub* that seemed to come from the very walls themselves. Watts reached out and placed the palm of her hand to the wall where she could feel the beat through the plaster. She walked on, trailing her hand behind her across the wallpaper.

She looked at the portraits as she walked the long hallway. They were all men, young and, she had to admit, attractive. The further Watts walked down the corridor, the closer to the present day she seemed to get. Renaissance portraits gave way to later eras, through the Victorian, Edwardian, and Georgian ages until paintings themselves gave way to photographs and the war years. She stopped suddenly at a formal portrait of a young dark-haired man in police sergeant's uniform. The eyes caught her first, bright and staggering. They drew her in immediately as Lewis'.

Her gaze dropped to the title plate at the bottom of the frame, Sergeant C.H. Tumnal. It was Lewis' father! She stepped on to the next photograph, the first in colour – of Lewis himself, then aged twenty-one at his university graduation. Watts stepped on to look at another portrait, to be met with Sarah's face staring back at her from the wall. And that's where the pictures ended, although the corridor continued.

Behind her, in the middle of the corridor, was an octagonal table with decorated fine marquetry of geometric patterns. As Watts stared down at it she saw in the pattern a stylised clock, but a clock of eleven hours. Eleven hours? Watts stared closely at the marquetry between the main eleven sections. Hours, or years? Her fingers traced the marks as the dividers of months and days.

'It's a calendar.'

Watts turned her attention to what was on the table. In the centre was a vase of hyacinths, dried but not by design, a framed photograph of an elegant woman in a long dress, and some books and sheets of music, together with a tin whistle. Watts took up the photo frame and returned it almost immediately. Too easy. It was Miss Leroy. She glanced over the books: Latin fables and fairy tales, but her attention instinctively went to the tin whistle and the music.

Lub-dub, lub-dub, the long hallway pulsed through her. Watts looked up and down the corridor. She found herself fidgeting with the tin whistle in her fingers as the room continued to beat through her. She looked down at the sheet of music and tried to remember back to those few music lessons she had had as a girl, before she had cut her hair short and discovered rock. She turned the sheet music on the table to face her and scanned the opening phrase, before placing her lips to the whistle and played.

It was all wrong. Watts pulled the whistle out her mouth and sunk to the floor. She put back her head and bashed it against the wood-panelling behind.

'That it should come to this.'

Watts heard the voice and looked up, blinking her eyes open. Matthew Leroy-Song stood a few feet away.

'The fate of the curious,' said Matthew. 'How are you going to get out of this?'

Watts looked up, remaining crouched.

'There has to be a way out. At one end.'

Matthew shrugged.

'Probably. Not that I've ever found it. The End, I mean.'

'What is this place?' asked Watts. 'Where am I?'

Matthew laughed and smiled to himself as he stepped closer to the table, looking cursorily at the objects it contained. Occasionally he tossed a wry grin at Watts.

'What isn't it, more to the point. A metaphor for life is probably the best way of describing it. It was my aunt's. She had it built.'

Watts scrambled to her feet.

'How far does it go back?' she asked, pointing back down the lines of portraits.

Matthew shrugged.

'Years. Never been to the beginning. It goes on forever that way too. There's no way out.'

Watts stepped up to him.

'You got here though?'

Matthew laughed.

'So, did you.'

Watts stared and scowled.

'There was a door when I came through. I didn't expect not to be able to go back.'

'You know how to leave,' Matthew said coolly.

Watts stared vehemently at him. She turned away and stepped back to the table and snatched the music nearer.

Ramming the tin whistle between her lips and ignoring the pain as it hit her teeth, she played the tune. Over and over she played the music, adding to the intonation and the rhythm at each repeat. It was a lively and folk-like tune, and it carried her along.

At first nothing happened. Watts stood in the corridor playing the tune and hearing the at times screeching metallic sound of a rarely-practiced instrument scraping down the back of her mind. After finger fumbling and mis-blows Watts landed on the rhythm, and the random collection of notes she attempted to play formed themselves into a dance, a jig, behind which the corridor itself pounded out the beat.

The gas lamps that lined the corridor flickered and caused shadows to dance and leap from the walls. Watts turned on her feet as she played, and the corridor seemed to turn with her. At her feet she found soil and leaves being kicked up from the tiled floor. Something reached out and touched her shoulder.

Watts spun round and found her face whipped by a branch that was reaching out from a tree. She spun around again and saw that where once there had been a wall, there were now trees. In front of her the table was a forest altar, shrouded in creepers and ivy.

Louis stood in the middle of the fair, surrounded by his friends, and with Kathryn clinging to his arm. Her eyes were fixed on the House of Mirrors.

'So, what happened to Watts?' asked Louis. 'Where did she go?'
Sarah looked up at her Dad.
'Nowhere.'
Louis stopped and looked at his daughter.
'You mean...?'

'It's obvious. So obvious we've been staring ourselves past it for months,' Sarah continued. 'Where's the one place that we can all go and never be found?'

Louis stared blankly.

'Nowhere. She's nowhere,' added Sarah. 'That's why she's not here now. That ride is some sort of portal – probably the same as the mirror in Taylor's room – and certainly at Song Villas.'

Kathryn closed her hand tighter around Louis'.

'The leaf monster that attacked me at the fair before – it came from–'

'From nowhere.'

'So, to find Watts–' began Louis tentatively.

Sarah nodded enthusiastically and encouragingly.

'–is to find Nowhere.' Kathryn finished.

Watts ran. The tin whistle still clutched tight into her fist, and dived through the trees, leaving the tiled corridor where it remained overgrown and pushed up by tree roots behind her. Branches seemed to reach out to hang onto her and hold her back as she ran, chasing torches in the distance, and the voices of Amanda and her student friends.

Watts caught a stitch and stooped to a stop, bent over double as she wheezed the breath back into her. Looking ever onward she could see the torches making off, and the voices fading into the distance. Clutching at her thighs she caught her breath and slowly straightened up to make ready to continue.

Either side and all around her, the trees pressed close. She had to push her way through, before the trees closed in on her. In amongst the thick forest it was dark as night, and claustrophobic enough to suffocate her. Watts found herself crushed, like she was at a rock festival. Her heart beat faster and faster as the need for breath – and fresh air – became greater. She felt the tin whistle clutched tightly in her sweaty fist. *Of course.* She lifted the whistle up and stared at its battered look. *It brought her here, so–*

The tune leapt out of the instrument as a dancing folk jig, and surprised even Watts with its rhythm. She didn't notice at first, but the trees were quick to react. Evening light poured in through the canopy, and with it a rush of air. Watts could breathe again. She continued to play as the glade widened, and the trees parted.

Kathryn raised her head to stay their conversation. Questioned by the others as to why, she shook her head and gestured to her ears for them to listen. Across the amplified beat of competing speakers, the continual drone of the generators, and the hum of voices, there was a song. Sparkling with brightness like a courting songbird, the folk rhythm of a tin whistle cut through everything.

'It might be nothing, but...' said Kathryn.

'It might be – something,' said Louis. 'Where?'

They all scanned the busy city centre street as rides whizzed and whirled about them, accompanied by screeches of delight and fear.

'There!'

Louis and Kathryn whipped round to see Sarah pointing through the crowds to where they could see a circle in the crowd forming. People were turning, facing inwards to watch where the music was coming from. Louis, Kathryn, and Sarah, dived forwards, excusing their way past people, and pushing their way to the front. In the centre of the circle, Watts played, entranced by her own song.

The song came to an end and Watts remained standing where she had been playing. In front of her, surrounded by many more anonymous faces in the crowd, were Louis and Kathryn and Sarah.

'You.'

Louis looked back at Watts.

'I know. It's me.'

Fifteen years earlier, and Amanda sat on the end of Lewis' bed on the eve of leaving home for university. Across the room, neatly stacked on the floor, were her bags – a rucksack, small suitcase, oboe case, and small daysack. Around her Lewis moved about the room, packing his bags and choosing between which books to take with him, before stowing them in between layers of clothes.

'You excited, Lewis?' asked Amanda. 'For tomorrow?'

'Terrified.'

'You don't see it as an opportunity for things to be different?'

'All the time,' said Lewis. 'It's my main reason for going to uni – to do things differently. To be different. Doesn't stop me being terrified by the prospect.'

'You want to go for a walk in a bit, down by the canal maybe?'

Lewis smiled.

'That would be nice.'

He crossed the room and retrieved some precious possessions from the top of his desk, wrapped them in scraps of bubble wrap, and tucked them into his case.

Later they both bounded down the staircase of Bevington House and crossed the hallway.

'Mum, Dad – Amanda and I are just going for a walk–' Lewis called out through the open doorway to the lounge, from where his father's Mozart records could be heard. Before his parents could answer, Lewis was pulling the front door closed behind him, and his

fingers were slipping in between those of Amanda's as they crossed the gravel path.

There was still a blue cast of light in the September sky as Lewis and Amanda walked down through Jericho to the canal.

Louis, then eighteen-years old, turned off the side street, down the narrow-cobbled lane behind the old boat yard. The high brick walls of old warehouses blocked out the last of the evening light, and he walked in and out of pitch black shadows as he made his way down to the canal.

He turned sharply left, and right again, and took a small flight of steps down onto the towpath. As he walked along the side of the canal, he watched a group of lads up ahead. His hands closed around the Sony Walkman in his hand, and his thumb nudged the volume dial up a touch on the Haydn trumpet concerto that came through the earphones.

A blend of evening light and street lamp illumination picked out the gang where they loitered around the next bridge. Louis knew them well – a couple were from the upper years of his school, but most, including Matthew Leroy-Song, were from the private school down by the river. Even over the sound of his music, Louis could tell that the gang's banter was dissipating as their gaze turned to follow him along the canal.

Matthew swung over the railings and jumped to land on the path in front of Louis. Louis stepped to one side of the path, and Matthew, dressed in designer chinos and ironed linen jacket, moved to block him.

'Oi, Tumnal, don't you ignore me.'

Louis kept his eyes fixed on the path ahead and moved to continue.

Matthews' hand shot out and pulled Louis back by his arm, twisting him around to face him. Louis glanced away, unable to return the fixed stare. Matthew snatched his outstretched arm and held the earphones off.

'It's rude to ignore your friends, Tumnal.'

Louis stuttered an answer and faltered.

'What are you listening to anyway?'

Matthew flicked the headphones off Louis' head and caught them in his hand.

'Hey!'

Matthew shook his head dolefully and, pushed one of the phones to his ear.

'Classical,' he said with a nod. 'Auntie would be pleased.'

'Give it back to me–'

'I prefer something edgier myself. The Doors, maybe. If you can't manage some classic Pink Floyd.'

'Give it back–'

'Come, come. You don't have to beg Tumnal. You just have to say the magic word,' said Matthew, before adding: 'Did mummy dearest not teach you manners?'

Tomorrow morning Louis was leaving Wren Hoe for university and a new life, away from the bullying and the loneliness. He felt anger now for Matthew souring any remaining joy in his last night in his hometown. He tried to reach forward and grab the headphones. Matthew thrust them further away and yanked the jack out of the headphone socket. The Walkman itself flew out of Louis' hands and skittered across the towpath.

The Walkman came to a stop under a firmly placed foot. Amanda Jones reached down and retrieved the cassette player, and passed it deftly back into Lewis' hands as she stepped between him and Matthew.

'Leave him.'

Matthew leered in front of Amanda and looked round her at Lewis where he was sheltered behind her.

'Or what? His girlfriend is going to get me?'

Amanda stood her ground firmly. She held out her hand and waited for the headphones to be returned.

'Since when did you have a girlfriend anyhow, Tumnal?'

Matthew glanced down at Amanda's hand where it remained held out. He took it in his own hand and lowered himself to press a kiss to it. At the last minute, Amanda snatched her hand away.

'Since when did you care anything about Lewis?'

With her other hand she reached out and snatched the headphones from Matthew's hand, and stepped back next to Lewis. Matthew looked up from his lowered head, and his body straightened to follow like an uncoiling snake assessing the situation.

'Are we done?'

Amanda, with a face like thunder, kept Matthew fixed in her gaze.

'Have a great life Matthew. You won't see us after tomorrow.'

Amanda clasped Lewis' arm as she turned and walked with him away down the towpath. Not once did she stop or turn back, and nor did Lewis.

'Louis?' Kathryn nudged him. 'Louis, what is it?'

Louis started and came back round from his daydreaming. He found himself looking into Kathryn's eyes close to.

'Just remembering.'

The others looked to their friend.

'Music?'

'It all comes down to music. The f-fair – Miss Leroy – she used to control me through music. Music was how my imagination was made real,' said Louis. 'And you remember, in your parents' house? It was music that almost led her to me.'

'It was music that allowed me to escape from—' began Watts. 'Wherever that was.'

Sarah shivered.

'It freaks me out. An endless corridor, with my portrait on the wall next to Dad's, and his Dad's, going back...'

'It was the life line of the Faery Queen.'

Louis shook his head, trembling.

'No, Louis. It is,' said Kathryn.

'I know,' said Louis. 'I just don't know how you can call her that – Miss Leroy – she was evil. She was no qu-queen.'

'It's who she is—'

'No!'

Louis shook his head.

'Was. It's who she was. To address her as she is, is to validate her continued existence. Miss Leroy – what she *was* – she *isn't* anymore.'

'But the corridor I was trapped in,' Watts added. 'That was pretty real.'

'It's just an empty corridor now. You said the portraits ended If *anything* was to continue, there should be another picture,' Louis continued. 'Last year my life should have been forfeit, and my imaginary son would have a friend and there would be a child to come.'

'You don't have an imaginary son.'

Sarah nudged Kathryn sharply in the side.

'He means me. I should be his son and have an imaginary friend. But—'

'It's all mixed up,' said Louis. 'You were thirteen, not eleven. It was all mixed up from the start.'

'So, the Faery Queen – she was doomed this time round from before I met with you?' said Kathryn.

'I think so,' said Louis. 'In the rose garden – her magic would never have worked.'

Kathryn reached out and squeezed his hand.

'I would still have died. Drowned, you know,' he added.

Louis felt the cool breeze of an early autumn night around his legs, and for a moment he thought he felt the rising of the water as it filled the pond in the rose garden. In his memories he could see the wave of water build towards him as it came across

248

the garden, Miss Leroy stood above him as she controlled the magic with Amanda at her side.

Leave him.

Louis heard Amanda's defence words coming back to him.

You are pathetic, bullying scum. Get the hell out of our lives...

Louis remembered Amanda fighting back all those years ago, and her love for him as unconditional as always.

'Dad?'

Sarah stepped closer.

'You're thinking about her, aren't you?'

Louis nodded.

'I can't help it. She – she was everything – and she loved me. She loved us. You were *ours*.'

'What are you saying?'

'You want her back, don't you?' asked Kathryn.

Louis shook his head.

'No.'

He took Kathryn with both hands.

'But I owe her.'

Lewis sat in his graduation robes, watching the tassel where it dangled in front of his eyes. Around him, names were called out and applause given. In his peripheral vision he could see the rows of students filing out into the aisle to go up on the stage. He kept watching the tassel dancing in front of him.

Lewis started. Next to him a fellow student was half out of his seat and ushering Lewis on. Lewis looked round to see the rest of his row almost out in the aisle already.

'Uh. Sorry.'

Lewis scrambled to his feet, and hurried down the row; catching his feet twice on the chairs, he straightened his tie and adjusted the graduation hat.

As Lewis was called up onto the stage, Amanda clapped enthusiastically from where she was seated with her part of the alphabet. From behind her auburn fringe she couldn't take her eyes off her boy, and she beamed with pride; and he was looking back at her for those few prized seconds of attention up on the stage that seemed to go on for hours. But then he wasn't looking at her, but beyond her, past her to the back of the hall.

Amanda turned her head. She stopped clapping as the smile faded from her face. Across the sea of mortar boards, and enthusiastically clapping parents, at the back of the hall, stood the headmistress from their old school.

4

Cloister's was a slick and modern wine bar, right in the centre of the city and located down a narrow passage cut through behind the shops and theatres. Surges of fairgoers kept on coming as they left the noisy fair that began just at the end of the passage.

Amanda laughed infectiously. Lysander was the funniest – a foppish clown with a wise-cracking sense of humour. She laughed with him and at him interchangeably in a way she had never, ever done before.

Lewis. She thought of him, and their life. They had laughed and joked, but she could still see that sulky pout of his if she had ever dared to laugh *at* him.

'Lysander, what?'

Amanda's animated faced turned serious.

'Taylor!' he called. 'What's your mother doing here?'

'Moth–' Amanda began. She turned her head, to see, standing by the door into the room, the tall figure of Miss Leroy.

Amanda stared, unable to speak. She turned back as Taylor entered the room.

'Miss Leroy is your mother?'

'Was my mother, yes,' said Taylor. 'She's passed, sadly.'

Taylor strode through the room towards the elegant figure in the corner.

'Hello mother, did you forget something?'

'She's dead?' Amanda hissed to Lysander. 'And mother?'

'Taylor's parents never married. He takes his father's name, Demetri.'

Amanda rolled her eyes.

'She's talking to him like she's...'

Amanda glanced round and leant closer to Lysander.

'She's a ghost!'

Amanda turned again, to look across the room as Taylor approached Miss Leroy to talk to her. She watched and remembered. Of looking back over her shoulder, the tassel from her graduation hat swinging in front of her eyes, and seeing Miss Leroy at the back of the hall. Applause rang in her head as the audience clapped the orchestra, and Amanda was standing on stage holding her oboe in front of her. She was beaming at Louis, but beyond at the back of the hall, Miss Leroy stood and watched.

Back in Cloisters, and Amanda shook her head at Taylor. She turned Lysander to face her and squeezed his hand into hers tightly.

'Get me out of here, Xander,' she said. 'I want to go home.'

A taxi cab pulled up in the street outside the gates to Song Villas, and Matthew got out. After the car slipped off into the night, Matthew unlocked the gates and slipped through onto the drive. His fast walking pace accelerated into a run towards the house. At the entrance his fingers fumbled at the lock and he was in, tearing across the entrance hall and down the corridors, round the corners to the servant's passage at the back, where he all but tumbled down the stairs into the cellar.

He burst into the furthest room and made straight for the corner. The girl-crone figure hunched in the corner shrieked with alarm and cowered further back against the wall.

'Enough!' Matthew shouted as he dived forward and grabbed the frightened figure by the wrist, dragging her to her feet. She screamed and fought to free herself, but Matthew's grasp held strong as he dragged her out of the cellar and forced her out of the darkness, and into the half-light of the stairwell.

'What are you still doing here?'

The words exploded from his mouth, his teeth bared.

'How did it go so wrong?'

'Matthew—' the girl simpered.

'It failed. You must have known it was always going to fail. Lewis was wrong—'

The girl-crone lifted herself up; in the body of Amanda she straightened herself into the pose of Miss Leroy.

'I—' she croaked. 'I loved him. I had to give him more. He had such creativity.'

'And it betrayed you.' Matthew snarled. 'It's all your fault.'

He forced her again, violently, up the stairs and through the hall.

'Matthew, no—'

Matthew pushed and shoved the girl-crone ahead of him.

'Get out!'

He pushed her through the front door and dragged her across the terrace, down the sloping lawn to the rose garden. Moonlight and clouds cast fractured shadows across the lawn, but it was darker still in the rose garden. Matthew pushed the girl-crone ahead of him, violently, and she tripped and fell under her twisted feet. She yelped with pain as she crumpled to the ground.

Matthew grabbed at her again and dragged her by the wrist to her feet.

'No!' he shouted. 'Get down them! In!'

He forced her on, and pushed her on to fall into the dark, stagnant opening of the first of the pools.

'Why, Matthew?'

The girl-crone looked up, pleadingly. For a moment, Matthew was touched by the girl-crone's beguiling face.

'Why are you doing this to me?'

Matthew stopped. He stared.

'You failed,' Matthew said through gritted teeth. 'You used to be strong. You promised stability, and continuity. You've failed me. You failed our people.'

The girl-crone stared back up at Matthew from where she was splayed in the pool. The expression on her face was timid and child-like – the girl in her; but her posture was that of the crumpled old woman that Miss Leroy had become.

Matthew shook his head and waded forwards into the shallows. He reached out towards the girl-crone and offered her his hand. She reached up gladly, before at the last moment Matthew withdrew his arm, closed his hand into a fist and knocked her down. She swayed and toppled face first into the pool.

'You're finished,' Matthew said. 'I don't need you.'

Matthew turned and walked away. He walked back out through the rose garden and up the lawn towards the house.

5

They had barely left the narrow cut-through of Friar's Entry, and escaped the southern-most reach of the fair where it surrounded the church of St Magdalen, and began their way down Broad Street, when it hit – a wrenching pain in her insides. Amanda gasped for breath and fell back; Lysander knelt beside her on the pavement and tried to wake her. Further back along the road the lights of the fair could be seen over the roofs of the college building, and the night pulsed with the booming soundtrack of other people's fun.

Her breathing was faint but still present, as he lifted her head gently, cradling her in his hands, and willed her to wake. Fairgoers passed them by and crossed the street to avoid them, assuming them to be just two more students having drunk too much.

It was into this scene that Louis stepped, rounding a corner from a side street, to find Amanda lying on the ground, surrounded by her student friends.

'Look at them,' said Kathryn. 'Another one had a skinful too many.'

She and Louis carried on along the street with Sarah, Caz, and Watts.

'That's not just—'

Caz pushed past Kathryn and ran toward the figures on the floor, calling Amanda's name. Kathryn and Louis looked at each other and rushed forward, arriving just after Watts, and landed on their knees at Amanda's side.

'What have you done?'

Watts lifted her head and stared directly into Lysander's face.

'I don't know. Nothing,' answered Lysander. 'She just suddenly went over, like a fit. I don't know—'

Back in the wine bar customers shrieked, and a crowd swelled around Taylor. He stood in the centre of the commotion with the crumpled dead boy of Miss Leroy at his feet. Around him views were being exchanged, and stories told. The manager was pushing his way through the crowd, and someone else was on their mobile to the emergency services.

That lad, he pushed her to the floor.

Taylor heard the words from where he stood, frozen to his feet. What happened next was a blur of slow-motion action; he jump-turned and pushed a nearby table in the process, flipping it onto its side as he broke into a run, twisting and turning through the crowd. Arms reached out to claw him and pull him back like brambles clinging to his clothes, but he broke free of them and slammed out through the doors at the front and onto the street. There he paused only long enough to break into a fast run down the street and around the corner.

In the next street there was the small crowd of people gathered around something on the pavement, and he slowed to a walk as he made the final approach. By this point a girl with short-cropped hair and porter's uniform was crouched over the girl on the floor, and Lysander was slightly further back. Taylor strode up to the gathered crowd and, as he passed Lysander close by grabbed him by the arm and yanked him along with him. At Lysander's protestation, Taylor silenced any comment with a look and a finger raised to the lips. He shook his head and walked Lysander on.

'Change of plan,' said Taylor.

'But, Amanda...'

'She's dead.'

Taylor walked him on, leaving Watts crouched over Amanda's body.

Watts knelt at Amanda's side. Beneath her skin there was a faint pulse, and the slightest rise and fall to her chest. Watts turned and stared at Louis.

'You've got to help her!'

Watts checked Amanda's pulse again, feeling for the slightest beat. She checked the airways to begin administering CPR on her friend. Around her the wind gusted fallen leaves in the gutter; another gust of wind swirled around the corner and lifted a pile of leaves into the air, whipping them to head height.

Kathryn took a step back and clutched tighter at Louis, wincing awkwardly as she felt a sting of pain stab through her.

'It's happening again,' she said, her voice winded. 'The fair. Miss Leroy's monster.'

The wind died down as the leaves fell again to the floor. Another gentler gust, and the leaves went scampering across the pavement, a rustle of tiny feet through the fallen leaves. The pile around Amanda and Watts grew, and another gust of wind blew a man-sized heap of leaves down the street. Again, Kathryn felt the sting of pain through her side and down the length of her arm to her hand. She pressed herself closer to Louis. In the distance they could make out dark figures moving along the perimeter of the broad street.

'Proctors,' said Louis.

'That's not what worries me,' said Kathryn. She watched the leaves on the pavement near to Amanda and Watts. The gusts of wind were stronger now, throwing the fallen leaves high in clouds of crispy autumn colour.

'It's him,' she said. 'He's back. The man of leaves and litter.'

'It's just the wind,' Sarah said.

'No. It's more than that.'

Sarah shook her head.

'They're just leaves, and you know what you do with leaves—?'

She glanced over at Caz and grinned. Together they both dived forward and kicked their shoes satisfying into the deep drifts of fallen leaves. The toes of their shoes were pushed through with a hissing like the static of a discontinued radio frequency.

'She's breathing!'

Louis and Kathryn heard Watts shout through the sound of wind and leaves. They looked to each other and moved forward. A wave of wind broke in front of them, and the face of a monster reared up, reaching out with veined arms of dry leaves. Kathryn leapt back as the monster slashed at her, and Louis yelped as he fought off a second creature. In the light from a Victorian street lamp, Kathryn could see the dark streak of blood on his cheek.

'Sarah, Caz, get out of there!'

'She's waking!' Watts screamed.

'We can't get to you!' Louis called back.

The wind blew stronger, flashing lightning streaks across the sky where the tram lines reflected the street lighting across the sky as the wind blew them taught and loose, and they sung with the whistling through the night. On the street, more monsters rose out of the leaves to surround Amanda and Watts.

Across the street, and in the quad of a neighbouring college, the dark outlines of the university proctors could be seen.

'Why?' Louis said, his voice panicked.

Sarah turned to her Dad and Kathryn.

'It's the faeries. They need a queen.'

'And – these—?'

Kathryn pointed at the leaf monsters, more scared than ever by them after her encounter at the fair.

'Defending the queen.'

'But she's not – not really—'

'I guess they don't know that,' said Louis.

Kathryn looked to Louis, and Louis looked to Sarah. Sarah was left weighing up the silence that lingered between the three of them.

'They need a queen, right?' Sarah said eventually. 'Tell me again how that was supposed to happen?'

Louis looked back at his daughter.

'You know that—' Kathryn began.

'Every eleven years an imaginary child is born to the son of the imaginary child. And as the child is taken, the Faery Queen lives on. Every eighty-eight years, the Queen must be reborn into the man's lifelong companion. That's what should have happened last time – both you and Amanda should have been reborn.

'But we saved you—'

Kathryn squeezed Louis' hand and fixed him in her gaze.

'And the rebirth couldn't be completed. The Faery Queen was left as that strange half being we saw in the cellar,' Sarah continued. 'I know how to end this, once and for all.'

6

Sarah led her father, Kathryn and Caz at a brisk pace back down Broad Street and across the road. Charlotte and Eleanor followed them as they headed down into the metro station.

'What about Amanda?' asked Louis.

'And Watts?' added Kathryn.

Sarah turned to face them as she slid coins under the hatch for her ticket.

'They'll be safer than any of us. Those creatures – leaf, or whatever they are – they aren't interested in harming them. Just determined to keep anyone else from getting to them. Amanda and Watts, they're protected now until this is all over.'

By the time the last tickets were being purchased their metro slid into the station and they boarded.

'So, what's the plan exactly?' Louis asked as he drew in alongside his daughter.

'Song Villas,' said Sarah. 'By way of home. I need you and Kathryn to get your instruments.'

'You're up to something,' said Kathryn.

Sarah said nothing. She just looked back at them while leaning nonchalantly on a pole.

After a couple of stops, they ran from the metro just north of where the fair was still a blaze of colour and noise. They cut fast through St Giles' churchyard and ran to jump onto a tram before it rattled off up Woodstock Road. Panting and wheezing for breath, they took their time to take stock until it was their time to ping the bell and alight from the tram. They crossed the road to where Bevington House stood, behind the high stone wall and the skeletons of autumnal trees. As the wind intensified behind them, they shut it out behind the other side of the front door.

'Flute! Oboe!'

Sarah barked her command to Louis and Kathryn. She didn't wait for a response before taking the stairs two at a time, two floors up to her Dad's bedroom. Lurching to a halt, she scanned the room before pulling open the drawers and rifling through them. Bookmarks, till receipts, and old train tickets flew through her fingers as she rummaged through pens, buttons, and odd coins from random European countries. And then she found it. She took in her hands her Dad's wedding ring, still on the gold chain from when he used to wear around his neck. She held the ring tightly in her fingers and stared at it, and remembered the past and simpler days.

A nine-year old Sarah stood at the side of her Dad's bed, which Louis sat on. He was bent over, staring at his wedding ring where he held it between the fingers of both hands.

'Dad...?'

Lewis didn't look up as he continued to turn the ring over and over in his fingers.

'Daddy.'

Eventually Lewis acknowledged his daughter standing by him. He beckoned her closer and slid off the bed to his knees in front of her.

'What are you doing?'

Lewis held a finger to his mouth and fixed her with his gaze. He reached out, and hooking his daughter's fair hair back over her shoulders, fastened the chain with the ring attached.

'Remember this, Sarah,' he said. 'It was your grandfather's, and his father's before him. One day I will give it to you, and you will know.'

'Know what?'

Lewis lay his hands on his daughter's shoulder.

'Just remember this. You will know.'

Sarah reached a hand up and felt the ring of gold where it hung next to her skin.

Sarah touched the ring to her neck. So back then, her Dad had been right. She had remembered – and she did know. She was about to fasten it around her neck when something made her change her mind. Her fist instead closed over the ring and its chain, and she stuffed it into a jeans pocket.

She picked herself up and walked from the bedroom, back across the landing, and down the stairs, all in a slight daze.

'Sarah, what's up?' Caz greeted her from the bottom of the stairs.

Sarah stared back blankly. Back on Broad Street, with the creatures of leaf and wind and with faeries running through the night, she had felt so certain.

'Song Villas,' said Kathryn. Both she and Louis held up their instruments cases.

Sarah nodded but just stood at the foot of the stairs.

'There was urgency?' said Louis.

'Yes,' said Sarah. She felt in her pocket, allowing her fingers to play with the ring and chain.

'We should...' added Louis. 'You know, be going.'

A makeshift gang of friends and family, resembling an oddball *Famous Five* with a miscellaneous collection of musical instruments and lanterns, were gathered in a loose circle in the tiled hallway of Bevington House. Sarah led the way again, out and across the garden, as they retraced their steps down Bevington Road to the metro line for Park Town.

When they arrived at the gates to Song Villas, they were in the time of the wild and unkempt gardens that grew through the ironwork and smothered the stone wrens on the crumbling pillars. The gates pushed open enough for them to get through and onto the drive.

'House? Or...?' began Kathryn. Her hands closed tighter around Louis' as they headed off across the grounds to the enclosed section of formal garden, with the series of interconnected sunken pools. Wild and overgrown, the roses were thick with weeds and other more voracious shrubs, and the pools were either dry or filled with a slurry of stagnant water and leaves.

Sarah dived forward immediately, and began dragging leaves and branches from the channels that flowed between the pools and freed the sluices.

'Play!'

Her head whipped round to face Louis and Kathryn. They staggered back and mouthed the next question silently to themselves. The decision though, when they readied their instruments, was instantaneous.

Caz began helping Charlotte and Eleanor position candles on the ledges around the main Italianate pool, and hung the lanterns from the tree branches. She stopped to watch Sarah for a moment when her friend was skimming leaves off the pond and fishing blockages out of the channels.

'Sarah, you're soaking.'

Sarah shook her head.

'I can't feel anything—'

Louis' and Kathryn's music played on into the night air. It wasn't the fragment of music with which Miss Leroy had bewitched and controlled Louis for so much of his life, but a sprightlier dance that was playful and lively. Every time either Caz, Charlotte, or Eleanor lit a candle or hung another lantern, a second seemed to appear elsewhere in the rose garden.

'You think they're helping us?'

Charlotte returned Caz's questioning with a shrug.

'I guess. They're playing faery music.'

'Good fairies though,' added Eleanor, as she lit another candle in a small alcove. Another light sprang up in the dark opposite.

Sarah continued to splosh and splash through the ponds, clearing them of debris so that the night resounded with the trickle of water running down the channels from pool to pool, with the candlelight twinkling back off the shimmering surface.

The splishing and the splashing stopped. Sarah stood on the far side of the pool looking down at the water. For a moment, only the gently running water disturbed the dark autumn night.

'Right!' she said. 'I think it's time.'

7

Louis and Kathryn stood at the head of the last pool either side of the narrow channel that fed it, playing the rhythm of music which the Faery Queen had bound her future lives with. Sarah held a dam board in her hands and moved forward with solemnity to push it down into the drain at the foot of the last pool. She turned again to face the source of the music.

Play on,
The faery music.

Sarah slipped her arms from her jacket and threw it to one side. She pulled her hoodie over her head and tossed it aside too.

I throw off my clothes.
Faery spirits I beseech you.

Sarah felt all the while for the ring on its chain in her jeans pocket. She felt her heart beating fast, and her body hot like an iron in the fire. The twinkling lights seemed to close around her and hold her fast. She reached up and felt the collar of her grass-green silk shirt, flicking open the top buttons. *It was working.*

.

As Roxburgh was my grandfather,

The north wind blows, sharp and cold,

Queen of Faeries, I am here.

And Sarah felt the wind blowing in from the north, accompanied by the jingling of fifty-nine silver bells hanging in the trees. She felt the water rise up her legs where she stood in the pool.

As Kathryn's oboe took the melody, Louis lowered his flute from his lips and took a step forward to offer the instrument to Sarah. She shook her head.

'No,' she said. 'It's different now.'

It was impossible to tell now if the water was rising or if she were sinking, but her fingertips at her sides were trailing in the water. The water – a flat calm – gently shimmered in the moonlight where it seeped over the stone sides.

Arms bent now, Sarah found the water rising up to her chest. The ring on its chain still held fast in the fist of her right hand. In front of her, her father lifted his flute to his lips again and echoed Kathryn's melody.

Sarah brought the chain up to her neck and slipped the catch to fasten it around her. A gust of wind swirled through the rose garden. The sky splintered with light and rocked with a thunder-clap onto the pools and the secrecy of the rose garden. Louis and Kathryn wavered in their playing but continued.

In front of Louis, Sarah rose up out of the water, standing tall, her blue eyes gleaming. Louis' flute dropped down in his hands to his side, rain running down his face.

'Sarah!' he screamed.

O no, O no, Lewis
That name does not belong to me;
I'm but the Queen of fair Elfland,
That am hither come to visit thee.

'No! Sarah—'

Louis thrust his flute into Kathryn's hands and dived forward into the pool, staggering forward as he sank up to his shoulders in shimmering water. Across the swelling pool, Sarah rose up in skirts of grass-green silk, and cloaked in a mantle of green velvet. She sat astride a milk-white steed.

'Sarah!' Louis shouted, his voice stretched thin.

Sarah leant forward on her horse and stroked the mane. She looked up towards her father, and her grin was the grin that Louis had always known.

'Stop your worrying Dad. We've won.'

She sat back and giddied her horse up. The strong, muscular legs of the horse reared up as Sarah steered it out of the pond, the water ebbing away. The fifty-nine silver bells now hung along the bridle. This was not now a steed of secrecy and deception, but one to be ridden openly and in plain sight.

Directing her horse out of the rose garden, Sarah broke it into a trot across the garden and into a canter to leave the park. Louis stepped out of the rose garden, followed by Kathryn, to watch Sarah head off across the garden, a garden that seemed to be reordering and tidying itself around them.

'What just happened?' Kathryn said hesitantly. 'Will she be back?'

Louis looked to Kathryn and nodded. He leant forward and squeezed an embrace from her, snatching a kiss as he took back his flute. As he remained standing there, holding the flute, his hands fingered at the keys.

He shook his head.

'I can't remember. It's gone.'

Kathryn glanced down at her oboe and tried to place her fingers on the keys. She shook her head as well.

'Sorry. Me too.'

The St Giles Fair was silent when Sarah cantered into the centre of town. The lights were off, and the rides boarded up. A few last ride owners were packing up their rides and sweeping up litter. Sarah swerved between the rides on her milk-white steed. She rounded the tall façade of Baliol College into The Broad and reared up to a halt in front of the creatures of leaf and litter.

Sarah dismounted, and stepped towards the creatures, in her dresses and mantle of faery cloth. This time there was no lashing out of clawed hands but a parting of them, as they broke apart and drifted into piles of russet and brown across the pavement. In the middle of it all, Amanda and Watts were kneeling, facing each other close in their arms. As Sarah stepped closer to the pair they both looked up together, like they had been interrupted from something.

'You came back.'

Sarah stood over Amanda, looking down at her. She wanted to hug her, like a child hugs her mother, but—

'Am I...?'

'Free. Yes,' said Sarah.

Amanda glanced at Watts, and grinned. They helped each other up, looking at Sarah at all times.

'Go, go on,' Sarah encouraged. 'Go home.'

Amanda stepped forward and embraced Sarah but pulled away just as quickly.

'Thank you.'

'Laters,' added Watts.

Sarah stood on The Broad and watched the two cross the street, to enter Turl Street and go back towards their college.

'Laters...' echoed Sarah, quickly and to herself. Around her a light breeze freshened the air, a contrast to the stormy wind that had proceeded it.

'I loved her, truly.'

Sarah turned to where the voice came from. Lysander stood now at her side, breathless, like he had been running.

'I know you did, sweet Lysander. But her love was not a love for you. Lysander, come - away with me. Tonight.'

From Sarah's other side Hermia approached them, and behind her Helena and Taylor followed.

'Lysander?' Sarah said again.

'Hermia, would you have me back?'

'I am here, aren't I?'

'Hermia—'

Lysander looked back across the pavement with big, wide, doleful eyes.

'Go. You too,' said Sarah.

Lysander took a couple of steps forward, and Hermia skipped towards him to clasp her hand in his. With a last look back at Sarah, they crossed the street.

Lastly, Helena stepped up to Sarah with Taylor.

'Helena, what troubles you?'

Helena looked round at Taylor and nodded her head to him.

'Taylor Demetri?'

'The Faery Queen – our ruler – she was dead. I sought only to keep order – be a regent to your power—'

'You sought power, Taylor,' said Sarah. 'I cannot let that go unpunished.'

Sarah turned then to Helena.

'Helena, it is for you to decide what you would have with your lover. You are of course welcome anytime into the faery kingdom, but Taylor must always stay behind.'

'I understand.'

Helena looked across at Taylor and offered him her hand.

Soon, Sarah was again left alone on The Broad. She wandered slowly, kicking at the leaves, back to her horse, and reaching up to his bridle, jingled a couple of the bells. She laid the palms of her hands to the saddle, as if preparing to mount, but instead buried her face in the horse's side.

'This *wasn't* what I asked for—'

8

Louis and Kathryn, with Caz, Charlotte, and Eleanor, were stood around in the kitchen of Bevington House. The kettle whistled to the boil, and on the side mugs stood ready; but nobody moved to do anything. Occasionally someone looked up, only to catch another's gaze, and they knew enough of what the other was thinking to not say anything.

The events earlier that evening remained lodged firmly in their minds, preoccupying each of them in different ways. Out in the hall the grandfather clock struck twelve.

Louis turned at the counter and drew a mug towards him. He lingered—

'It's a bit late for coffee,' he said. 'Hot chocolate, anyone?'

Kathryn agreed.

'With a dash of rum.'

'I should be going really,' said Charlotte, moving only inches from where she was. 'I'll never get up in the morning.'

'Same,' said Eleanor. 'Shall we?'

Louis looked up at the two friends.

'If you're sure.'

'We can make up a bed?' added Kathryn. 'For you too, Caz; it's too late for you to go home tonight now.'

Caz nodded thanks. For a moment, Charlotte and Eleanor looked like they would agree too.

'She's gone, hasn't she?'

Louis turned to Caz, holding his hands out, plaintively.

'I don't know. I really don't know.'

'She must have,' said Kathryn. 'The Faery Queen was to take Louis' life, and he would have ceased to exist. Tonight might have been a year later, but she's still gone in his place.'

'Miss Leroy is back then?' Louis said.

Kathryn shrugged.

'I don't know. There's not a precedent for this,' she said. 'You made that hot chocolate yet?'

Louis was left looking blankly at Kathryn. She nodded at him, and the mugs in his hand. He turned back to the counter and flicked the kettle on to re-boil, and set about fetching out a jar of cocoa. Kathryn wandered out of the kitchen, to return a few moments later with a bottle of dark Estonian liqueur.

'Couldn't find the rum, but this will do us nicely.'

She lifted it up towards Charlotte and Eleanor.

'You sure we can't tempt you?'

Louis and Kathryn leaned into one another on the sofa in the lounge, cupping their mugs in their hands on their lap, and finally beginning to relax. It was just like before; when they had first met, and they had these quiet nights in...

Except, of course, for Caz, tired and sleeping in the armchair opposite. It could have been a scene from a few months ago; before Amanda had returned to their lives, and disturbed their unconventional family unit of father, partner, and imaginary child. It could have been Sarah, as she then was, asleep across the room, were it not for the daringly purple-blue dyed hair that distinguished Caz from her best friend.

'We've never actually met her parents, have we?'

Kathryn turned her head from where it lay on Louis' shoulder.

'I mean, she was Sarah's best friend,' continued Louis. 'You'd think we would know more about her.'

'Like your parents knew everything about your friends—'

Louis shot Kathryn a stare to cut her off.

'Okay, bad example,' Kathryn backtracked. 'Although it's a good point. She was normal. She would have friends that you wouldn't have known anything about, much less the parents.'

Louis let Kathryn's words hang and turned to stare off into the middle distance. He squeezed Kathryn gently closer to him.

'I miss her already, Kathryn.'

The moments because minutes, and the minutes became hours. The mugs were now on the coffee table, and Kathryn was herself asleep in Louis' arms. He sat awake, just idly gazing across the room; not at anything in particular, but musing over things.

'Sarah was my imaginary child, Kathryn.'

Kathryn mumbled under a cover of light snoring.

'What if Caz was Sarah's?'

Kathryn dreamed on in her sleep.

She watched Caz through the window of Bevington House – forward and back, forward and back, Sarah swung from one of the trees just as she had when she was younger. Now she was clothed in the green silk dress of her new life. She looked fondly on at the other world inside the house. There was Caz - ever-dependable Caz - and there at the forward swing was her Dad, with Kathryn asleep in the crook of his neck. Back, and there was Caz again with her blue-purple hair Forward, and there was her Dad again. Sarah wanted to go in to the house now and return to her family, but she knew it had all changed. She had changed. Everything had changed.

Sarah swung from the tall tree just as she had done years – no, not years – before. To swing from the tall trees in the garden of Bevington House *was* the most natural thing in the world, and she was sure she must have done so when she was little, except that she had no memory of it. Forwards and back, forwards and back, the ropes squeaked where they rubbed on the branches. When Louis got up from the sofa and crossed the lounge to examine the source of the squeaking, the swing was empty, and just drifting in the wind.

'Louis?'

Louis turned away from the window to where Kathryn had woken again.

'I thought I heard someone in the garden?'

'You mean Sarah?'

Louis nodded sadly.

Kathryn frowned. She offered out her hand.

'Come on. It's late.'

Louis nodded down at Caz.

'You think she'll be alright?'

''Course,' said Kathryn. 'She's slept over how many times with – Sarah.'

She retrieved a blanket and carefully laid it over Caz where she lay sleeping. Louis and Kathryn retreated from the room, switched off the lights, and headed upstairs.

Sarah stopped. Crouched over some books in Louis' study, she heard footsteps on the stairs and voices crossing the landing. Quickly, she flicked off her torch and held her breath. The footsteps and voices moved away, and up another floor. Sarah breathed again and flicked her torch on again. She moved to Louis' desk and began hunting through his files of story notes and first drafts.

She found an early draft of *Flyht* and enjoyed the striking imagery, if simplistic writing. Looking further back, there were other half-abandoned stories. And then she found it. The story of Louis Tumnal - author, photographer, living with a loving partner who worked in publishing, and—

—Sarah turned the pages over and over, then more hurriedly, flicking forwards and scanning the words. No daughter. In Louis' perfect life, there was no - Sarah.

Sarah snapped the books shut and placed them down on the pile in front of her. She pinched herself, and knew that she at least was real.

9

Morning came, and Amanda and Watts sat opposite one another in the college dining hall eating their breakfast. Watts sat with her buttered toast and coffee as Amanda enjoyed a bowlful of cereal, fruit, and yoghurt.

'I had such a curious dream,' said Amanda, and she told Watts, as well as she could remember them, of all the strangeness of her life. When she had finished, Watts reached across the table and took her friend's hand.

'It was a curious dream, certainly. Awful even. You can't have known who you were.'

Amanda laughed.

'I know. To think that I might have a husband and everything, a daughter even—'

Watts grinned. It was a ridiculous idea for the present, but she did look across the table now, and imagined a future. Her hand squeezed Amanda's tighter, before relinquishing it to let her finish her breakfast. Out of the corner of her eyes, she saw movement at the High Table and signalled Amanda to it.

'The Master doesn't look well,' said Watts. 'Like he's had the future ripped out of him.'

'Ironic, really, considering that, maybe for the first time, I feel so alive.'

They continued to watch as the Master was brought his breakfast. He looked tired and haggard, aged beyond his already elderly years. Matthew Leroy-Song sloped into the seat next to the Master, himself pale and awkward in looks and composure.

'College finances must be taking a tumble,' quipped Watts.

'He looks pretty lonely too,' Amanda said, pointing across the room to where a tall, lanky, fair-haired student was sitting alone towards the end of one of the long dining benches, spooning porridge from bowl to mouth in an endless, repetitive cycle.

'That's Taylor Dimitri,' said Watts. 'Rich father. He's the son of an MP, and one of the governors. He normally has a harem of girls around him.'

'Looks like the Master's not the only one to have lost something this morning.'

'If it's brought him down a peg or two, then so much the better.' Watts laughed. 'He's not pleasant to the porters, and least of all to his scout.'

Sarah stood across the road from Wren Hoe County School, watching as pupils arrived for the start of the school day. She had got there early and seen teacher's heading in. She had watched as Miss Vernal's old metro had lurched and stalled into the car park. She knew that Caz hadn't yet arrived. She knew her daily pattern because it had been the same as her own for as many years as she could remember; so she watched and waited, determined to speak to her friend. A clique of girls sashayed down the street, swishing their hair periodically in a coordinated murmuration; they passed Sarah like she wasn't there, but that was not unusual. Next, a couple of kids, grunting words to one another as they stared passively at their phone screen walked by;

one of them clipped Sarah with a sharp elbow, and she had to steady herself from falling into the traffic.

'Hey!'

No answer.

The rate of children arriving at school increased, and still Sarah waited; until, eventually, she saw her. Caz.

She was heading towards Sarah on the same side of the street and looked straight at her. Sarah waved and called out her friend's name as she launched herself forward. Caz appeared not to have noticed as the lights changed and she accelerated her pace to cross the road. Sarah reached out to grab her friend's arm, but her hand closed around nothing. At the school gate, Caz greeted Beth Vernal, and exchanged a short conversation, into which Sarah tried to contribute, but it was like they couldn't see her.

'Guys, what's up? Stop playing games—'

But Caz was now walking across the car park, talking homework with Miss Vernal.

Sarah stomped away and threw her hand down beside her, as other children jostled past her to enter the school.

'Just ignore me then.'

Sarah turned and walked away, glancing back with a little regret before quickening her pace across the car park. Or she would have had it not been for the lurching, growling mustard yellow car that swerved into the entrance and almost knocked her flying. She turned and stared as the car lurched to a halt with the engine running, and a cloud of exhaust belching out the back. The passenger side door swung open, and the slender figure of Polly Lynn got out. Sarah turned and began walking briskly away.

'Sarah!'

For a moment, her stride hesitated before quickening.

'Sarah Tumnal!'

Polly's call was that of a teacher, and caused Sarah's escape to flounder and fail long enough that she found that she had to stop and turn back, and wait for Polly's approach.

'I forgot my homework,' she lied. 'I thought if I ran home now I'd get back—'

Polly shook her head, and Sarah knew that her concern wasn't over whether she was skipping classes or not. The little mustard yellow car was still sitting, idling in the middle of the car park, but now the tall, gangly Tom was approaching them too.

'Mrs Lynn...?' Sarah began to say, in her best school pupil's voice.

'Cut it out, Sarah,' said Polly. 'We know who you are, and that you're not here for school.

Sarah shifted awkwardly from foot to foot as she tried to work out Polly's intentions.

'We know who you are, Sarah,' Polly added, smiling.

'I'm not, really,' protested Sarah. She found herself shaking as she spoke. She knew who Polly and Tom thought she was, and it made her angry. 'I'm not like her!'

Tom reached Polly's side and looked about to speak, just as Polly began to answer.

'She bewitched the innocent and stole their souls—' Sarah interrupted both aof them. '*She* was evil. I am the queen of good elfland.'

Polly reached forwards.

'I know you are,' she said. 'And you know how I know? You have taken your kingdom out of love, not hate. You took it not because you wanted it, but because it was the only way to help others.'

For a moment Sarah didn't feel like the queen of elfland that she now was, but the schoolgirl that she had been, being told that everything was going to be alright.

'You know there's someone else you have to go and see now,' continued Polly.

Sarah shook her head.

'I can't,' she said. 'I mean, I want to, but I don't think I even can...'

Polly frowned. For a while the three of them stood in an awkward silence on the edge of the school grounds. Sarah glanced round, wondering how she could excuse herself.

'I should—'

Sarah saw the last few children arriving for school.

'You should...'

She began to edge away.

'Wait a mo—'

Polly began rummaging in her shoulder bag to find a small notebook and a pen. She scribbled something down, and tore the page out before offering it to Sarah.

'You should go. He deserved to know.'

Polly proffered a smile.

'In the meantime, if you need to contact us, anytime...'

She nodded her head, in an encouragement to have the paper taken. Reluctantly, Sarah took the paper and stuffed it into her pocket.

'Laters!'

Sarah cast them a wave as she turned and headed off. Tom stepped closer to his wife and slid a strong arm around her waist, squeezing reassurance back into her.

'If only she knew, Tom,' said Polly. 'Really, I mean. That this was only just beginning for her.'

10

Kathryn sat at her desk in the basement classroom of the local college, with her work spread out around her and Louis' camera and notebook next to her, with his satchel marking a place on the chair. She couldn't help but laugh and snigger to herself as she watched Louis across the room. He had decided to sign back up for the classes, and, no sooner than he had entered the room, the class bore, the elderly and opinionated Colin, had cornered him on the other side of the room. Occasionally Louis would throw a plaintive look of despair back across the room, but there was nothing that Kathryn could do without herself getting caught up in another conversation about yet another flashy and pointless bit of camera kit or app.

After the session had finished, and Kathryn and Louis had managed to escape the photo lab without further extensive *Colin-versation*, Louis challenged her on her support.

'I thought I was never going to escape—' he said, as they hurried down the corridor for fear that Colin would come after them with 'just one more thing.'

'I know,' Kathryn said. 'I wanted to help, honest. But there was no way, without two of us getting Colin-ed.'

'I'd forgotten what an insufferable bore he was,' said Louis. 'Argumentative, opinionated. Impossible.'

They emerged from the stairs into the foyer and left the college onto the small open plaza squeezed between the front of the building and the busy West End junction. They crossed the street via the crossings and rounded the corner into a street busy with bars and restaurants, unaware that they were being tailed by a small figure in a hoodie, with the hood pulled over their head firmly.

Louis and Kathryn turned abruptly and entered the pizza house, where the lights from within bathed the pavement in a warming glow. Inside the restaurant they were shown to a booth overlooking the street – the same booth where they had had their first date almost two years ago. The waitress took their drinks order and Louis ordered a bottle of wine. As they studied the food menus, over the cubical backrest Amanda and Watts entered the restaurant and were shown to a table in another part of the restaurant.

At Louis' and Kathryn's table they ordered their starters and mains, and the waitress took back the menus. When she headed back to the kitchen to turn in the order, the figure in the hoodie slipped in to the restaurant and into their cubicle, taking a seat next to Kathryn.

'Hey, what do you think you're—'

Louis raised his hand to summon the waitress. At this point the figure pulled back their hood and flipped out her fair-haired ponytail. Sarah's joyful, grinning face revealed itself to them.

'Hi ya.'

'Sarah!'

Sarah shrugged.

'Why the surprised face?' she said. 'You didn't think I was just going to disappear, did you?'

'I don't know what I thought—' Louis stuttered, suddenly unsure of himself again. 'Miss Leroy was going to take my life to perpetuate her own. I didn't know what was going to happen to you. When you rose up out of the pool in that dress, with that horse, you were so different.'

Sarah laughed.

'I am different. But I am the same Sarah, too.'

Kathryn was turned towards Sarah.

'What happened? After you left us?'

Sarah left the question unanswered. She excused herself out of the question, partly by the waitress bringing the bottle of wine over. When asked if she was joining the table, Sarah was quick to rattle out an order for a Hawaiian.

'Are we having dough balls too?'

Food order amended, the attention turned back to Sarah, and she felt the weight of Louis' and Kathryn's stares. She shook her head.

'I wasn't born into this,' she said. 'And nor were you.'

She looked across the table, eye to eye with Louis.

'The Faery Queen picked you out, Dad. Miss Leroy, she made you something - but it wasn't your destiny,' said Sarah. 'That's how you were able to break the spell.'

'We weren't though,' said Louis. 'Not in the end. You—'

'I said it wasn't your destiny,' said Sarah. 'Just like it's not mine. And that's why this is different. I took this because I wanted it.'

'So, what happens now?'

Sarah acknowledged Kathryn's answer and flicked her gaze forwards and back between her and Louis.

'Whatever we want to happen. You have Kathryn,' said Sarah. 'And for my mum - Amanda - her memories will come back now of the person she could have been, before she was dragged into this twenty years ago by Miss Leroy's gift to you and your imagination.'

'And you?'

Sarah shrugged.

'My life I guess, it's my own but with some additional responsibilities. Miss Leroy after all held down her job as headmistress and pillar of the community for how many years?'

Across the restaurant at another table, Amanda and Watts sat opposite one another. They clinked wine glasses and drank to their future.

'I remember now, Watts,' said Amanda. 'Primary School. You and I. We were best friends. What happened there?'

Watts shook her head.

'People drift apart. Children especially. Doesn't have to be forever.'

Watts leant down to the satchel at her side and pulled out a slender notebook that she slid across the table to Amanda.

'I got you this,' said Watts. 'So that you could write down your memories.'

Amanda took the notebook in both hands, opened it, and stroked the luxurious quality to the paper.

'It's gorgeous. Thank you.'

Amanda chewed on her lip as she considered her notebook, and Watts opposite her.

'When I used to read fairy tales, I used to imagine what it would be like if I were in the middle of one. And as soon as you start thinking that, you start to think there ought to be a book written about you.'

Amanda closed the new notebook and laid it down alongside her.

'And now, in this, I can write one...'

'Will I be in it?'

Amanda smiled, coyly, and reached across the table to touch Watts' hand.

'I hope so.'

Watts' fingers opened to let Amanda's hand in.

'In my other life, I always felt that without him I wasn't real,' continued Amanda.

'And while you were chasing him, I didn't feel like anything more than an imaginary friend.'

'With you though, we're not imaginary friends,' said Amanda. 'We both can be real.'

Amanda stood up from her chair and leant towards Watts.

'Thank you,' she said. And pressed a kiss to Watts' forehead.

Watts looked up, through her big, round, blue eyes, and beneath her fringe of fair hair. She pushed her hands up across Amanda's shoulders and through the thick curls of Amanda's auburn hair. She pressed a second kiss to her lips.

They breathed. Their gaze was locked to each other's eyes, and they slid back down to sit alongside one another on the bench seat, Holding each other in an embrace, they kissed again.

11

The next morning I stood again on the doorstep of my parents' house in the leafy northern suburbs of the city. But this time, I stood with Watts next to me. I pressed my finger to the bell and waited.

After a few minutes the door opened inwards to the demure, harassed figure of my mother, Dr Amelia Jones.

'Hello moth—'

My tone was bold, if apologetic in tone. Even so, I never got as far as to finish my greeting.

'It's you,' Amelia said brusquely. 'You had better come in.'

'We won't stay long,' I began, as I followed mother into the hall. Watts followed me and closed the door after us. I was halfway across the hall on my way to the drawing room, when Mummy led us instead over to the staircase and began to lead us upstairs.

'Mummy? What's happened?'

Amelia continued across the landing, where Lord Kennet, the Master of Woodiwiss, was in quiet, urgent conversation with the softly spoken, short and affable family doctor. As we passed the two men, their conversation ceased, and they greeted us both gravely.

'Dr Jones. Miss Watson.'

Watts and I moved on, following Mummy into my father's bedroom. I stopped inside the door, unprepared for what I saw. Behind me, Watts stepped closer, and reached out to take my hand. It was warm and comforting to have that connection, as in front of us, propped up on pillows in his bed, my father was an ashen-faced shadow of his former self.

Mummy nodded me in the direction of the chair next to the head of father's bed. Hesitantly, I stepped forward, glancing first to Watts, and sat on the edge of her seat.

'Father?'

Professor Jones, his breath slow and broken, took a moment to answer. I'll remember what he said next for the rest of my life, not because they were spoken through a dry, husky, and cracked voice, but for their simplicity. And their unusualness. He apologised.

I'm sorry.

Those weren't my father's last words to me, and it wasn't the day my father died; but it was the day that he and I finally understood one another. We talked that day like we never had before. I wouldn't say that we are friends. He has his world in the college and his research, and I have my own career in publishing. And I also have Watts.

Alice Watson. It turns out father was not surprised. He never thought my relationship with Lewis was real. I'm not sure if he approves, but it doesn't matter. If I'm honest, I don't know where this goes – between Watts and I. All I know is that, for maybe the first time in my life it feels right.

Mummy completed her monograph last summer. Apparently, my publishers – yes, I'm still working at The Press – have accepted it. It seems that she was just beginning to relax from it when my father's ill health took hold. I'm still not sure of the exact dates, but he has been fading fast over these last few months. The episode that has struck him down now though was that night of the fair. If that's a coincidence, then there's nothing I can do about it. I sometimes wonder what deals he struck with Lord Kennett and Miss Leroy. Whatever they are, he's not telling.

I'm writing this in the notebook that Watts gave me, in my rooms at Woodiwiss College. Yes, I'm still living there, and I've made it quite the home for Watts and me. I have my plants around me again – pots on every window sill. I'm expecting Watts home at any moment, and then she will cook dinner. It turns out that I still can't cook. That was always Lewis' domain, and now it is Watts'.

It's hard enough being Amanda Jones.

CODA

Afterwards

lacrimoso

A porter walked the circumference of the quad outside The Bod as night fell on a fog that had not lifted all day. He lit the gas lanterns that surrounded the buildings – the Clarendon House and the Sheldonian. On Broad Street, a man talked in one of a row of phone boxes opposite Blackwell's Bookshop, under a flickering, failing electric light

Thirty years have passed, and Kathryn Summers, acclaimed photographer, was stalking the Wren Hoe streets with her camera – a 35mm film camera. Times have changed since those days of plenty when she grew up. She moved stealthily through the city streets, hunting out her latest photography project; a culmination of a career documenting the lost and the dispossessed.

She took the steps into the compound outside the Sheldonian, and proceeded through the fog, then instinctively she stopped. She lifted her camera up to her eye and rotated the focus and exposure rings. Slowly two children come into focus. She clicked down the shutter and lowered the camera away from her eye; the children were gone; like forgotten friends.

ACKNOWLEDGEMENTS

For the entire time that I was writing Mr Tumnal, the book that precedes this one, I thought that it was a standalone novel. But I soon came to realise that the story was not finished. I've never had an imaginary friend, much less married one, so, I'd like to thank Louis Tumnal, and Kathryn, Amanda, and Sarah, for making me realise so much more about myself.

Thank you also to everyone at ALLi, especially the endless encouragement and support of Debbie Young, Dan Holloway and Orna Ross, and the infectious enthusiasm of Joanna Penn. Lorna, Laura, Lucy, Luke, Anna, and Alan, thank you for your support, and Jane, you've not been as involved in this story, but your encouragement has always drawn me on. I'd like to thank everyone who has shown their support for my books, you know who you are. Lastly, but by no means least, I'd like to thank my wife Emma, for putting up with my many funny little ways, and my always active funny little brain when it comes up with the weirdest of things too late at night.

Talk about this book with the hashtag #MrTumnal @shepline

Lightning Source UK Ltd.
Milton Keynes UK
UKHW03f1346110418
320874UK00001B/80/P